Naomi and the Purloined Journal

THE WILD MARCHMONTS #1

ALICIA CAMERON

To all the Wild Ones out there, and those who would like to dare.

Contents

The Marchmonts

The Royal Family

Cedric Marchmont, The Earl of Tremaine, 45, known as The King

Agatha, his countess, 46

Charles Marchmont, his brother, 40, The Crown Prince

Eliot, his middle brother, 30, The Black Sheep.

Dorian, the youngest brother. A rake, 28, The Princeling

Queenie (Clytemnestra), his sister, 25

Ophelia, his sister, 21

The Wild Marchmonts

Mother Lady Eleanor Marchmont, 46, Scottish, peaceful but quietly forceful

Richard, 24, dark and brooding.

Roseanna, 22, pleasing, reserved, dark.

Naomi, 20, humorous, cynical.

Phoebe, 19, dark, wild beauty.

Stephanie, 16, Crazy auburn hair. Sporting. A *fait accompli* expert.

Tabitha, 12, Prodigy Engineer, Quiet, keeps secrets

Berthe, 8, Too honest.

CHAPTER 1

The Invasion

Eliot Marchmont returned to Tremaine Towers at around nine that evening. Though his family had been resident here for ten years, since his brother Cedric had succeeded to the earldom of Tremaine, the vast house still did not seem like home, as Marchmont Hall once had. Dinner would be over, he knew, for the Earl kept country hours. He was glad, for he had no desire to see his family this evening. Some of them would, at this hour, be in the withdrawing room to the left of the hall, so naturally he turned to the right, to his sanctuary.

'Godwin, have some food sent to the library, as well as some tea. I'm thirsty, make that ale. No need to inform the family of my arrival, I'll see them all tomorrow.'

Godwin the butler wore a wig against his loss of hair, but it was of a very different type to that of the six footmen, being a tall, albeit decrepit, bush, and lacking a trailing queue. He wore an old-fashioned frock coat of dark grey and had a dignified frost in his manner.

'Mr Eliot sir, but I *should* just mention ...'

There was a gleam in the butler's eye that Eliot was too tired to analyse. 'Tell me tomorrow, Godwin.'

He'll find out before then, thought Godwin. He nodded James to the kitchen to inform Cook and lingered in the hall to see Mr Eliot open the library door, 'Good God!' was his exclamation, rather better than Godwin had hoped for.

The sight that met Eliot's eye as he entered the quiet of his sanctuary, was emblazoned there in a second, for pondering later. A pile of bodies, arm and legs everywhere, lay before his fire.

It *was his* sanctuary, for his only general order in this house was that a fire should be lit in the library on the days when he might be expected home. His sister Ophelia had teased him over this shocking expense — for the fire often lit an empty room if he turned up a few days late, but since they both knew this expense would not pay for one of her many petticoats even, he knew she was being sardonic.

There was a lady sewing in a chair by the fire. *His* fire. She seemed to be around the age of his sister-in-law, the Countess of Tremaine, mistress of Tremaine Towers, who he knew to be 48 years, but he could not be certain, for he was paying more attention to the pile on the floor. There was a male figure at the centre of it, and his stocking feet were on a little brass guardrail before the hearth. His head was cushioned on someone's leg, and a dark haired child had her head on his chest. One of his hands rested on the child's head, while the other held a book that he read, while the little person on his chest was engaged in cutting paper with long, perilous seeming, sewing shears. Another child, perhaps older, had her light brown hair splayed on the man's leg to his other side, feet flat on the floor, with a book against her knees. Yet another female head lay on a cushion, a figure whose legs were over the man's lower torso, and *her* feet provided a pillow for a red head of unruly curls. The young lady who was curled around his head, one of her legs providing his pillow, was also dark, but not the darkest head of the group. She was on her side and Eliot could only spy her shapely back and hips and that one of her feet was in the hands of another dark girl, reading on her back. All this he had observed in that flash of shock.

When he gave his exclamation, the youngest child turned her head to see, but her male companion placed it back on his chest firmly, not otherwise stirring. A female figure, whose feet had made a pillow for the redhead, jumped up, tidying her dress and hair, and made him a curtsy, as an 'Ow!' sound came from the direction of the red curls.

'Roseanna! Now my head is cold!' said the childish voice of the redhead.

Eliot turned to the lady sewing, who had not risen and was gazing at him mildly.

'Madam, we have not been introduced,' he said with as much politeness as he could muster. 'I am Eliot Marchmont. Might I inquire—?'

But it was a piping child's voice who answered, 'Oh we are the *other* Marchmonts. Are you from the *shiny* people? You do not look as shiny as them.' She pulled herself away from the young man to sit up. He sighed and continued to read.

'*Berthe!*' said the lady who had been sewing in the chair, whom he supposed to be her mother.

'This is Roseanna,' the child said, pointing to the standing one, 'and I am Berthe, and that is Tabitha, and that is Naomi, and that is Phoebe and that is Stephanie. She's the easiest to remember, because of the red hair. And in the middle, there is Richard, and he is the true earl, you know.' The child prattled.

Eliot, astounded, looked at the true earl, who continued to read his book, the other child, Tabitha was it? now hiding her head in his shoulder, her full back on display only.

'Berthe! Come here!' said the quiet but deadly Scottish tones of the mother. Berthe came forward and stood quietly opposite her seated mama. 'Since you overheard that piece of information, *what* did I say you must do?'

'Be silent about it, Mama.'

'Go to your room now, Berthe. You will breakfast there and lunch there too.'

'But I may *freeze*, Mama!' protested Berthe.

'Dinner too, then,' said the mother, raising her lilt a little. 'Go now.'

Berthe left the room, her riband falling from her waist length black curls. Eliot picked it up and handed it to her.

'Thank you,' she said in a depressed voice. 'Very happy to meet you.'

After this hiatus, the mother intoned 'Sit!' Eliot automatically looked to the chair she was seated on, because it was his own, to obey her. But it was evident she meant her children. They rose and found places to sit, one, he thought balefully, behind his desk. The young man stood behind his mother's chair, eying Eliot indifferently.

'I must present you formally, sir. I am Eleanor Marchmont,' She smiled at him faintly and Eliot bowed his head. 'These are my children, as you may have gathered, and *you* must be the earl's middle brother Eliot Marchmont, I suppose. My son Richard is my eldest, at twenty-four years,' Richard made a bow which Eliot returned, both faces without expression. 'My daughter Roseanna is twenty-two now,' the pretty, neat lady in the seat opposite her mother — she who had got up first when he had entered — stood and curtsied demurely. 'Naomi, who is twenty years,' the young lady behind the desk might have curtsied, but Eliot missed it, 'Phoebe here is a year younger than Naomi, Stephanie is fifteen, no, sixteen now, and Tabitha there is yet only twelve. Eight-year-old Berthe you met already,' A very dark girl, with even wilder hair than the child, curtsied with a glare (Phoebe), a red haired girl-child made an elaborate, but ironical he felt, curtsy fit for a king (Stephanie), and the twelve-year-old with long brown tresses, made a schoolgirl attempt and unbalanced, blushing furiously (Tabitha). 'I have given them to you in order, since it must be trying to have so many introduced at once.'

'You are on a visit here, madam? Am I to understand we are relatives?'

'Your brother told you nothing? Poor you!' said a less than sympathetic voice, low and with a rasp, from behind his desk. This was Naomi, he recalled.

'My deceased husband would have been a fourth, or perhaps fifth, cousin of yours. I should not lead you to believe that the relationship is close. Our *present* plan,' the lady said carefully, 'is to make our home here.'

'Your home?' Eliot was astounded, but a foremost thought was voiced, before he could stop it. 'This room is mine.' It was damnably rude, he knew, and he flushed a little.

'I quite thought it a library,' said the raspy voice from the desk. He did not look at her.

'I understand completely,' said the mother, evenly. 'This is your private retreat.'

'I did not suppose the *rest* of your family know how to read,' said the darkest one with the wildest curls.

'Phoebe!' said Roseanna, appalled.

'I beg your pardon, sir.' The dark wild thing continued, in a voice that denied the sentiment, 'I only meant, one can be reasonably assured that there will be no one else in the library. Before you came.' She seemed to enjoy adding.

'We shall restore the room to you tomorrow evening, Mr Marchmont. I must ask that we remain here this evening, since Godwin has not seen fit to obey my instructions to have fires lit in our rooms. And as the west wing has long been unused, it is particularly cold. There is a room there equal to become our sitting room eventually. I shall have the bed taken out and add some sofas and chairs where we can find them. It had a larger fireplace and it will be better for us.'

'The second earl's room, as you describe it,' said Eliot, remembering his tour of the house years since. 'Tremaine put you in the west wing? Doesn't it leak?'

'Well, if it does, it must be set to rights. We have not had rain as yet.'

Her air of quiet authority perplexed him. If this was some outlying family of Marchmonts who were here as poor relations he might believe it, for their gowns, and the gentleman's raiment, were not fashionable in the least. Indeed, very dull. Their appearance was unkempt generally. Girls with hair down their backs when past the age to do so, wild and disarrayed, were as unlike his own family as could be. But this small Scottish lady had the air, not of a beggar for boons, but of a matriarch in charge. It was quietly done, not ruling the roost as his vulgar sister-in-law, the countess, did — throwing her authority about by being unpleasant to the servants — but still, it was strange.

There was an interruption.

'Your food, Mr Eliot. I brought it in myself in case there was anything else I might do for you.'

Eliot was not deceived. Godwin had arrived to view the damage. 'Put it in the green salon. After I eat, I will see my brother.'

'Yes sir.'

'By the way Godwin, Mrs Marchmont has ordered fires in the chambers in the west wing. See to it.'

'The master ...' he began, then looking at Eliot Marchmont's raised brows, said, 'yes sir!'

Eliot turned to the lady, 'It was interesting to meet you, ma'am, but I shall not disturb your family more this evening. I must eat, then go and see my brother.'

'Oh, I believe he will be in his study. I set him a task to be achieved before breakfast tomorrow.'

'*Set him a task...!*' said Eliot, once more astounded. 'Very well ma'am, I shall see you tomorrow, no doubt.'

When, eventually, Eliot found his brothers Cedric and Charles, they were in the earl's seldom-used study. The duties and the responsibilities of such a large estate were many, but business was not something Cedric deigned to stoop to: Eliot supposed the earl believed the study itself might take care of the estate papers mechanically, behind its closed doors.

'Ah, Eliot! Just the man!' said the florid and portly Charles. 'Have you any unpaid bills? Drop 'em on the pile!'

'I do not.'

'Course you don't! *The Black Sheep,* indeed. Never mind,' he drawled in his affected manner, 'mine will do in compensation.'

Eliot saw the papers on the desk, of disparate sizes, which were piled upon two covered books of folio dimension, which he recognised as the estate accounts. 'What do you need them for?' He was looking at his elder brother, who was rummaging in a drawer, moving papers about.

'Do ring for Godwin, Charles!' the earl drawled, his drawl twice as languid as his preening brother's. 'It is tedious, but I remembered the tailor's bills. Jean-Luc has them.'

There was an air of action about his elder brother, despite the drawl, that Eliot had hardly seen.

Charles got up from the edge of the desk where his plump rear had been resting, 'Oh, Franks will have mine, too. Just as well you remembered, Cedric, or we should have missed out!' he gave a start before he pulled the bell. 'As well ask for your wife's bills, too. I suppose she'll have kept some from you, women always do. And the girls. Their fripperies *never* seem to be covered by their pin money,' Charles lamented.

'What *is* this?' Eliot demanded.

'A windfall!' Charles clapped hands together in gesture of childish glee. 'All our bills paid, but only if we can get it to the lawyer who is coming tomorrow before breakfast. At seven. *Who* visits at that hour?' he looked aggrieved but sighed. 'After that, there is no second chance.'

Godwin came in. He tried his best as a straight-faced butler, but Eliot always saw the interest, not to say *fascination*, in his eye. He was instructed to go directly to the valets and lady's maids and bring every unpaid bill to the study immediately. 'And tell the maids not to worry,' said Charles, as an afterthought, 'for their mistresses are not in trouble.'

'You sounded almost *compassionate*, Charles,' said the earl with distaste.

'Do not be ridiculous, Cedric,' said Charles, replacing his posterior on the desk and touching lightly at his pompadour, to check its perfection, 'it is just that we must wheedle out all the bills *now* or they'll fall on *you* afterwards.'

'What *is* this?' demanded Eliot again. 'Who were that family in the library, and what was that about the *true earl*.'

The Earl sat up suddenly, 'Be quiet, you fool!' he said, forgetting to drawl. 'Do you want the servants to hear you?'

'It is *true*?'

The Earl sat back, a feeble hand to his head. 'Explain, Charles. I *really* cannot.'

'Well, it is not decided, but you and I *may* be out of the succession,' Charles pouted fleshy lips, playing with his cuffs.

'I never considered myself *within* the succession,' Eliot replied, 'so that I don't care about that. But *why*?'

'Well, *I* care,' said Charles, '*I* was next in line, for there are no children in my way, after all.'

'Seek my death if you like, dearest brother, I am close to it anyway...' said Cedric, in that affected, feeble voice that always set Eliot's teeth on edge.

'I still do not understand.'

Charles explained, 'The husband of that Scottish woman was the sixth earl's son. The one that could not be found and was eventually presumed dead. It delayed the succession, you know that. But in fact, he was in the East Indies, or perhaps *Africa* or some such, and then in Scotland, and only heard after Cedric was appointed Earl, those three years later, though we are but lowly fourth cousins to the previous earl. So I suppose, with the father dead, that surly boy *is* the earl by primogeniture. But there are legalities. One cannot get rid of Cedric that easily.'

'How long have they known?'

'Oh *years*, apparently! Or at least, the parents did. Once the father was dying he wrote to Cedric to have his family live here.'

'For the son — Richard was it not? — to take his place as earl?' Eliot was reeling.

'*My* place, Eliot.' Cedric's smooth voice sounded less feeble. 'In law.'

'But if they chose to dispute it...!' said Charles.

'The agreement is that they will not.'

'In order to live here? It seems ridiculous.' Eliot looked at Cedric, 'You believe they will not fight you, and so you keep them near to ensure it? I do not remember that you have the compassion to keep a poor family, even if they have some claim on you. Nor with your own want of economy, the funds.'

'I know they *look* it, but it seems that the other Marchmont family are not at all poor. The Scottish woman has already paid the servants wages for last year, and now she will pay our debts. But *only* if we present them before breakfast.' Charles sighed, 'but God knows what we will do about Dorian's!'

'She has indicated,' said Cedric with distaste, 'that her lawyer has already visited Dorian for that purpose.'

'But Dorian's bills must be—!' ejaculated Eliot. His brother was the foremost rake and gambler in town.

'Indeed!' sighed Cedric.

Eliot thought of Mrs Marchmont saying that the roof must be put to rights, and began to understand her quiet authority. 'And what of *Richard* Marchmont? Has he no ambitions to be Earl? His family evidently has the money to challenge your position in the courts.'

'He *claims* he does not want it,' said Cedric, simply. 'But his mama ... of that I am *not* so sure! She tells me that she may ask that Richard be appointed my heir, since I have no issue.'

'Precious little chance of that now.' Charles said, carelessly. 'But that *would* blight my hopes.'

The earl shot Charles a look of fatigue but made no remark about the hopes based on his demise, and by a brother only five years his junior, and said, 'Now that you know, Eliot, you should take yourself off. Pleasant to see you again, of course.' He waved a dismissive hand.

Eliot began to leave, but Charles moved more swiftly than his bulk usually permitted and took his arm, he said in a low voice, 'No need for the ladies to know, of course.' He frowned. 'But if Her Ladyship don't shut her mouth at meals, she will provoke the Scottish woman to tell her.' He patted Eliot on the back. 'Don't worry that you'll see much of them. Breakfast and dinner is all. The Scottish woman insists on the *children* being there, too. Isn't it *appalling*? But they absent themselves afterwards and they have their own wing, so we seldom see them.'

'The west wing must be *foul*!' protested Eliot.

'I hear the Scottish woman had it put to rights,' said Charles disinterestedly. 'Quiet voice, but it carries weight, I've heard.'

'Stop calling her *the Scottish woman*,' ordered Eliot, 'or *I* shall begin to refer to her in public as *the Dowager Countess*.'

He opened the door while Charles was saying, in a panic, 'I say, Eliot, you can't let the household hear that!'

Godwin was in the hall, and Eliot wondered, not for the first time, whether he had a listening cup to place over doors secreted in his coattails. He rather hoped he *had* in this case, perhaps it would stop him from disobeying Mrs Marchmont's orders. It looked like she had earned his obedience, whatever his brother might think.

What an appalling situation. He wondered what brought the family here. *Were* they uninterested in the succession, or did they have another purpose? Mrs Marchmont was putting all to rights, it seemed. But why pay his family's debts? That, as he knew, was an everlasting pit. There must be another motive.

He went to bed, disgruntled because his haven had been invaded by another nation, and because he did not understand the situation. This last was the more annoying — he liked to understand.

The next morning, before breakfast, when Mrs Marchmont's lawyers were to receive his brother's bills, he was to find out a little more. Because when retrieving a favourite volume of Donne from the shelves, he saw a glimpse of red behind it. He had to remove four more books to get to it — a Morocco leather covered journal impressed by a gilt NM.

Eliot settled himself behind his desk, and when he looked at the first entry, without any sense of shame, he found some partial answers to his present questions, as well as much amusement. After a paragraph, that put a half-smile on his face, he leaned back on his chair and put his feet on his desk, ready to be entertained.

CHAPTER 2

The Purloined Journal

It is fortuitous that I have had to begin a new journal, for the world I now inhabit bears no relation to our other life. I feel pity for the inhabitants of Tremaine Towers who have had to take us in. Had they extended a warmer welcome my pity would have been a tad more sincere, but as it is, I strive for compassion. I only wish, for my mother's sake, that Cedric Marchmont, great Earl of Tremaine, would do the same.

The Earl is elegant, effete, with long white hands and an even longer white face. His drooping eyelids seem heaven sent to look down on the world, and he heartily obliges. He did not rise as the seven wild beings were shown into his presence, but merely raised his head a little, shuddered, and looked back at his book.

'I do not see why it is my business to house you all,' he said in such a tone as Berthe used to whine in when she was three years old, 'why on earth can you not house yourselves?'

My mother stiffened and stirred, but he did not move me. We older siblings all knew why it was his business. Perhaps he said so believing Mama would have told us naught, and that we would feel oppressed, but he was wrong.

'Godwin will show you to your - ah - accommodation.' A hand raised like a languid king's, and he waved us away.

Before the door closed on us, Berthe said in the loud carrying voice of a child, 'Who was that peculiar gentleman, Mama?'

I looked over my shoulder and caught the earl's expression. It would be a future delight of mine, I thought, to put Berthe and Lord Tremaine in the same room as frequently as possible.

Eliot, reading this, gave a sudden bark of laughter at the wickedness. He read on.

After his description of our quarters, I expected us to be housed, dormitory fashion, in a barn, perhaps. But we were merely taken to a wing of the house obviously not much used. Ideal, I thought, but Mama had other feelings. In her quiet voice she said to the superior butler, who was prepared to look down his nose as much as his master, 'I see that the corridors here have neither been swept nor dusted.'

The butler was shaken. Mama's regard was steady. He had been taken in by our somewhat shabby appearance. He was now being challenged by a lady about the state of the grand house that he was responsible for. While it was the housekeeper's remit to see to these duties, the man was still humiliated. A slight change in his colour denoted this.

'This wing has been unused for years, madam,' he said coolly, but even reluctantly an apology sounded in his tone, 'I believe that the bed-chambers have been well attended to.'

He led the way, and it was, for the most part, true. Certainly a duster had been passed across surfaces, and there was fresh linen on the beds. Mama's room was particularly handsome, with a huge bed dominating the space.

'It was once the second countess' chamber, Mrs Marchmont, in the days when this wing was the house alone.'

'I see.' She turned and smiled at Godwin suddenly. Mama's smiles have felled dukes in her day, and Godwin, though his face stayed immobile, was not immune.

'Goodnight ma'am. I shall mention the other matter to the housekeeper. The prepared apartments for your family are those with open doors.' He bowed and left us and we all, with a great sigh, set out about destroying the order of mama's coverlet by throwing ourselves onto it in a pile. Richard, who nowadays strives to exhibit maturity, had to be pulled down by Berthe and Tabitha both.

Our play was interrupted some time later by the entrance of a housekeeper by the name of Mrs Peters. She was tiny, with a respectable mob cap, the face below wearing a sour look. She tried to come the higher hand, but mama quietly reminded her of her duty and told her that she expected cleanliness and order by the time she came back from dinner. Mama's quiet voice worked wonders. Its sheer certainty and its call to guilt (if one deserved it) worked better that my cattish remarks might have.

That night at dinner, warned to mind my tongue, I consoled myself with saying those cattish remarks only inwardly.

The company in the drawing room before dinner was elegant indeed. All the members of the other family, it seemed, were very fashionable, and I must admit that entering on this glittering array, I blinked. The word that occurred to me about the fashionable ladies' dress was dribbling. It appeared that London fashion required the dresses to dribble on the ground at the back, like tiny trains. Each glittering dame dribbled across the floor as she walked, very upright even in their own home. Their hair was carefully arranged and bejeweled, and the eldest lady also wore an ostrich feather, dyed to match her gown.

I regarded the carpet. Perhaps the ladies' fashions were thus designed to help relieve the maids of their duties, since the three Marchmont ladies swept the floor for them as they walked in a stately fashion around the room. If the ceilings were lower, that ostrich feather might have dusted the candelabra while they were about it. I wondered if their walking clothes dribbled similarly, or their pelisses? I suddenly wished to see them on muddy paths.

We had tidied ourselves at Mama's request, but we were dull, dull indeed, by comparison.

Berthe said it for us all. 'Aren't they all shiny, mama?'

A stifled laugh came from one of the Marchmonts, and I turned my eyes, prepared to like him, but I saw that it was a sarcastic laugh only. He had his hair in a tall pompadour, and though in elegant black evening attire, wore rings on his fingers, a great ruby on his cravat, and fobs that clinked on his waistcoat. (He was just the sort of man who, if born sixty years ago, would have worn a mile-high wig and covered his lead-white face with patch.) If this was his country dinner attire, I could hardly wait to see him in a ballroom — for where else could he add adornment? I imagined a tiara on his startling coiffure and laughed inwardly.

In the general introduction I found he was Charles Marchmont, whom his sister, the elegant, light-haired Ophelia, introduced as the 'Crown Prince'. She called her eldest brother, the handsome effete who had greeted us, 'King' and her youngest brother Dorian (who was not present)'Princling'. None of her family seemed amused by this. It was her sister, a lady who was even stiffer than the others, with elaborately tended ringlets at her brow, tight like her anxious face, whom she called Queenie. She had a middle brother (also from home) whom she referred to as The Black Sheep. I wondered how much more dreadful than these people he could possibly be. She did not look at me, but I quite liked her, only for her humorous descriptions.

There was a Lady Tremaine, too, the Countess. No special name was attached to her, making her seem like the outsider, in Ophelia's world at least. Lady Tremaine had never been a beauty, I fear, but she might have appeared better if her pride had not required her to look down from afar. She had fair hair and grey eyes, nose a little large and lips surrounded by tiny lines, which was the result, I envisioned, of pursing them too often. Not all her silken adornment or elegant surroundings made her content, it seemed. Her husband (the King) bore the attitude of terminal boredom each time his wife spoke, and once interrupted her conversation with her brother-in-law by saying, 'Must you, My Turtle Dove?' The tone was bitter, the endearment dripping with sarcasm. The countess flushed, and I felt sorry briefly, until I saw that her way of coping with being despised by the husband she appeared to admire, was to despise others around her.

'It pains me to mention it, it really does, Mrs Marchmont,' said that lady in a haughty voice, 'but I heard that today you directed my servants.' I underline this latter phrase as her voice had underlined it in speaking to Mama. She smiled in the manner of her husband, 'Pray, in the interests of domestic and family harmony,' she added significantly, looking down her long nose, 'do not.' She preened. 'It is already a great deal too difficult to house you ... though,' she smiled slightly, 'you are, of course, welcome here.'

'She says it is difficult to have us, Mama. Should we go home now?' asked Berthe, bringing the talk around the table to a halt.

'I do not know, Berthe, should we?' said Mama calmly.

I thought I should help this along, for the earl and his brother were looking suddenly chilled.

'Why do you wish to go home, dear one?' I asked my little sister, disingenuously.

'The shiny people seem cross, Naomi, and not happy that we are here.'

'Children should be seen and not heard!' intoned Lady Tremaine, awfully.

'Why do the younger ones have to eat with us at all?' complained the bouffant Crown Prince, holding a napkin to his nose as though some stink came with us. (The general tone of all of that family's voices requires underlining, I find.)

'My children,' said my mother's quiet, assured voice, 'always eat with me.'

'Always!' said Berthe, strongly.

'Shut the child up, for goodness sake,' uttered Bouffant.

'How rude!' said Berthe's wonderfully clear voice. 'Mama, did you not say it is rude to say, "shut up"?'

'I did, my dear,' Mama agreed firmly. Charles looked wrathfully.

'It is also rude to tell the rude how rude they are,' I said in an explanatory tone to Berthe, 'and useless too, for they are generally too silly to understand you.'

Mama gave me an admonitory but resigned look at this. My sisters emitted repressed giggles as one, even the shy Tabitha. I had said as much for their sake. Not all of them are accustomed to this kind of disdain. Some are more sensitive. Berthe is, of course, impregnable.

My eyes met the consternation of Charles, the Crown Prince, and I smiled. He did not know that

I saved him from wrath worse than mine. If he had succeeded in rousing Phoebe...! We had come prepared to be on our best behaviour, but not to be provoked. All other Royals at the table eyed me unpleasantly, and only my brother and mother continued to eat unaffected. My mother, I suspect, because she had expected as much; my brother Richard because he gave not a whit for anyone's opinion.

Silence reigned.

'<u>You</u> are not bad looking, though your coat is atrocious.' I nudged Richard, who had not been much interested in these proceedings, to let him know he was addressed. Charles Marchmont continued, 'If we give you a new touch, you should not disgrace us in Town.'

Richard's eyes swept over the bouffant hair, the round face and fleshy lips, the high shirt points that were currently digging into the meat of CP's cheeks and the profusion of fobs on Charles' waistcoat, and scoffed audibly, returning to his meal.

'Not <u>one</u> of you,' said Lady Tremaine venomously, 'show the <u>least</u> bit of gratitude to be invited, I find it extremely vulgar.'

My mother looked at the Earl who seemed not quite so comfortable as he wished to appear. 'Then you should discuss things with your husband, countess.'

'If I have asked you <u>once</u> to be quiet at dinner, My Cherished One, I have asked you a <u>hundred</u> times,' said the earl to his wife in that whining voice, but with an extra bit of meaning, I thought. 'You know the par-<u>tic</u>-ular tone of your voice is painful to my ears. As a consequence, I now have a sick headache.'

All of my family were shocked by this, for we had never heard a husband address his wife so in public, and we looked askance at the countess, whose face was flushed, but immobile. But if it stopped her being rude to Mama...!

'You do not look sick. You look—' we all held our breath as Berthe sought a word, 'cross and ugly.'

I had to swallow my hiccough.

'I am sorry, my lord,' said Roseanna, my sweetest sister, anxiously. 'We tell Berthe she looks ugly when she is cross, and that stops her tantrums.' She laid a gentle hand on Berthe's head. 'She is a vain little thing, you see.'

My waspishness dearly wished to finish this with a more biting observation.

'I think, ladies, that you should leave the table now,' this sickly-sweet tone of the head of the house was a disguised threat, and Richard raised a brow at him. It didn't do to rile Richard — even if he was slow to anger, he could be deadly, like my papa before him.

'If you do not care to dine with us in future,' the earl's voice was getting fainter, 'I should be happy to see that another salon is equipped with a dining table.'

'That will not be necessary,' said my mama, in that quiet voice that brooked no argument, 'we shall all become accustomed to each other soon.'

Their eyes met for a moment. It seemed to me that Mama won.

'I very much doubt it,' sighed his lordship, as though from his deathbed.

Eliot put the journal down, then returned it exactly where it had been hidden, and laughed. That searing pen had seen off the earl, countess and Charles. That she liked Ophelia showed even more discernment. Though Ophelia was often frivolous, he liked his sister, too. He was anxious to read what the diarist thought of the others, and of himself, of course.

NM. That must be *Naomi* Marchmont, the one who had sat behind his desk, whose shapely back had been to him on the floor, her leg a pillow for her brother's head. Dark Brown untidy hair, slender (but with those shapely hips) and large eyes was all he recalled. Hair cut around the face, wavy but unkempt. But at least she put it up, unlike some of her sisters. Phoebe and Stephanie, wasn't it? Only Roseanna and Naomi wore it up, albeit that Roseanna's was respectably neat, while the other sister's was careless.

At breakfast the next day Eliot told the other Marchmonts that if they wished to find or replace books, he would not be in the library during the day, but only after dinner. Mrs Marchmont said happily that would do, their sitting room was *being seen to* at this very moment, and they could very well take their books there in the evening.

'*Your sitting room?*' cried the Countess, much put out. She was a mean, vain woman, and Eliot had no time for her histrionics. He felt for her under Cedric's tongue sometimes, but she turned it back on others, just as the journal noted.

He looked at the half-smile on Naomi Marchmont's face. The earl put his hand on his wife's arm. 'I have already said that Mrs Marchmont may do as she will with the west wing, Light of My Life. Did you forget?'

Of course, thought Eliot, the lawyer will not yet have paid the no-doubt exorbitant bills.

'I was merely inquiring, my lord,' replied her ladyship, flushed. 'I do not even know what is occurring in my own house. I feel all household decisions ...!' her husband's gaze was cold. 'Of course, my lord. If *you* ordered it so...'

'Yes, Mine Own, but may we *not* have household management over breakfast?' He waved a weary hand. 'Too, too, vexatious.'

'Perhaps it might be easier for all concerned if you consider the Towers *your* home, your ladyship,' said Mrs Marchmont, in her cool voice, 'and the west wing *mine*.'

'I *beg* your pardon?' for once Eliot did not blame his sister-in-law Agatha for her shock. He did not approve of Mrs Marchmont's assumption of authority on this point.

'Only because we shall likely come to bandy words daily. I have a great deal to do there, and I am sure you, too, have much to occupy you, countess. Too much to bear with all the arrangements that must be made to suit my family. The men shall see about the roof next week, I believe.'

The flush on Agatha's cheek turned purple. '*You expect the earl to squander...!*'

'Not at all,' said Mrs Marchmont calmly.

'Then you have *funds*?' said Ophelia, suddenly agog.

'Indeed.' The lady said.

'Then why,' said Eliot's sister Queenie, almost without her volition, 'do you *dress* so?'

Phoebe, the dark haired Marchmont with the long curls she did not put up, and the very definite, dark, but somehow attractive, eyebrows, said casually, regarding Eliot's elaborately dressed and coiffed sister, 'That is what *I* wanted to ask *you*. Why do *you* dress so?'

'Phoebe!' remonstrated Mrs Marchmont.

'I should not have said so if *she* had not, Mama,' said Phoebe, unrepentant, 'but I did *wonder*...'

Berthe said, in her bell-like tones, 'But Phoebe, remember that Mama told us *we* should not be rude even if the shiny people are.'

Eliot put his napkin to his mouth. Assuredly breakfast would be more interesting these days.

Mrs Marchmont rolled her eyes at this and said to her hosts, 'My girls, beyond Roseanna, are not much interested in clothes, and we have lived rather simply in Scotland.'

'But your neighbours must think you *impoverished*!' said Lady Tremaine.

'I do not believe so,' said Mrs Marchmont, smiling faintly.

Ophelia looked narrowly. 'How *large* is your house in Scotland, compared to the Towers?'

'Oh, not *quite* so large. I expect the Castle might have a few fewer rooms, though I have not made a count.'

'It was Mama's home, you know, as a child,' said the sweet voice of Roseanna, though apologetically.

'Your father was ...' pursued Ophelia, hot on a trail.

'Oh, the Duke of Clashmore. The title became defunct, unfortunately, after his death. Some Scottish titles can continue on the female line, which I consider an excellent thing, but not ours, as it happens.' As she said this, Mrs Marchmont was engaged in stopping Berthe's sleeve go into the butter as she reached for a roll.

'Then you are *Lady* ...' Charles was saying, aghast.

Eliot was enjoying this. He exchanged a look with his sister Ophelia, who obviously was, too.

'*Lady* Eleanor, if you must,' the Scottish lady said lightly.

'Then you inherited the wealth of the Scottish estate...' said his sister-in-law, breathing heavily.

'Well, *estates*, you know,' corrected Lady Eleanor in her quiet Scottish voice, 'And not all are in Scotland.' This was not a boast, but only that she was evidently a female who valued precision in speech.

'But that is not all,' said Phoebe, obviously relishing, like Eliot and Ophelia, the established family's discomfort. '*Papa* left us very wealthy too.'

'But your papa did not inherit...!' protested Charles.

The dark-haired brother Richard, usually silent, spoke at this, 'Something he professed himself glad about, since he said it would have made him lazy.' One side of his mouth lifted and he seemed to be reliving his father's presence.

'Oh, but Papa was an inventor, you know. He made machines,' said Tabitha, the twelve-year-old. She had been quiet, almost withdrawn, but at this she showed some animation. Only because Eliot sat near her did he hear her next mumble, 'There is nothing here to play with at all.'

'I suppose,' said Lady Tremaine, overhearing this mutter, 'there may be some toys in the nursery.' Although her voice was unpleasant, Eliot was amazed she had ventured so much.

'She means *machines*. There are all sorts of mechanical parts dotted about the castle,' said Stephanie, the redhead. 'They don't interest me much.'

'Tabitha and Richard make things, too.' The diarist spoke at last, and Eliot looked at her again. There was a great deal of humour in her eye, but most of it, he suspected, was wicked. He hoped to read more of her wickedness tonight, if the journal remained in place.

'The point is, father made patented improvements to many machines used in textile production, for instance.' Richard said informatively.

'He always said he had the freedom to invent since he met a rich wife,' said Phoebe.

'He was a *wonderful* man!' breathed Lady Eleanor.

'I heard that he tinkered ... I hardly believe it!' protested Charles. One could always depend on Charles for expostulations.

'So,' said Cedric, with an air of great distaste, 'your husband was *in trade.*'

He said so as though the deceased patriarch had sinned against decent society. What did Cedric think his stocks and shares were, if not trades? It was a distinction made by the gentry that Eliot had never understood. It was as well the earl knew nothing of Eliot's own movements recently, he thought.

'At any rate,' Lady Eleanor was saying, sipping some chocolate, 'if I live here, I shall set the west wing to rights, beginning with the roof. My family need not live with a leaky roof. So, since the cost does not fall on the estate, there is no need for us to discuss each matter that arises in that regard, is there, countess?'

'Why do you smile, Miss Marchmont?' Naomi Marchmont inquired of Ophelia, arching a brow.

'Why do *you*, Miss Marchmont?' demanded Ophelia, arching her brow in return.

Before Eliot could find out the result of this battle, the Scottish voice began again. 'That brings me to another point. I shall give the earl and countess their titles, of course, but it seems to me there are a deal too many Mr and Misses Marchmonts. Why do we not all, as we are family, dispense with formality and call each other by name?'

'Certainly!' intoned the earl faintly, 'but there are so *many* of you that it may make some *years* until I remember you all.'

Lady Eleanor eyed him, 'Strive to do so more quickly, my lord.'

As usual that pleasant tone had something else in it and Eliot was not surprised to see his brother avoid her eye as he drawled, 'Certainly, dear lady!'

'Crown Prince,' said the awful child in her clear tone, 'pass me the rhubarb preserve.'

Charles sat back, defeated.

CHAPTER 3

Barclay Arrives

The spine of the journal was at a different angle, good! Eliot took it from its place behind Donne's poetry, and read, putting his feet on the brass guardrail as Richard Marchmont had that first evening, having to lay back at an angle in his chair to do so.

Another of the Royal Marchmonts arrived last evening and was astonished at our reading habits. I suppose we look more like a pack of hounds than the gently bred descendants of a Scottish Duke and an English Earl. But it was cold in the library, even with the fire. Despite our Scottish blood, we are all "cold rife" as they say in the Highlands. Thus like a pack of hounds we lay, all atop each other, a sight poor Mr Eliot Marchmont has never before witnessed, I imagine.

Are the Royal Marchmonts even permitted to <u>touch</u> *one another? I fear it would impinge on their dignity so much that they might combust, like darling Papa's failed air-blast engine.*

Mr Eliot looked, despite his curse on entering the room, different from his brothers. He was neither insufferably languid, like the King, nor a trussed up popinjay, like the Crown Prince. After his shock, he looked a little surly, to be sure — we appear to have stolen his retreat. I quite see that one needs a place of respite from such a family, so I was almost sympathetic. His hair is wavy like mine, but somewhat lighter. It is thicker even than Richard's dark thatch and is brushed back from his head rather carelessly. But the height his brothers painstakingly concoct on their own hair is given to him by nature (though not as high as the ridiculous dandy's). His face is rather more like Richard's too, in that it is handsome, chiselled from fine marble by the ancients, almost.

Eliot paused. He stood and looked at himself in a mirror. Handsome? He? Chiselled by ancients? He worked his square jaw from side to side, stunned. He sat back down to see what else she might say.

His brows are low over green eyes. His face looks stern, but I cannot help wonder how his brows might look raised in animation, whether that fine, but rather sulky mouth might look better with a smile. At any rate, another difference from the faces of his brothers is that there is no discernible affectation on his. He is a man and not a fribble, at least, as Richard later remarked to me.

We have agreed to leave his sanctuary to him in the evening. Phoebe protested later, but I was heartily in agreement with Mama. We like each other very well, us wild things, but we are too rich a feast to foist on the more prosaic Mr Eliot Marchmont. I enjoy foisting us on the other "Royals" for the purposes of observing their diverting disgust, but the casually dressed Mr Eliot does not yet seem to deserve our becoming an irritant.

As I read this back, I see that I have written a great deal on the subject. Might I be forgiving his stiff politeness too easily because of his overwhelmingly handsome face? Am I such a low female as to be moved by that, and therefore forgive discourtesy and dullness? I hope not. Perhaps in future I shall dip my pen in red ink while I peel away the layers of Mr Eliot Marchmont.

Eliot considered "overwhelmingly handsome" with "discourtesy and dullness". He thought of himself as neither handsome, discourteous nor dull. The last rankled. He could have an acid tongue when riled, but he had not yet been discourteous to *the wild things*. Like Naomi, he was biding his time to see if acerbity was required. Did he thus appear spiritless and dull? He looked back at the journal. There was only half a page more.

It was a diverting breakfast, with the "Royals" shocked by our wealth, and Papa being "in trade". Papa never mentioned this himself, except to his dearest friends — but what was a genius like papa to do with his inventions? He had to see them made, of course, and patented (a very difficult business) and thus he profited when companies sought to license from him, almost by accident. Mr Gavin McLeod was his lawyer friend, and Uncle Gavin undertook all the business of selling, as well as all of the pa-

perwork. Papa said he, too, was a genius, but in the field of business and the law. Now Uncle Gavin still sells and licenses Papa's machines, some of which are not yet overtaken in design. And he oversees the lawyers who look after the estates for Mama.

Eventually Papa, too, enjoyed business I believe, and was good at it. He was no fool, and those who sought to cheat him, thinking him pampered member of the Quality, fancily dressed, found out differently.

I think, too, that Mama's wealth was a factor in Papa's acceptance of "trade" — vulgar as he, as a gentleman, had been brought up to believe it to be. But Papa was not a man happy to live off a rich woman.

Queenie made the mistake of criticising Phoebe's dress. Actually, I acquit her of being cruel. She said it without thought. But when one pokes the bear it thrusts its claws at you, and so it was. Phoebe remarked on Queenie's dress, too, and the poor woman was humiliated. She is not, like her sister and brothers, a confident person. I instantly felt sorry for her.

She is quite a plain lady, for all her adornment. That she *bore the name Queenie, when by rights the King's wife (the countess) might have been thought to do so, had me surprised. But the amusing Ophelia did not give her sister-in-law any other epithet, and generally ignored her. Queenie is, I think, rather older than any of us. So she ought, as these things go, to be married. She wears the finest French muslin, and silk in the evenings, and all her dresses are over-trimmed and elaborate, in colours that do not complement her, so that it seems to exaggerate her plainness. Her hair, too, has so many tightly controlled ringlets surrounding her face, so many braids with entwined ribbons, so many silver roses or bows that it makes one's head spin. The face beneath the dark hair is long, with a tightly held, prim mouth. Her maid has shaved her eyebrows which must have been thick and dark, (for we can see the shadow of them still above her rather pretty, but spiritless, eyes) and drawn thinner brows in somehow. Her complexion is dark, rather like Phoebe's, but someone has tried to lighten it with powder, then add colour to it again with rouge. But the whole is a failure of artifice, and I wish I could see her unadorned.*

As this pitiful, insecure person was trembling beneath my sister's tongue, I suddenly recognised that actually, she resembled Phoebe. If her brows were on her face they would be the same definite shape (I would hazard, seeing their shadow), they both had that angular face and jaw, those fine eyes. Queenie's lips are thinner and tighter, her nose a little longer, but it is the artifice that separates them, I think. Phoebe is a wild beauty. Queenie is a trapped, painted, unhappy, bird.

Eliot frowned, seeing his sister anew in his mind's eye. She was twenty-five now, and had been pressured by Cedric (before the succession) to find an advantageous match. There had been someone in her first Season, he remembered, whom she had not been permitted to marry, and she had cried a great deal. She had been eighteen and Eliot had been twenty-four. He had been sorry for her without knowing the details, for they had never been close, and he had clumsily tried to comfort her. But he accepted Cedric's dictate that she had fallen for an ineligible man without perhaps investigating as he should. Afterwards, his sister-in-law and his brother Charles had taken charge of making her look like a *lady of consequence*, to throw her into her next Season improved in elegance. The results of which had been Cedric saying in that dreadful drawl, *"Better, but one cannot, it seems, make a silk purse from a sow's ear."*

It was cruel, but it was his little sister Ophelia, then only thirteen years, who rescued her. 'Well,' she said, 'I think she looks like a queen.' And so, ever after, Charles had ironically called her Queenie, and since her true name was so dreadful — Clytemnestra — it had stuck. She answered to it readily. Charles' satire on her sister had caused Ophelia to satirise the rest of the family in revenge, for even in her youth she had more spirit that her sister.

But now Eliot thought, the journal having brought poor Queenie to the forefront of his attention. All of his family were overdressed, besides Ophelia, who looked the part of a Greek goddess and was permitted to pursue this simplicity, since it was, after all, fashionable. But he saw Queenie now in his mind's eyes, always anxious, undefended against the tongues of the others, dressed up like an expensive doll in clothes that did not become her and made her uncomfortable. Worst still, she would not fight it, and her own opinion would remain unasked for.

Eliot was not a powerless child anymore, he should do something for her. But then, he was often from home and she would be left with the rest of them when he was gone. Could he recruit Ophelia to the cause? Perhaps, but although Ophelia's wit gave her some protection, she, too, was powerless against her elder brothers. She might laugh at them, but she was still at their disposal, and she knew it. He frowned, and eventually returned to the last part of the entry.

There was not much else notable over breakfast, except the general discomfiture of the Royals that we are not in fact, poor relations, but instead, wealthy ones. One would think this would be a cause for celebration since we would not batten on the earl — but this is to be disingenuous, I know very well why they dislike it. Mama has been uncowed by them since the first, and now they think they know why. Actually, with Mama's character it is unlikely she would be cowed in any case, whether wealthy or not. She is a remarkable woman.

So too is Phoebe, a force to be reckoned with. Do I hope the Royals continue to poke the bear, simply for my own entertainment? Phoebe does not attack, but claws back instantly. She brooks no insult. She worries about no consequences. She does not fear blood and bone. They have no idea as yet.

I can control my tongue, though I do not always choose to. I can write away my annoyances within these pages. I can laugh at the absurdities of arrogance and vanity in my head. But Phoebe cannot. Phoebe lashes out instinctively, without thought, leaving the blood to splatter where it may.

Mama has a plan in being here. It includes a London Season for Roseanna, Phoebe and me. This is dangerous ground for Phoebe, I feel. I suppose the two Royal sisters will be there too. Perhaps Mama hoped we might learn how to act in London from the Royals but in my opinion, and probably hers now too, it is only how *not* *to act that we might learn here. Best take our cues from the only true lady in the house, my mama.*

Mama has other plans. I do not know what they are, I only know that they are for the best.

Eliot admired Lady Eleanor Marchmont more than many of his own family, at least what he had seen of her. However, he was a trifle anxious about her *plans.* If she decided to claim the earldom for her son, and was successful, then things may be bad indeed for his sisters and brothers. Cedric had already mortgaged Marchmont Hall (his family's original estate) to the hilt, to subsidise his follies, and the estate itself had gone to wrack and ruin. Having gained his place in society as earl, he had begun to *spend* once more, having his family dress finely as befitting their positions as residents of Tremaine, and funding his own excesses elsewhere. Debts had accrued, and though Eliot had no direct knowledge of it, he feared that money for the upkeep of Tremaine Towers was diverted elsewhere. Without the Towers estate, if Lady Eleanor decided to fight for her son's rights, his family might lose all they had.

No doubt the care of his sisters might fall to him, at the very least. This he would not resent, but there would no doubt be emergency needs for his brothers' relief at times, to save the family reputation. He ground his teeth at the thought. Eliot had an annuity from his father, as did Charles and Dorian, while of course Cedric had inherited the Marchmont estate. His brothers had simply refused to live within their means. The girls were left very small dowries only, and nothing at all to live on. Eliot had also been left his grand-mama's money, which turned out to be equal to his annuity. But the girls could not live as they did now if Eliot were to be responsible for them. He could not give himself the expense of a Season. Without Tremaine House in London, it would be too ruinously dear. He could dress them, but not to *London* standards. Marchmont would now pay little, due to Cedric's poor management, so Eliot and the girls could expect nothing of him. Since the Marchmont estate had been neglected, Cedric would also be pursued by debtors soon enough, if he were no longer to be the earl. As it was now, even the most rabid of debtors could be appeased to wait to quarter-day payments from the earl's substantial estate.

It had occurred to Eliot now that ruin might happen anyway. Cedric's idea of consequence, his profligacy, required a larger fortune than even the earldom possessed to support it. Something Eliot had understood was that the entail on Tremaine Towers had protected it from mortgage. Cedric could not use the Towers to garner money, or he would have by now.

But as a result of the journal entry and his cogitations, there was one matter he might address.

Eliot spoke to Ophelia. 'Is there not something to be done about Queenie's dress?'

'Have you just noticed, dear Black Sheep?' said his sister cynically. 'Dreadful isn't it? All chosen by Charles and Agatha, who think themselves adepts, but are plainly *inept* instead.'

'Can you not help her?'

'Ah, you approve my taste, dear brother!' Ophelia said in the same sarcastic tone, then sighed. 'I tried. Charles and Agatha considered me impertinent. Queenie is ever pleasant to me, but on the subject of dress and hair she will not listen. She says that I have no idea what lengths one must go to when one is *not* pretty. It takes her maid two hours and a half to do her hair in the morning, but since my curls are natural, she knows it is minutes only for mine. She threw my beauty in my face. She is not *envious* of me, she is not so ill-natured, but she thinks me disqualified to comment by being naturally pretty. Therefore she listens to Agatha and Charles who are, she thinks, making the best of what they have.'

'*Charles* is? She's delusional.'

'So said I, but she says that he covers his corpulence with his tailor's skill, and enhances his thin locks by hair products and careful *coiffure*.' Ophelia looked at him, 'But why, all of a sudden, does this concern you?'

Eliot would not mention the journal — though he believed Ophelia would enjoy it — for it was his own purloined delight. 'Two things,' said Eliot, 'First, after not seeing you all for so long, I noticed that Queenie seems much more unhappy than I remember her. And second, it occurred to me that she bears a strong resemblance to Miss Phoebe Marchmont, whom I would account as a beauty. Not a usual, sweet beauty, like her sister Roseanna, but a beauty nonetheless. And if Queenie resembles her, why is she not accounted *pretty* at least? In her first Season, I remember her as quite presentable.'

'Quite presentable! Do not *gush*, brother dear, I pray. And how would you describe me?'

'Also presentable.'

'I'm overwhelmed.'

'Anyway, if Queenie were dressed more naturally, I think she would look better and be happier.'

'The shaved brows!' Ophelia said, considering it. 'Perhaps I *might* order her maid to desist, and get Queenie to agree, seeing that those definite brows looks so well on Phoebe.' She looked at Eliot closely. 'This is the first time you have remarked on a woman's appearance to me. And it is about the dully dressed Marchmonts. Two of them.' She arched a brow, 'Which of them has stolen your heart, my deadly dull brother?'

'Neither. A hell-cat or a compliant, do I look like someone who would admire either?' He frowned. 'And I am *not* dull! You are the second person to tell me so in two days.'

'What? Has the dreadfully honest child struck at you, too? She does not seem to admire us *shiny people* overmuch. I confess I like her.' She smiled at him, 'And you *are* dull, Eliot. For you do not go to gaming houses, or keep mistresses—' he called her name as reprimand. 'And you do not bankrupt yourself at the tailor's or keep ten carriages, or run up debts, or flirt, or—'

'Yes, yes, The Black Sheep indeed.'

'If I had your independence,' she said more quietly, 'I should behave too, I think, for it makes one anxious to know that all this,' she gestured to the grandeur around her, 'could collapse at any time.' She then put on her usual rebellious smile and said, 'But for now there is nothing more to do than buy frivolities and flirt a great deal.'

'Dorian once said something similar to me. Cedric has been a bad example.' He grinned at her, 'and lest you be too disappointed in my lack of family vices, my dear Ophelia, let me tell you that I have just made the greatest wager of my life.'

'Brother!' cried Ophelia, grasping his sleeve with comical outrage, 'How *could* you?'

He was amused to see she disapproved, his frivolous sister. 'Don't worry,' he told her, 'I only wagered *half* my fortune.'

Ophelia gasped, then threw her head back and laughed in shock.

'Still think me dull?' he inquired.

Her eyebrows raised, 'That rankled, I see. Oh, my very careful, dull brother...' and she laughed again, and he joined her, and they were discovered like this by Charles.

'Don't laugh! Have you *seen* them?' Charles sounded unfeasibly disapproving, 'They are *running in the gardens*!'

Eliot and Ophelia looked to see the formal beds (a geometric pattern of low box hedges surrounding flowers with gravel paths separating) and a crowd of the dully dressed Marchmonts running between in some sort of pattern. Eliot and siblings looked on from the window, amazed.

The other Marchmonts were carrying a variety of thin branch sticks each, each about three feet long, from which strips of tattered fabric flew. They appeared to be sticking them in, perhaps as markers, when they passed certain points, and now the formal gardens were adrift with twigs and flags, giving it an unkempt air. As they watched, the only male figure, Richard Marchmont, was removing flags from one decorative bed, and a shout went up from the piercing voice of Berthe Marchmont, who charged at her brother to grasp at the flags. Her cries brought the other sisters, and also (Eliot realised with a gasp) the dignified Lady Eleanor, all running to Richard who was holding aloft the twigs from Berthe's jumping grasp. Soon he was surrounded by a throng of females, and laughing as they cried foul at him in words the window viewers could not hear.

Eliot was amused to see Phoebe Marchmont climb onto her sister Naomi's back to reach, and the other females held onto the struggling Richard as the tippling twosome grasped the sticks from his hands — quiet Tabitha having had the insight to tickle him under his arms, loosening his grip. The unstable Naomi finally toppled, and Phoebe fell to the ground too, running off with the twigs onto the central path, not seeing the carriage coming towards her, or hearing because of her family's din. All three watchers from the window held their breath, but the phaeton was halted at an angle, the horses jumping in their traces in protest, one horse's head in the bushes that bordered the carriage path.

The driver jumped down as the groom took their heads and ran forward to the fallen girl.

'Barclay! You have shown your skill this day,' said Charles Marchmont to Sir Osbert Barclay, the handsome driver of the sporting carriage that had narrowly failed to kill Phoebe. He was a member of Charles' set in Town, but more because he was also a country neighbour from their days at Marchmont Hall, Eliot felt, than any real closeness of taste. Someone they had all met infrequently over the years. He was not such a dandy as Charles, but he was fashionable: he had a sportsman's build, artfully windswept hair, a strong jaw and humorous dark eyes.

'Yes *indeed*, sir!' gushed Queenie.

He bowed at this, and as all the Royals had gathered in the green room to greet him, he smiled generally. The wild ones had sought entrance, too, but had been refused by Lady Tremaine, the countess adjuring the girls to make themselves presentable before greeting guests.

Phoebe Marchmont growled, but the voice of her mama stopped her. 'Yes girls, it would not do to meet Phoebe's saviour in our dirt. The muslins, please!'

The girls had gone up stairs and Richard had stopped Barclay before he entered the salon on Charles' arm. 'Sir! We have not been introduced, but I thank you on behalf of my sister.'

Barclay had stopped and bowed, saying, 'Not at all! It put my skills to use, at least. I have only previously needed to use them in absurd bets, you know!' he smiled charmingly, and Eliot had seen Phoebe Marchmont pause on the stairs and look over her shoulder, before picking up her skirts and running towards the west wing.

When the girls came down in a few minutes, the children, Tabitha and Berthe, were missing, and Eliot wondered why briefly. It would, of course, be usual in most families, to keep the children from visitors, but the other Marchmonts generally disobeyed this custom. He was disappointed to deprive the visitor, who was basking in the admiration of the room, of the benefit of Berthe's remarks, but then perhaps, Eliot thought of himself, he was a little sour for some reason.

But before Eliot had this thought, he had been amazed what five minutes could do to affect change. The simple muslins worn by Roseanna, Phoebe, Naomi and Stephanie, plus the silk worn by Lady Eleanor, were all in darker shades of violet, with black ribbons. He saw it dawn on all his family that the dull dresses they had seen before were, in fact, as displayed by these more delicate versions, half-mourning. These dresses were not in the first fashion, being decent in the number of petticoats and having necklines protected by translucent, gathered shifts below, several inches above the bodices — giving them the look of Renaissance paintings Eliot had seen abroad. Rather Italianate in style, he felt. Neither Stephanie nor Phoebe had gone so far as to put up their hair, but they had at least removed the grass and leaves to be found there earlier, and Phoebe wore a purple ribbon band which hardly kept her turbulent curls in check. Of all the Wilds, these two most resembled Medici women, but all the Wild girls looked, he thought, a little strange and other-worldly, but still charming.

The Countess affected the introductions colourlessly, and Barclay was casually charming to them all. Lady Eleanor gave him her hand and thanked him on behalf of her daughter. Eliot grew bored, and watched out the window as the remaining disfiguring flags were being removed by footmen from around the decorative flower beds, as Cedric had ordered that *ugliness* to be gone from his view.

'Oh,' said Naomi Marchmont as though to herself, 'Now we shall never know who won!' She was evidently looking over Eliot's shoulder.

'It was *I!* Richard cheated,' said Phoebe with certainty.

'You were playing an amusing game, ladies—' said Barclay, smiling.

'We were, it is a racing game, and because we all start at intervals, giving the children some advantage on us, and making up for Richard's long legs by keeping him back, we must prove we have passed the alloted points by laying out markers,' Stephanie informed him.

'In *my* garden. And such *ugly* markers,' complained Lady Marchmont. 'Why not use ribbons?'

'I doubt we have so many ribbons among us!' laughed Naomi. Her tone suggested an absurdity and was therefore bordering on insult to the countess.

'We shall keep such ugliness away from the *front* of the house in future, countess,' said Lady Eleanor.

The countess' sour face indicated that she did not like the tone of this concession.

'You make a prolonged stay, Charles informs me, Lady Eleanor,' said Barclay pleasantly.

'Perhaps,' said Lady Eleanor, in that gentle Scottish burr. The slight accent might sound a trifle provincial to London ears, but Eliot saw that her bearing and air impressed Barclay.

'Shall you stay longer this time, Sir Osbert?' asked Queenie, rather ardently.

Eliot frowned. Obviously, his sister was *very* impressed by Barclay, but that gentleman's polite response was a bland, 'T*wo days only*,' and he did not keep her eye.

CHAPTER 4

Richard Snaps

The journal described the event of the race with verve, underlining Richard's perfidy in theft most amusingly. Stephanie, she reported, would surely pay him back soon. Stephanie, it seemed, did not like to lose at any game. Eliot sipped his warm wine, given to him by Godwin because a maid had heard him cough and had then reported it to Cook below stairs. Cook had come with them from Marchmont, and had known Eliot as a boy, and thus he sipped the wine that had been warmed by a hot iron and by the servant's affection. He stretched out, anticipating the world view of the wicked diarist as he continued reading.

The carriage was almost upon Phoebe before we noticed. It was only a continual scream from Tabitha that alerted us, for after the fall we were punishing Richard, who was using his superior height and strength in the most despicable way, picking us up one and another, using first Roseanna's body to shield him from our buffeting assaults, her legs dangling in the air, and then when she had escaped, he lifted me — but Stephanie had jumped upon his back, and we were winning. Then the terrible noise from Tabitha, who had, in her mind I think, already pictured Phoebe beneath the wheels of the oncoming carriage. But the driver stood and pulled the horses around (in a way that might have ruined their mouths, I fear) and stopped them some feet in front of Phoebe's prone form. He had jumped down before we all could move, and Phoebe was some distance from us by this time, having run off with the markers from my brother's hands. Richard's back was to the path, and hearing the cry, he turned with Stephanie still on his back — but seeing Phoebe untouched, he ran to Tabitha, holding her gently, stifling her sobs.

I held Berthe's hand, and we watched as the hero, running to the fallen maiden, was confronted not by a female shaking and sobbing in distress, but by the laughing, unfettered thing that is Phoebe, rolling on her back in glee.

'Madam,' he said, surprised but amused, 'might I help you rise?'

Phoebe grasped his outstretched hand and rose energetically, but instead of thanking him, she turned and held the twigs aloft. 'I win!' she called back to us, and we all ran forward as one, laughing our alarm away by arguing with her.

Mama, recovering first, gave a bow of her head to the gentleman in gratitude, and said, 'Shall we meet at the house, sir? Then we might be properly introduced.'

With a gesture she herded us back through the beds, as he, smiling, turned to the carriage and got back in, straightening up to drive to the stables.

Berthe said to me, 'That gentleman is shiny, too!'

I could not quite follow her logic, since the gentleman had been wearing a dark driving coat and buckskins, and even supporting a Belcher tie rather than an elaborate cravat, so I raised my brows in query. She looked up, saying 'Boots!'

Ah, she was quite right, his white topped riding boots shone indeed. Mama instructed us to shiny up ourselves (in more Mama-like words) and we went willingly enough. The hero deserved our neatness, at least.

Tabitha was still clinging to Richard, and upstairs he suggested to Mama that he stayed with the littler ones, since he had already said his thank you to the baronet in the hall. Berthe was disposed to come with us, but Tabitha's distress intrigued her, and she stayed to help Richard be absurd with her sister, drawing her out again. We all knew what had made Tabitha, of us all, so anxious, so we left Richard to his charge.

I could look at the scene in the green salon with some attention. First, we saw the Royals all agog at our dress. Roseanna looked particularly pretty in the palest violet, with darker sprigs of green, and it was evident that Stephanie was fast blooming into a young lady too, though she would hate the thought. Mama had chosen a purple that prettily displayed her hair, the dark red curls and her pale, freckled skin. I wore the plain violet I had chosen, rather darker than Roseanna's, and Phoebe's was a rich pansy coloured fabric that Mama had chosen well. Her hair was still to her waist, she refused the formality of even a coil — but it was true that many experiments with pins had failed to keep those wild dark curls in check: she infected them with her rebelliousness, and they frequently fell out all around her. She looked at Barclay with interest, I thought, but she was not particularly grateful, somehow. Her interest stemmed not from the general appreciation and attention being given him (by Queenie, the CP, the countess and to a lazier extent, the King), but simply because he was a fine figure of a man, with laughing eyes.

Ophelia's eye lacked admiration, I noted, and she looked a little bored. Her gaze crossed mine for an indifferent moment, but I had seen something else there as she regarded the baronet. Of all the Marchmonts, her reservation about him made mine.

As I said, Sir Osbert is obviously a sportsman, and to add to that, he is tall. His manner is superior to my taste than most of the Royals, in that it is more relaxed. He appears to be self-denigrating, but I am not so sure. Behind his charming face, there is something a trifle self-satisfied, but then his looks were minimised by standing too close to the Black Sheep. The baronet's face does not send one to look for a sculptor, as does Eliot Marchmont's. His figure, too, though imposing, is inferior. Close observation shows that Eliot Marchmont's shoulders are an inch broader at least. The baronet's riding dress is from a fine tailor, and the hair beneath that beaver he had been wearing while driving had turned out to be carefully tended — so that the Black Sheep's beauty, in a less sharp coat and a carelessly knotted cravat, looked effortless and infinitely superior by comparison.

Eliot stood again, to look at himself in the mirror over the mantle. His *beauty*? He should stop reading the paragraphs that mentioned his name, he was becoming self-conscious. He had felt, as he had looked at Naomi Marchmont's slender form in the dark violet dress, that he had blushed — a thing he had never done previously, even in his youth. He was glad she had not observed it. He would have been afraid at how she might interpret it. He was beginning to feel an intimacy with Naomi Marchmont that *she* could not possibly share. It was built on knowing her feelings, albeit retrospectively, and the ability to anticipate her views on things. He had caught himself trying to catch her eye, as he might Ophelia's, at some absurdity of Charles'. She did not see it, fortunately. She had no idea he had any fellow feeling, or guessed her views. He ought, he really ought, to feel guilty for reading her private thoughts. But her family's invasion of the library had made him vengeful in the first instance, and later it had seemed that her wickedness did not deserve (or invite) his discretion.

He felt, however, that her opinions on him, or his form at least, were something he ought not to know — she would certainly prefer to keep such things to herself. He understood, from her general demeanour, that even if she admired a man's looks she would give little away. She had professed no interest in Barclay in public, though she evidently did admire his looks to an extent.

Eliot had seen more of a gleam in *Phoebe's* eye when she regarded the baronet, but the gleam there turned cynical as he asked after her injuries (perhaps hoping to be thanked again), and she had laughed him off. There was something of their mother in all the Marchmont ladies, something not easily impressed.

He read on, a little afraid of more praise, which he might have regarded as flattery, except that the words were never meant to be openly expressed. Somehow, that they were her true thoughts was more frightening.

Or is my preference for a stern, unsmiling face (that calls out for a marble replica) instead of a mobile, charming visage, some sort of bizarre obsession?

The Black Sheep looked at me for a second. There was no telling his feelings or thoughts. Did he despise my dress, or approve? It is nowhere as fine as his sisters', but better than our more comfortable wear. I must ask myself, why should I care for his opinion? Not because of his handsomeness, or because he is the only male Marchmont who intrigues me, but because, unlike his siblings' faces, where distaste and disapproval are not disguised, he alone is a mystery.

Eliot smiled. Thank goodness he had not given his stolen knowledge away. He must strive to be even more distant in Naomi's company.

He laughed again at the shiny boots. It amazed him that there were those of his friends who seemed to avoid splashes on their fashionable riding boots. Mud seemed to stick to his own boots the *moment* he was on a horse or driving his curricle. He suspected Naomi would prefer the splashes to the shine. He shook himself. He did not suspect Miss Naomi Marchmont of having a *tendre* for him. She was not so foolish. But this appreciation of him as a work of art (and he doubted her taste in that regard) rather than as a human being, was not pleasant. He was still, he supposed, a man of *"stiff politeness, discourtesy and dullness"* to her.

No, he would not mistake her interest as anything more than inquisitiveness on her part, or her aesthetic appreciation as anything more than a lack of exposure to the superior attraction of other gentlemen, caused by her limited acquaintance. She had not, after all, had a Season.

That evening it seemed that Barclay, who had been pressed to stay for some nights, had another appointment. Eliot had heard about the cockfight in a village two miles hence, and presumed Barclay had come less on a visit to Charles than to place bets on the illegal event. Charles and Cedric, both gamesters, were too squeamish to attend such places, Charles bemoaning his one visit to a cockpit where as well as witnessing the gruesome spectacle, he had had his purse filched by a professional.

Thus, it was only the Wilds and the Royals who were to share the dinner table.

The two families saw each other only at breakfast (which was generally a short affair) and dinner, meeting briefly in the salon beforehand. There was little talk across family lines, beyond greetings. All the young ladies sat, but the dark-haired child wandered around, restless. Eliot watched as the countess, obviously concerned for her Sèrves, called, '*Do not touch!*' frequently across the room, as exploring little fingers headed for a porcelain figurine. He looked to see how the Wild family took this, but the mother seemed merely amused. Richard had entered, warmed himself at the fire, then taken a seat on a sofa between his mother and Tabitha, draping his arm carelessly over the young girl's shoulders.

Ophelia, who Eliot came to sit by as usual, glanced over at this intimacy that had seldom been offered *her*, then looked away, murmuring 'How quaint!' but with some sarcasm.

However, Eliot had already noted that being with his *Royal* family seemed like a form of torture to the little girl, who seemed, outside her family, to be shy and retiring. He wondered if her mama noticed, and if so, why she put her through the unnecessary pain of these dinners. But he believed she *did* notice, and that she was, perhaps, trying this enforced intimacy with his family as a practice for Tabitha going forth in the world beyond the wild ones. He must remember to make some casual, undemanding remarks to the child.

The King, as Eliot now called Cedric in his head (following Ophelia's invention and Naomi's amusement) was ignoring all, slouched (regally) in a chair, gazing at the pages of a book. The only remarks that crossed the divide were a disinterested and distant remark from

Lady Tremaine about the great number of workmen employed on the roof of the west wing. To which was replied an equally uninterested 'Yes!' from the mama. In tricks of great ladies, Lady Eleanor was even more proficient. But Eliot knew from talking to the workmen on his walk today, that the workers had been required to note any obvious deficiencies in the *whole* roof and do emergency repairs there too. It made him wonder more about her plans but looking tonight at Lady Eleanor's ever-neat appearance in half mourning, not a hair out of place in her simple coil, he felt that she might simply be tidying up.

Berthe, the terrible child, said to the earl, in that carrying tone, 'You must be the *slowest* reader in the world. You *never* turn a page.'

Eliot found Ophelia's lips were twitching, for they both knew that Cedric held a book before him to prevent intercourse with anyone he did not choose.

Cedric touched his forehead as though in pain. 'Do not approach me, child.' He said. It was a faint tone, but it held some threat, which the child ignored.

'But you *don't...*'

'*Really!*' exclaimed Lady Tremaine. 'Restrain your child, Lady Eleanor.'

It was Phoebe who said, 'Berthe, come here darling!' and talked to her quietly.

Eliot said in a lowered tone, to Ophelia, who had been declaring herself bored and longing for town, 'Why do you not speak to the other family's females? They are around your age.' It was said idly, but he was interested in her response.

'We have *age* in common, but no *interests,*' said Ophelia. 'I did ask Phoebe Marchmont what she had done all day yesterday and she said, *Oh, we just went out and played, you know!*' Ophelia looked arch, 'Can you *imagine*? I don't suppose I have ever *played* in my life.'

It was true, Eliot thought. He had been eleven years her senior and often from the house. He had imagined that she must play in the nursery, if at all. Clytemnestra, or Ness as they called her before she had become Queenie, was four years older than Ophelia (a lifetime in child years), and merely took her for a walk occasionally. Was it jealousy that made Ophelia hold back from the other family, or a real sense of superiority, like Charles and Cedric?

'I don't see *you* engaging them in conversation, either,' his sister remarked.

'Ah,' said Eliot, 'but there is a *particular* reason for my unfriendly reserve.'

'See?' said the voice of the terrible child, who seemed to have sneaked up to the side of Cedric's chair and now looked over his shoulder. Her finger pointed to the book, her face close to his. 'You were at page a hundred and thirty-two ten minutes ago.'

Eliot saw Cedric give a faint twitch, then raise his hand negligently. The back of his palm connected to Berthe's chest, and he pushed her from him so that she took a step back. Eliot did not see Richard move, but in half a second Berthe's brother had grabbed the seated Cedric by the cravat and pulled him forward until their noses were inches apart. The earl paled in shock, but his face was otherwise immobile.

'You *touched* her?' Richard Marchmont growled.

His mother cried, '*Richard!*' but now Charles, with a weather eye on Richard's vicious expression, was attempting to tear him off, by grabbing at an arm and pulling, 'Here! *I say!*' he protested. Richard's arm stayed at the earl's throat, eyes locked.

Lady Tremaine screamed, the servants froze, and Eliot walked forward, putting a hand on Richard's shoulder. 'Marchmont ... Richard! Do not! He meant no harm.'

If only Cedric would apologise, he might be released. Richard Marchmont's body was tense for violence, Cedric, whose throat was constricted, squawked 'Godwin!' and the butler looked to the footmen. This was an escalation not to be wished for.

It was Berthe who saved the day, 'Richard!' she called to her brother, 'Richie-Rich! He was just *playing*, *look*!'

Both Richard and Eliot looked down. Cedric's free hand had been a claw on the arm of his chair, but somehow the child had prised it off and now held it between both of hers and waved his arm, playfully smiling.

Richard let his hold go, and stood. '*Never* lay hands on my sisters again.'

Cedric did not meet his eye, but took his hand gently from Berthe's, to adjust his neckcloth.

'He will not,' said Eliot for him. The other Marchmont girls sat back down as Richard strode from the room.

'Violence! I cannot have *violence* in my own rooms!' said Lady Tremaine.

The laugh that greeted this was cut off and might have come from Phoebe or from Stephanie, he was not sure which.

'Indeed, you are correct,' said the calm voice of Richard's mother. 'But you have seen yourself that my son is of the *words will never hurt me* opinion. He has ignored all the insulting remarks made to his sisters over this time and has only intervened when he saw a hand laid on Berthe. I do not agree with his reaction, but Richard is moved by the *sticks and stones* phrase in the proverb too. He is peaceful, but protective of his sisters.' She turned to Cedric. 'My son may have been crude in behaviour, but I do not disagree with his sentiment. By all means, reprimand where you see fit, my lord, but laying a hand on my children is not something you have a right to do.'

Cedric stood. He had fully recovered his urbanity, and he said to Godwin as he left the room, 'Tell the kitchen that dinner must be delayed a half hour. My cravat is quite destroyed...'

'But I'm *hungry*!' objected Berthe, unaffected, it seemed, by the recent drama.

The earl did not look around. His wife went to follow, but was gestured away.

'Well,' said Ophelia. 'This was the most entertaining evening I have ever spent at Tremaine.'

'How dreadful!' said Queenie, faintly. 'I hope there will be no such incidents again.'

Phoebe Marchmont laughed. 'Oh, I don't think there will be. Everyone has received Richard's warning, have they not?'

'As ever,' said Eliot's sister-in-law, voice dripping with outrage and disgust, 'no *shame* seems *possible* from your family, and no apologies from you, ma'am. I suppose a *Duke's* daughter is not accustomed to apologise!'

Lady Eleanor appeared to think about it, 'I suppose not!' she concluded.

Ophelia laughed shortly.

Roseanna, the polite and gentle sister said, 'It is just that Richard loves the younger children so. I expect your brothers were like that too, Queenie, when you were little.'

There was really nothing to say to that, thought Eliot, a trifle sadly. There had been no such thing for the child Clytemnestra, or for her sister Ophelia. He, Charles, Dorian and Cedric had never been protective in the least. He supposed that if he had seen a sister assaulted, he might have made a push to stop it, but for the slight move such as Cedric had made on Berthe, he would have made no efforts. The child was not at all hurt. Queenie blushed consciously. There was a silence.

Charles murmured, 'I have never been so *shocked* ... and to put back *dinner*...!' in a complaining tone.

'Never mind,' said Naomi Marchmont in her quiet, lilting voice, 'I expect your shock will be superseded soon and that tonight will serve to accustom you.' Charles fairly growled at her, but she continued reassuringly, 'But I shall have a word with Richard and command him to delay any assault he wishes to make until sometime *after* dinner in future.'

'Enough now, Naomi!' said her mother. 'As dinner is to be late, I shall take you, Berthe, to have a word in an adjoining salon.'

'Can I come?' asked Tabitha in a barely audible voice.

'Very well,' said their mother, and held her hands out so that all three moved out together.

CHAPTER 5

Interesting Encounters

Eliot had to wait a whole day to read Naomi's thoughts on the incident, and he sat down with brandy at his elbow and prepared to enjoy. If she hadn't been such a diligent journalist, he would have been disappointed dreadfully. She described the incident in the drawing room, obviously missing the moment her brother had moved as he had, but only describing the wastage of Cedric's neck cloth.

The Royals were shocked, as we all were — but for our side it was for just an instant. Richard is slow to anger but completely protective. It has been almost a mania for him since Papa died. As Mama said, he does not care about words, he hardly hears them. He cares not at all for the world's opinion, and he assumes the same of us, I think, though that is not universally true. Some of the sharp words do reach us at times. But as we are female, he will let no one touch us in anger. It was a light push that the great earl delivered to a child, but it was full of contempt. Richard understood this and could not support it.

Earlier in the evening Richard and Eliot Marchmont had stood before the fire, facing away from each other. Richard gazed towards the window while warming his coattails, Eliot conversed with his seated sister, Queenie. They looked like they would make a handsome pair of marble book ends, both with chiselled jaws and cheeks, and full heads of hair that would render well in stone. But Eliot Marchmont has the energy, however reserved he is, of a man who is noticeable, present. Sometimes my darker brother seems to be absent to any except the children. He withdraws into himself in company, while however little EM may speak, he is an alive, powerful presence to all.

But when Richard's hands were at the King's throat, they all knew suddenly that my brother was a man of power, too. I, personally, was thrilled. The large bulk of the CP intervened and tried to move him, but the Black Sheep was more sensible. He sought his attention with a hand on Richard's shoulder. It might be warning, but it was comfort, too. However, it was Berthe who managed our brother, by taking the earl's hand and playing with it. Our beloved child is a genius sometimes.

In the general complaints afterwards my Mama mentioned insults, and I could see the recognition in the eyes of most Royals. She was telling them she had noticed but ignored. That she had not acted but might. All of them realised, though the women are not sure how, that Mama has a hold on the King. It is frustrating for Berthe's "shiny people", who wish to crush us with their disdain.

This entry was less amusing, but it was informative. Eliot regarded the bust of Aristotle on the mantle. She spoke of him as marble once again. Did she even note that he was human? But then he read the last paragraph.

I worry a little for Roseanna and for Tabitha. Unkind words and actions affect them more than the rest of us. Even I do not like it when EM's eyes cross mine as though I am not there. I see his mouth twitch with his sister Ophelia, in their whispered conversations, and I know at least he has some humour, though it may be only sarcasm. I still long to see him smile. Richard's infrequent smile changes his whole face, and I suspect EM's would too. But I shall never see it, I fear.

When had he last truly smiled? Eliot was shocked to know he could not remember.

How to approach her, to reassure her there was no dislike at all, without divulging his knowledge? For it hurt him, those lines, *as though I am not there...* He was aware of her, he realised, even when she was not in the same room. To be so distant was becoming a lie, but he needed to keep reading, it was to him a daily solace in this place. So, he could not let her guess.

The next morning, he implemented his plan, although somewhat by accident, and in a way that almost made everything go wrong. He had followed the wild ones into the hall after breakfast and heard the mother bid Richard goodbye with an admonition not to go to a hotel where he might meet ruffians, but instead to *Grillons* in Albemarle Street, where he should, at least, be safe.

'A fashionable hotel? Not I, Mama. I would feel out of place.'

'Do not make me worry, my dear.'

The other Marchmonts stood in a clump in the hall, and Tabitha took one of Richard's arms. 'Do not worry Mama, brother.'

He looked down, and as ever when he looked at his two youngest sisters, his face softened. 'I won't. But Mama, you know I have travelled the country and never come to any harm.'

'With Papa ...!' said Naomi, then obviously wished she had not.

But Richard said blandly, 'Not always! I have been sent out on my own many a time while we were away. And I have frequently travelled to Edinburgh, and if you think there are no ruffians in Edinburgh...!'

Roseanna, looking at her mama, whose face was still calm, but pale, said, 'Hush Richard, or you will not be permitted to go to Edinburgh either!'

Eliot moved forward to them and said, 'Forgive me for overhearing, but if you visit Town, Richard, you might want to stay at *The Black Duke* in the city.'

Charles had eventually left the breakfast table and now entered the hall saying, '*The Black Duke*? How can you say so? It full of a bunch of cits.'

'Really?' said Richard, looking over at Charles impudently, 'That sounds more interesting than a bunch of dandies.'

'It welcomes businessmen, certainly,' said Eliot in a calming voice, 'Manufacturers and engineers may take rooms there. It should cater to your interests,' he turned to Lady Eleanor, 'and is very respectable, I assure you.'

'Thank you, Mr Marchmont,' said Lady Eleanor, simply.

'Yes, thank you, Marchmont,' said Richard.

'I thought we had decided to be less formal, Lady Eleanor, my name is Eliot!'

He saw Naomi Marchmont smile from the side of his eye, but her sister Phoebe frowned, and Roseanna was looking over her shoulder again at Charles.

'Why do you look cross?' said Berthe to his brother Charles, who looked down at her, annoyed.

'Never you mind.' His gazed moved to Eliot, now visibly among the wild ones, and said, complaining, '*I* have to make them *fashionable* for the coming Season! How can I do that if you put M— *Richard* in the way of meeting a lot of cits?'

'I'm going for a walk,' said Eliot, ignoring his brother. 'Have a good stay in town, Richard,'

Richard Marchmont nodded.

Eliot strolled out, feeling eyes at his back.

It seemed that some of the females were staying behind to watch their brother go off in the postchaise that Godwin had had summoned. That left Eliot sitting on the bench surrounded by an informal hedge, where he had decided to wait for, and then follow the family, to seem to come upon them by chance later.

When they appeared, he moved behind the hedge. Only Phoebe and their mother were missing, and the others headed off down a path to the river, at first at a walk, then with some apparent teasing, it became a chasing race. Roseanna, Tabitha and Stephanie held sketching bags, Naomi a book, and Berthe nothing at all. Berthe ran through his sister-in-law's flower beds in a way that made Naomi catch at her. She had watched her feet, however, and didn't seem to have done much damage. But Naomi, who found it hard to control Berthe's squirming, called for help and Roseanna laughingly obliged, the two older sisters lifting her bodily and depositing her on the grass, with looks that were teasing threats. Stephanie had disappeared, but he heard her laugh and saw that she sat above on a tree branch, kicking her legs and jeering at Berthe's predicament. As they released the captive, the redhead jumped down without warning, from far too high, Eliot considered. It must have been a normal occurrence, for it provoked no particular reaction in the sisters, except Roseanna adjuring the wild Celtic princess to let down the skirts she had kilted up to climb.

Eliot followed them on, amazed. Never had he indulged in this kind of horseplay with his siblings, or with anyone else. He had done a little drunken carousing in his extreme youth, to see what his brothers liked about it, but even with Dorian's aid, he had felt it empty very soon.

Tabitha took up a position beneath a tree and took out her sketching block, and so did Roseanna — she commenced a pastoral river scene, looking at the view. Stephanie climbed a tree again with consummate ease. He had once climbed that tree himself to rescue the young scamp Dorian and had finished by falling off with his brother on his back, breaking his own leg in the fall. The memory made him catch a breath, but he saw that Stephanie was more monkey than human, and she settled herself on a branch near the top, her sketching bag abandoned at the foot of the tree where her sisters sat. Stephanie was bonneted, a simple straw with a very large brim in front. The child invariably wore it outdoors, her Mama's protection for pale skin, he thought. Berthe dawdled around on the river's edge, gazing in as Eliot had done as a boy, picking up sticks and generally poking around.

Naomi chose the largest oak, some way back from the river, and took out her book, soon engrossed. Her feet were outstretched and crossed at the ankles, her old velvet pelisse falling apart to reveal the navy cambric below. She took off her bonnet, as did the other sisters except the redhead, and sat with no more protection from the late spring sunshine than the leaves from the trees. The females of his own family would be bonneted and parasol-ed against the awful effects of the sun on the complexion, and neither would they stretch out beneath trees, legs crossed and relaxed. He was coming nearer to Naomi's tree, wondering what casual remark he could make to greet her.

She was bent over the book, but seemed to hear him before he had a chance to speak, and not looking up, she held out an arm, making questing movements in his direction with her hands, 'Oh come and look, do! It is so amusing.'

He took her hand in a daze, and she pulled him down, leaning her shoulder towards his, pushing the book in front of him. He glanced at it, but could not focus at all, for to get nearer she had moved her arm, bent at the elbow, on his back, her hand cupping his shoulder, reading, '*Rectitude is our only recourse, Benjamin, for I may never marry you in this life time!'* She had spoken it with ironic drama and turned to him to share the amusement. He moved his head to her's at the same time, still in shock, and found their noses were only two inches apart. '*Eliot Marchmont!*' she breathed, shocked, then she pulled away abruptly, so that he had to reach out and grasp her arm to save her from falling in the opposite direction.

'It is I!' he agreed with an attempt to sound laconic.

'I thought it was *Richard*,' her husky voice said, distracted, '... but of course, he has *gone*...'

'*Yes...!*' said Eliot.

Her large eyes were locked on him in shock, and he said, amused, 'I do not think much of your taste in literature.'

'I love to read dreadfully written books sometimes, to encourage myself.' She was talking, he thought, automatically, still dazed. Though she had moved a little distance away, they were still sharing the trunk of the tree, shoulders close.

'Encourage yourself?' he queried, just to keep them talking somehow. He, too, was shaken, but he tried to appear nonchalant.

'Oh, if people will read *this* they may as well read *my* writings.'

'You write and seek publication? That is a trifle unusual.'

'Yes. For what is the point of writing so much and have few people read it?' He looked off, silently agreeing, thinking of the wit of her journal. She smiled. 'And I'm glad you did not add *for a young lady*.'

'I *thought* it,' he admitted wickedly, 'but did not say it.'

'Ah!' she said in the same tone, 'you disappoint me.'

'You should rather be disappointed with the *World*. It is evident that ladies have had some success in the literary field, but hardly in the number of men—' She glared at him, and he added quickly, 'because gentlemen publishers do not choose to so encourage them, I am persuaded.'

She sighed. 'Like *you*, you mean, *Eliot*?' It was evident that she was trying out his name in her mouth, rather rolling it about.

'Yes *Na-omi*, I am ever a discouragement to female ambition.'

She laughed. 'Because we should all be pursuing female accomplishments, like Roseanna.' She gestured to her sister who was concentrating on her drawing and had not seemed to register the distant presence of Eliot Marchmont. 'She dearly wishes to achieve the expected virtues, but has no talent, unfortunately.'

He looked over at the figure with the sketching block on her lap. 'Not necessarily — her shoulders are too stiff. She's trying too hard.'

'Is *that* it? I confess my own lack of artistic talent produces the same result. I am tense all day when I try to sketch, and the outcome is *shocking*.'

'You must be like your sister then. It is evident that her muscles are too tight, and that indicates *thinking* rather than seeing. *Thinking* never produces a good result with any form of art.'

'I take it you are an artist yourself?'

'I enjoy sketching at times, yes.' They were silent for a while that might become too conscious and awkward soon, so, still gazing at the tree with the two sisters beneath, he remarked as casually as he could, 'Do you worry about Stephanie falling?'

'There is no use in that. She does not respond to anyone's worry, and seldom comes to real harm.'

He looked up at the tree, where one of Stephanie's legs dangled from the high branch. 'Does she wear *buckskins* beneath her gown?' He heard himself sound shocked rather than sardonic and cursed himself beneath his breath.

She laughed, 'Yes, though you ought not to mention it. They are an old pair of Richard's and almost come to her ankle. Mama thought them a suitable solution to the scratches that Stephanie frequently has on her legs from climbing. Mama is having some pairs constructed in a thicker cotton now. Pretty, in case anyone should see them. In Scotland the buckskins were fine, but here...'

'Too many eyes, as well as judgement. Some might wonder that your mother does not just forbid climbing.'

'Like Phoebe, it is hard to forbid Stephanie anything. But Mama forbids her children very little, if they have facility for it, and it does not harm others.'

Eliot's eyes dropped to the foot of the tree again, glad that the awkwardness caused by their closeness was being relieved a little by this conversation. 'Your sister Tabitha draws too. But she never looks at her subject. Has she not received instruction? Does she still draw from inside her head?'

'Now that I look, I *do* see that Tabitha is more relaxed than Rosie,' then she turned her eyes to him briefly, sharing her amusement, 'No. Tabitha is not drawing what she *sees*, but what she *imagines*.'

'Still as a child, then?'

'No.' Naomi's lovely smile crossed her face for a moment, and inconsequentially, Eliot trembled. 'Tabitha draws gears.'

He made a sound of inquiry.

'There were machinery parts all over our castle home, and Tabitha loved them, even as a baby. She drew them all the time, as soon as she could pick up a pen, and Papa explained their use to her for hours on end. Richard, too. I think it was her special time with the men in the house.'

'And yours?' he wondered.

'Oh, I shared other things, but many. We shared books and writing and all of us know *something* about machines that will one day change the world — for that was Papa's pet enthusiasm and much talked of around the dinner table. But he was a gentleman too and was able to converse about books and art and music, or even bonnet trims, with ease. He was a warm and witty man, and we all miss him.' Her eyes had lit up talking of her father, and then was replaced with sadness that she hid by dropping her lids.

'I see that you still share your love of books with Richard, or I should not now be sitting here.'

She blushed again, adorably, Eliot thought. 'Why did you approach me, sir? Was there something—?'

'It was only to pass the time of day with you girls. I confess I find mealtimes a little fraught with tension between our families, and seeing you all before me walking, I thought to strike up a less strained conversation.'

'That was polite of you!' remarked Naomi, eyebrows raised.

'Your family rather fascinates me, as mine does you—' he remembered that he should not know this, and added as smoothly as he could, '...I imagine.'

'Yes, indeed. Our families are very different. I thought *you* may also disapprove of us.'

This was not quite true, Eliot knew. She had held out a little hope for him, as she had stated in the journal. She was looking for amplification. 'Why should I? I do not particularly approve of my *own* family, however.'

'How can you say so? I should defend *mine* in front of strangers to my death.'

'I am not a stranger — and you have already revealed your sister's lack of artistic talent to me, after all.'

'But I don't *disapprove* of it!' she cried.

'Mere sophistry! Because *I* may, for all you know. I might consider that all young ladies should have this attribute and then I would have disapproved of Roseanna, all because *you* betrayed her secret.'

'It is no *secret* once you look at her pages...' murmured Naomi, in a pet.

He smiled widely, perhaps wider than he might have if he had not read the words in her journal about wanting to see him smile, but it still felt natural, for he was amused. 'You are an unkind sister.' Her expression matched his and for a moment they remained so, until he turned away. 'But watching you all earlier was like watching a litter of puppies playing.'

He thought she would continue to castigate him for his choice of phrase, was looking forward to continuing to spar with her, as he did with Ophelia, but she said, turning her chin in line with her shoulder, '*Jealous?*'

This question shook him, because he saw it was true. He *had* been jealous of them — even while being amazed that first evening, as he had seen them atop each other. A family that wanted — and found it *easy* — to be this close to each other spoke of an intimacy he had never known. Her question was pert on the surface, but inquiring, nonetheless. He looked deep into those knowing blue eyes.

'Yes!' he breathed truthfully, making her blink.

They both looked away but remained seated for a minute in silence. He sighed at last. 'I had better take my stiff-rumped-self off, and let you get back to your book.' He got up and brushed himself off with his hands.

She tried to look with insouciance, but she flushed a little, consciously. 'Very well, Eliot.'

'I'll take that path,' he said with a gesture behind him, 'so as not to disturb the other puppies.'

He moved off, thinking with relish that she might make him pay for that remark later. They had begun a connection, and so there *would be* a later.

It had been too quickly intimate, too physically close, not casual enough. But since she had smiled twice, and since she now knew he did *not* disapprove of her, he did not regret it.

Eliot walked off, content, confused and slightly uncomfortable. As he headed along the riverbank, away from the two artists and Naomi, he thought of his aim for today — to begin to connect with Naomi so that *she* did not think that *he* thought ill of her — or that he was made of marble. He had achieved this, but rather too well. When she had pulled him down, he could have resisted, no — he could have failed to take her hand in the first place, but it had been such an imperious, demanding little hand that he had taken it and knocked himself off-kilter. The physical proximity had jumped their relations from early acquaintance to more. He was wondering about *what* more. It would not do to seem as though he were pursuing her and was almost sure he had not. They had sparred a little, as friends or even family might, that was all. If they could get over the consciousness of their closeness, things had gone perfectly, if a trifle quickly. And possibly their touch had little meaning for the girl whose whole family lay together like hounds. It was just that for *him* touch was rare, and he had felt it more. That was all it was. He thought back, believing he had hidden his reactions well.

He became aware of a couple ahead of him somewhat, by the riverbank. It was Phoebe Marchmont, and only a yard apart from her stood Sir Osbert Barclay.

It had been a happy coincidence that Barclay had gone out last night, away from the Towers. Eliot had heard this morning at breakfast that Barclay was to leave in the afternoon, to return to his home. Thus, the baronet had not witnessed the between-families altercation of last evening, and Charles, though the baronet's friend, would never stoop to tell him.

However, over breakfast, Barclay had paid a deal of attention to Phoebe Marchmont, but she had pretended to ignore it. Eliot had seen her watch Barclay, though, when he was talking to his sisters, charmingly teasing, as was his wont around young ladies.

Now the baronet stood laughing down at Phoebe, who did not smile in return. But even from this distance Eliot could see the rapt attention in her serious gaze. He almost wanted to shout out, to warn — but warn Barclay, not Phoebe Marchmont. She, with her old velvet cape and dull walking dress, her black curls almost to her waist, looked somehow more dangerous than the man who towered over her, in his immaculate boots, buckskins and fashionable coat. Barclay narrowed his eyes and stepped towards Miss Marchmont in a practised move, no doubt to give her the first feelings of proximity, something that would make a young lady shake, shudder and withdraw, all the time showing his power over her. No doubt, thought Eliot, he wished only to play with a pretty girl, like the practised flirt he was. It could be the start of something, or nothing at all. Eliot was poised to move, but loath to intervene without cause.

Phoebe Marchmont said something to the baronet that Eliot could not hear, and she did not move away, but at Barclay's answer, she stepped forward, held him with her gaze in a way that knocked the smile from Barclay's face. He reached forward to touch her cheek and, before Eliot could move to intervene, Phoebe's hand came over the baronet's and she turned her lips to kiss his palm, passionately.

The baronet staggered back. He looked down at her astonished, then reached out to grasp her shoulders.

'Phoebe!' called Eliot, moving forward, 'Naomi is looking for you,' he gestured behind him.

Phoebe turned to him, looking happy, but with some fire still burning in her eyes. 'Oh yes ... Eliot!' she too trying out his name, 'Good day, Sir Osbert!' she said over her shoulder. She walked, head held high, along the riverbank to find her sisters — one outstretched hand caressing the tall grasses at her side playfully as she wandered.

Eliot approached the baronet. 'What behaviour is this, Barclay, and with the family of your *friend*?'

'Hardly *close* family, I understand!' said Barclay laconically. 'Some sort of distant cousins you've had foisted on you, Charles said.' Ah, thought Eliot, Charles had cast the other Marchmonts as poor relations, by inference at least. 'And if you saw what happened a moment ago, Marchmont, you must also know that it was Miss Phoebe Marchmont who did the kissing.'

Eliot could not deny it, but said cynically, 'With the right encouragement, I'm sure.'

'Still,' laughed Barclay, 'I did not expect it.'

'No, you sought to flirt and give a young lady some hope of your affection, did you not? I repeat — *not with my family*, Barclay.'

'Oh, do not worry! I shall not tell this tale abroad and ruin Miss Phoebe Marchmont's reputation.'

'I have no such worry. For if you did, you would die.' He gave Barclay a derisory look. 'I am within an ace of calling you out now. Only the fact that Phoebe Marchmont shocked you off your feet is stopping me.'

Barclay's expression froze and he turned away, after bowing his head ironically at Eliot's unsmiling face.

It would be better for Phoebe if he did not pursue this, Eliot reflected. However, there might be a card game, or a carriage race soon where Eliot could arrange for the impecunious Barclay to lose some more money, at least.

CHAPTER 6

The Guilty Reader

Eliot had only just made it through dinner. His awareness of Naomi was extreme, and he wanted to find the journal immediately, to find out her thoughts about today. It was wicked, he began to feel, to impinge on her privacy this way, but he was as addicted to the words inside the red Morocco binding as some poor devils become to the Chinaman's pipe.

But at dinner he could now permit himself a slight smile, or a glance her way, when Charles said something ridiculous, perhaps, or the terrible child was amusing.

That evening's remark was to Charles, 'Crown Prince, you look less fat today ...' Charles looked alarmed to be addressed, and then relieved, for this was not Berthe's *worst* random exclamation — but he was nevertheless about to reprimand her when she added, '... but more *squished*!'

Since Ophelia knew that Charles' new patented corset had arrived just that morning, she gave a shout of laughter at this, then covered her mouth with a napkin — an insincere display of remorse.

'Do you encourage your child to say exactly what she wishes, madam, no matter how *rude*?' asked Charles to the calm Lady Eleanor.

'Oh, she needs no encouragement,' said Naomi before her mother could answer, and Eliot exchanged a mock-chiding glance with her. She flushed a little, and he felt the heaviness of his awareness again, trying to shrug it off.

The mother spoke reprovingly, 'Berthe, you are past the age of making personal remarks. Apologise!'

'*Am I*, Mama?' said Berthe with interest. '*When* did I pass that age? You did not say so on my birthday!'

Lady Eleanor looked across at Eliot's family, ranged on the other side of the table, and raised her brows ironically. 'Do you see? Even with *me* Berthe is frank to a fault.'

'To a *fault* is correct,' whined Charles. 'There is no point in *telling* a child like that. She needs to be *punished* to remember.'

'It is as well that my brother Richard does not hear that!' said Phoebe in a challenging tone. Charles gave her an unpleasant look in return.

'Shall my dinner table *ever* be peaceful again?' said the Earl in a drawling, but warning tone.

Roseanna tried to pour oil on the troubled waters, her gentle voice saying consolingly, 'Berthe does not *mean* to be rude, dear Charles. *Really!*' she smiled at him and added encouragingly, but deferentially, 'And if one is around her for a while, one begins to find her comments amusing — and sometimes *insightful.*'

'*Really?*' drawled Charles, offended.

'Really,' said Roseanna, her dark eyes wide open, meeting his candidly, but then realising the import of what she had said. Her face fell. 'But not in *this* case. You do not look squashed *at all*, but *very* elegant...'

Charles flushed, and then nodded, but only to stop a flood tide of worse back-handed compliments from the well-meaning, but inept, Roseanna.

But Roseanna, worried that he might still be offended added, '... and you only creak a *little* bit.'

Ophelia's elegant reserve broke entirely at this, going off in a paroxysm of giggles that made Charles and the countess look at her disgustedly. Roseanna was confused and apologetic at once.

Eliot had looked once more to Naomi, who was comforting Roseanna, while trying to keep herself falling into the state of Ophelia.

'You are *unwell*, Ophelia!' the countess informed her coldly, 'Go to your room!'

'Oh, I *will*, excuse me!' Eliot's sister managed, still holding a napkin to her mouth, taking herself off in a flurry of yellow muslin.

'I'll attend her!' said Queenie, for whom this whole interchange had caused tension and worry.

'Do not do so Clytemnestra!' said the countess, for Eliot believed she did not wish another loss to her ineffectual army, and therefore be outnumbered by the wild ones. 'She will be well presently.'

Queenie sat miserable, but Roseanna said, noticing, 'I have been meaning to ask you, Queenie, I mean Clytemnestra, what is the name of that trim on your gown — it is perfectly *lovely*.' As one, Eliot and Naomi regarded the trim. It was a pleated silk, he supposed, but overly pleated and too deep, and it stood out around Queenie's bosom (a place on his sister's body that needed no exaggeration) in a series of trumpet shapes, looking unwieldy. As one, he and Naomi looked back at each other, as though amazed. Naomi's smile broke through at him, brows raised, and Eliot almost reciprocated, but he had done much thinking. Friendly interchange and no more. He must be *careful* here.

'*Please* call me Queenie — everyone does, Roseanna, and I prefer it to my dreadful Christian name. I do not think the trim has a name, does it Charles? Just pleated silk you know.'

'I designed it *just* for you, my dear sister,' said Charles, smug.

'Charles is *so* kind,' smiled Queenie.

'Oh *yes*!' agreed Roseanna, 'and always so *elegant* himself!' Charles preened at this.

Naomi raised an eyebrow at Eliot. He had not seen that mobile brow before, and it amused him. His lips twitched despite himself, then he looked away. Their intimacy was such that he was now afraid. He must read the journal and discover her thoughts on the day. It would not do to encourage her interest beyond the normal — he was not such a cad as Barclay.

Charles had told them of Barclay's departure, and Eliot had seen Phoebe's surprise and confusion. It was evident that she had not known of his leaving, and that she was not happy. Perhaps she had truly been touched by the man. She had a passionate nature, that much he had seen, but it had looked, however shocking, like such a *natural* action that it had thrown all Barclay's practised routine into stark relief. She was true to herself, but Barclay was a false god, Eliot believed. And perhaps Phoebe, roused by his undoubted charm, was too inexperienced to notice his practised suavity. He was sorry for her.

If he were to describe the event to others, she would face criticism and derision, but he had *been* there. He had seen that Barclay's actions were deliberate, his smile winning, and the young lady's response. She had responded not to his *actions* probably, but to the words he spoke that Eliot had not been able to hear. Her behaviour was wild, it was true, it was outside the bounds of proper feminine reserve. Perhaps he should warn her mother — for if she were to be observed conducting herself like that again, she might pay a heavy price, and her sisters, also. But he had seen her fiery nature these days too. She was not stupid. Having been fooled once, he did not believe she would repeat it. So, Eliot would stay silent about today's event.

Phoebe looked unhappy, but also a little fierce. She was only a little more silent during the meal, and perhaps only he noticed her saddened state.

If he had not read the journal, perhaps he would have been appalled by her behaviour. But he *had* read the journal, and he understood her.

The journal was, to his relief, in its habitual position. He took the brandy bottle and sat down, seeing his hands tremble as he opened the pages. How ridiculous!

He began to read, and it was an account of Berthe at the dinner table, told with glee. Eliot looked down the page for his own name, disappointed. It was not there. He turned the page and noticed it at last. He wanted to read that part but chastised himself for his lack of restraint. He would wait. But he was annoyed. It seemed that the ranking of their remarkable encounter was lower in Naomi Marchmont's eyes than Berthe's nonsense, while to him it had suffused his day.

...as usual, Roseanna's attempts to diffuse the situation were kindly meant and badly achieved. But I will not laugh at my own sister. There was something wrong with Phoebe also, she seemed a little cast down at dinner, which I only noted due to her muted reaction to Berthe. Ophelia found it so absurd she was reduced to leaving the table. I find I like her. She does not care to know us more deeply, and she looks down on us a trifle, but she is more human than the other Royals.

But Roseanna's compliment to Queenie's ridiculous dress had consequences. The first one was that He sent me a look of amusement — how can his face remain stone still, and only his eyes smile? It was natural, I suppose, to exchange the glance. I had looked to him to share, too.

How was this accomplished in only a day? The cause, I suppose, of my careless mistake earlier in the gardens. But it made me tremble inside afterwards, because of its very naturalness.

Eliot looked up. He *was* in the entry earlier than he had thought. Designated with a "he", but with a capital letter. He was uncomfortable at this, even more uncomfortable than her admission of trembling after their gaze.

But so began the most ridiculous friendship in the world, Roseanna and Queenie. I had been wondering if any crossing of the Great Divide between the Royals and the Ruffians would occur, but I never thought it would be so futile. The ridiculous trim on Queenie's dress was admired by Roseanna. Had I been talking, to say so would have been stooping to sarcasm — but Roseanna has no taste at all and was quite sincere. In the withdrawing room, while we awaited the frightful gentlemen and Him, my sister and Queenie sat together talking. Phoebe eventually awoke from her low spirits enough to give a look at me in awe. Roseanna was gushingly asking for fashion hints from the worst dressed woman in the Towers, even including our own half-mourning.

That is a ridiculous expression, now that I write it down, for how could we half-mourn the best man in the world? But apparently my dull dress does it for me.

Charles caught on to the conversation when he arrived and showed a desire to take Roseanna under his wing, too, but Mama thanked him and told him it would not be necessary. 'No trouble at all,' he said portentously, 'we must spruce your girls up before the Season. Can't be seen with them like this!'

'I pray you not to concern yourself,' said Mama calmly.

'Charles is right, Lady Eleanor,' said the countess, stiffly. 'You do not know London. Edinburgh society cannot be compared! The girls' clothes must

be seen to, as must their manners, or the Family will be utterly shamed.'

'We shall strive not to stand anywhere close to you in public, my lady,' said Phoebe with sickly sweetness, 'I assure you that would be a relief for <u>*all*</u> *concerned.'*

'That is quite enough, Phoebe,' said Mama. 'But it is true countess, that you need not concern yourself with my family.'

I regarded Roseanna and Queenie, who were looking on, tense and uncomfortable, both. They exchanged a look of fear. What a ridiculous friendship! I had previously considered that all amity must be thought a good thing, but seeing them together, I understood that this was naive. My sister Roseanna is kind and beautiful, but has acquired, unlike the rest of us, a desire to fit in wherever she goes. I often wonder why her self-esteem is such that she wishes to be as others — but it is so. She was quite comfortable with us all on the library floor that evening when we first met Him, for example, but as soon as she sniffed disapproval, she instantly sought respectability. That is Roseanna. And now she wants to fit in by admiring Queenie Marchmont, of all absurd creatures...

Eliot bristled for his sister at this last phrase, but he could not, in fairness, dispute it.

...if she had admired Ophelia Marchmont, it may have been to some purpose. She might really have learned something from Ophelia's elegance, and been made a little braver perhaps, by association with her stronger nature, or perhaps taken some influence from her easy social manner — but no,

Roseanna chose Queenie. Queenie, with the dreadful fear of everyone, even larger than Roseanna's. Whose desire to please is just the same, whose taste is appalling, whose self-deception is enormous. It merely exacerbates Roseanna's own weakest traits.

For Queenie too, this is fatal. She now has someone who backs up her belief in the style that she has been forced into, I previously believed, by Charles and the countess. It may be comforting in the short term to have this approval, but it is like a sickness to be given more security to follow the wrong path. My own worst inclination is to find all this absurd, and thus enjoy it in my wicked heart, but I must not. I cannot see what is to be done. Roseanna will not offer Queenie an incitement to be brave, but only to be more fearful, in the long run. She will not offer her strength, or a way to stand against the infliction of ideas from stronger personalities (such as a friendship with my sister Phoebe might have given her) but Roseanna will instead only increase Queenie's compliance. It is not a friendship, but a comic tragedy for both.

Yet how is one to recommend the end of friendship to a dear sister? If Ophelia would talk to me, I might discuss it with her — but it seems to me that she has rather abandoned her sister to her fate.

He might talk to me, perhaps, but He may laugh at my concerns — which are, of course, insulting to his family. It would also be to expose dearest Roseanna. Mama is busy, but I think she noticed tonight. If she has, all is well. Mama is a marvel with knotty problems.

The business of Mama at present is putting the west wing to rights. She began to order the housekeeper, Mrs Peters, to do so, but she admitted to me that it was an imposition indeed. So she sent to an agency in London to find girls, and persuaded a canny maid to recommend more girls from the village.

She ordered us all to begin to clear the attics, for it kept the children amused. There were both treasures and rubbish in the attics, as well as a great many spiders, but we all of us, including mama, enjoyed the rummage. The treasures — very old clothes, a sword (which thankfully Berthe was not able to raise) old account books and papers wrapped in oilcloth, some damaged items such as a pretty music box and a painted, but chipped jewellery box, that excited Tabitha (because in need of repair) Mama stopped her from taking away a rather fine old chair, sadly broken, and told a footman to carry it off to get it fixed in the village. Frankly, I think Tabitha could have managed it. She was appeased by finding a load of crude mannequins and a discarded puppet theatre, which mama said she could rescue. Berthe began to sneeze and was sent off out for a walk with Stephanie, 'But don't fall in the lake!' adjured Mama.

The children have been everywhere of course. The kitchens (which we could tell by the powdered sugar around Berthe's mouth) the stables (which we could tell by the smell) but it is evident that Berthe has toured the entire residence, unknown to us. Phoebe told me that He had emerged from his bedchamber with Berthe beneath his arm suspended in the air like a board, for she had stiffened herself in response to his picking her up by the waist, and he held her perpendicular to his body in a manner that Phoebe laughed over. He adjured Phoebe to take the shameless brat away and inform her that if he found her once again in his chambers, he would beat her with a switch.

I remarked, in an offhand way, that it was good that Richard was absent, but Phoebe said that the way He held Berthe was as Richard might himself, if she were being too rowdy. And somehow, she thought our brother would have approved. The Black Sheep had put Berthe down and then laughed when she assured him that she would not enter again, as she still had a great many rooms to visit if she wished to see the whole house. He had recommended that she did not visit the earl's rooms, unless she wished to be severely punished, but Berthe replied that she had been in there already and thought the room was a great waste of silk that might better make girl's dresses. 'I dearly want a silk dress, but Mama says it is not for little girls.'

I made a mistake today. It does not seem possible as mistakes go, being so utterly stupid. I was beneath my reading tree, a good deal away from Roseanna and Tabitha, who were sketching. I was reading an amusingly awful passage, and when I heard someone come up towards me, in my distraction I thought it was Richard, and held out my hand without looking around. There is no way to explain this. We had just seen dear Rich off on his travels. I knew it. How could I make such an error?

Someone grasped my hand, and I pulled him down to share the book. I even leaned in further and virtually forced him to be close to me. Suddenly, it felt strange. I turned my head, and it was Eliot Marchmont, His face turned too, only inches from mine.

Eliot put the book down. He needed a moment before he could read on, and his conscience was roaring that he had no right to know what came next for her — but there was no way, there was really no way, that he could put the book away now.

My heart stopped and I'm ashamed to say the shock had me nearly fall over, but his hand stopped me. He spoke amusingly about my choice of literature and then it seemed natural for us to tease each other. We were rather closer together, against the tree trunk, than would be usual. Indeed, apart from Richard or Papa, I have never been so close to a man. It was different, and somewhat breathtaking, though I tried to hide it. It would perhaps feel so with any gentleman, but looking into Eliot Marchmont's eyes upon occasion, I began to doubt it. There is no question that he is, aesthetically, very beautiful. Like the wonderful portrait of my grandmama in her youth that hangs in the green salon, one could look at him for hours — if only he did not notice. But the teasing carried me through, and I felt I could meet him again at dinner without having given too much of myself away.

Berthe's nonsense had us exchange humorous looks throughout dinner. I feel that beyond his good looks, I <u>like</u> Eliot Marchmont. Perhaps we are becoming friends. I would welcome it, but I *fear I am too inexperienced. I have never before had a male friend of my own. And somehow it feels dangerous.*

With this, Eliot agreed. He should not know, and had never before known, that a female found him "beautiful". It was a strange word to attach to himself, and it somehow related to his being a marble statue once more. He had determined to go beyond featuring in her imagination as a statue, but he had succeeded rather too well for his own comfort. He had wanted, and then relished, becoming someone she could share her wit with, in *person,* rather than through the page. But now he had achieved this small goal he realised it came with pitfalls he had overlooked.

As their eyes met, he *knew* her. Knew her well. And it placed her at a disadvantage that he was ashamed of. And then, her laughing with him in the flesh affected him more than he had realised it would. Her candid eyes, her smile, the messy hair he had wished to push back behind her ear as she talked, her closeness, had all affected him.

He had plans, and she did not feature in them. No female did — not for some time, at any rate. Why was he panicking? She had evinced a desire to be his friend, that was all. Surely, he could make friends with the woman whose words had amused and educated him all this time? He could allow himself *that*, in any event. He wondered that if he did not know his effect on her, if he had not read the journal, whether that might have happened eventually in the course of things, without containing the threat of more. But probably not. He would have avoided her and her family like the plague, simply on the basis of their different rules for living, so obviously displayed at their first meeting. No doubt Berthe would have foisted herself upon him in the same way as now, but to the rest he would have remained indifferent.

He would have missed her entirely. She was not the prettiest of her sisters (Roseanna) or the most arresting (Phoebe), though she was more than pretty enough. He might have noticed a wry aside and appreciated it over time, but not so quickly become entangled with her. The stolen journal was to be blamed. That entertaining, incisive look at the world, and therefore at her own personality. It had drawn him in before he knew it. It led him to look at her more frequently, and to descry the meaning in the look in her large eyes. He saw her intelligence, wit and appreciation of the absurd, even when she masked her face in a remote look when in the presence of Eliot's family.

He looked on at her from a distance sometimes, seeing her open face within her own family, her joy, laughter not tinged with cynicism, her playfulness. He had sat on a rise the second day and watched her read seriously, and imagined the face he could not see. He had watched her walk with the family, walks that turned into runs, or play-fights. Even once he had seen her go off alone and was fascinated, but not surprised, to see her twirl in a solitary dance as her outstretched hands touched the tall grasses around her, as Phoebe's had on the day of her kiss with Barclay. Naomi's words had made him a trifle obsessed. He resolved to put some distance between them — and in order to do so, he believed, he should no longer read the purloined journal.

Eliot Marchmont no longer spent his evenings in the library. He had begun to order a fire in the green salon after a day or two, following his resolve to no longer purloin the red Morocco journal. For he had twitched during those first evenings before the library fire, nose pointed to a book, but attention inclined behind his back to the shelf of volumes where the journal was hidden.

But even when he removed to the green salon, he had to retrieve books from the library, and his fingers had itched towards it ...!

It was ten days before he gave in.

There were some unusually short entries, as though the writer was a trifle weary of her daily account, which now contained little amusement. The last entry would probably, he guessed, have been written today, and there seemed to be a new resolve back to the honesty that had characterised her previously. It terrified him, but it was irresistible, too.

He pulls away from me, I can see it. I worried at first that my admiration of His beauty would be evident in my face, but it is not that. It is the incident at the tree that has changed things. I am not really His family, so what should we do with a friendship where we tease each other as we did that day? And, to some extent, at dinner that evening. But breakfast the next day, and all our meetings for the days following, have been different. He does not look at me.

Perhaps, like me, He does not know what to do with a such a friend. It is possible. The direst thought is that He thinks me inclined to him as a woman to a man. I cannot, as a connoisseur, but admire His looks. Everyone must. Phoebe said to me that she had never seen such a handsome man, excepting our brother. Actually, we have met one or two — but they all seem, unlike Richard, or Eliot Marchmont, to be aware of their good looks and seeking to use them to advantage. I think that Phoebe admired Sir Osbert Barclay, perhaps, but he, too, seemed such another to me. Richard and the Black Sheep are the more attractive because they do not notice or care about something so shallow as mere beauty. And thus, I admired Him. So unlike his brothers who preen their less attractive feathers to little result.

But I am humiliated if He thinks a little teasing to be something I took as encouragement to pursue a romantic connection, or even an arranged one.

It is good then, that He acts this way — it gives me a disgust of him, for he is deliberately denying a natural connection of temperaments. We find some of the same things amusing, and that might have been a beginning for better relations between the families — for a start, with his sister Ophelia, at least. But he, like they, does not wish this, evidently. They keep themselves apart, even from each other. But in his case, He has self-awareness. And so that makes him merely a coward.

The west wing is becoming ever more habitable. On the floor beneath the attics there is a room that mama has set up as a kind of munuments room. She is arranging some of the attic's treasures there, as well as some odd things that only the children found precious. Tabitha had made the old marionettes work, and repaired the Italian puppet theatre too, and has made a tableau of it - Roseanna even sewed new curtains for it. It was better, she told Berthe, not to play with it since the cords seemed to tie themselves in knots again with every touch. But Berthe was only mildly interested with this artifact, being more concerned that Mama should send the sword away to be sharpened. Which Mama completely refused to do.

I wondered a little at our making this room at all, but Mama said these things were relics of Papa's own family, and therefore we might spare them some attention and care. If the countess found out, no doubt she would despise the presumption, but Mama, when Roseanna worried this aloud, said that she did not mean to remove them from the house, so what harm was she doing? It was true. Mama even admitted a scholar one day who examined the documents found and advised on the best methods for their preservation. Mama has ordered a carpenter to make a map cabinet, capable of housing the oldest papers in shallow drawers. To be made out of cedar, to keep away the moth. Stephanie was only interested in the ancient, mostly broken, sporting equipment. She was allowed a space of wall to display a racquet from the ancient game of tenis, too fragile to mend, and found (goodness knows where) someone to repair the archery equipment. An old bladder ball (that King Henry the Eighth might have kicked in his prime) Stephanie insisted on display-

ing. She was especially delighted to find a cross-bow, which has now, worryingly, disappeared.

The coming and goings of persons in the west wing evidently concerned the countess greatly, but the earl not at all. He remained indifferent to us.

There had been a standoff between Mama and the countess about the new maids mama employed and housed in the attics of our wing. These maids are dressed neatly and identically in grey dresses and white linen aprons, distinguishing them from other servants. Lady Marchmont objected to feeding them, and she also complained that they were not under the housekeeper's regulation, but Mama had said that costs would not fall upon the household, and that she had not wished to give Mrs Roberts more work than she had already, with too little staff. Cook too would be recompensed for her extra labour. The countess, said Mama sweetly, need not worry.

There was another fuss about the men renovating an old barn on the estate for reasons Lady Tremaine could not guess and Mama would not yet inform her of, talking only vaguely about some future use. Also, the countess objected to the further individuals newly employed to clean out the stalls in the half-empty stables. Mama had herself visited the chief groom, and he had succumbed to her manner, and had not objected to the invasion of strange workers putting things to rights in the unused part of the stable block.

I did not witness each encounter of Mama and Lady Marchmont, but the work continued.

Soon the other rooms in the west wing were polished and clean, the windows too. It becomes a cosy place. The glass at the side and back were mullioned and old, the wainscoting revealed to be a warmer coloured oak than we first thought, once it was cleaned. The west wing had once been the main house, and it had an old-fashioned comfort once mama worked her magic. Chimneys were swept (and repaired in some cases), and old linen washed and patched, for mama had a great appreciation of the stitching of the past and treasured the work of the ancients. I found her caressing an embroidered coverlet. 'Women's work,' she said, sadly, 'is never as treasured as men's.'

So her daughters and she treasured it. We could all sew, even Stephanie, mother had seen to it — but Tabitha was excused the task, and Berthe's skill was not yet fitting to repair ancient threads and match the colours. Mama found a brown linen sampler, set by a "Maria Marchmont, 12 years", that must have been a hundred years old, and gave it to Berthe to repair the torn threads and to turn the edges neatly for remounting.

The west wing, the parts that we inhabited, became comfortable. Mama caused a great many extra pillows to be made to replace dusty hassocks, adding a touch of modern. It saved our posteriors on the hard old oak. But she did have some elegant sofas delivered from London, one for each of our rooms. Modern upholstery was definitely superior.

I found a desk that I moved to my room, and Mama set up my quill and pens and inkpot there with a smile, but I was not yet accustomed to it, and still wrote most often in the library, when it was empty during the day.

Our own beds have fine new linen, and we were as comfortable as Mama could make us. The horses began to arrive. Some sent from London by Richard, and one or two favourites sent all the way from the Highlands. Mama's mare, Duchess, Richard's favourite hunter, named Duke after his grandfather's title. I can ride again, on a roan I named Precious, and soon I might drive too, for Richard was no doubt tasked to bring home carriages, also. The renovated barn would house them, I guessed.

'You could,' drawled the earl, 'have ridden horses from my stables had you wished, my lady!'

'My family is so numerous, Lord Tremaine, that it might be seen a burden upon your family. Or interrupted their pleasure. We tend to ride together, you know.'

'Yes,' he laughed, disparaging and bored at once.

The countess, as usual, looked upset. There was nothing to reprove Mama of, for none of the expenses of Mama's changes fell on the estate, and everything she did benefited the property. But the countess felt the presumption.

Mama is, of course, presumptuous. No one but she could have set about her task so quietly, industriously, meticulously, and unashamedly as Mama. She did not seek permission before she acted, did not apologise to anyone. She simply did what she saw fit. I was still not entirely clear what being here, to the evident ire of the other family, was for. Something to do with Richard, perhaps, or with launching us girls on society with the earl's help? I could think of little distinction that such a man could confer on us, apart from rank. Mother's own family status would surely have been enough to launch us adequately. None of us, including Mama, I believe, seek status. We sisters all, I think, must choose a man we could respect if we are to take a husband.

Recent events have made me more fearful of marriage. I may not marry at all. But the prospect of London has, for us all, more attractions than wedding alliances to offer. I will like to dance, I'm sure. We will enjoy the play and the opera, and many usual town distractions. But there are also foundries for Tabitha, and new sources of mischief for Berthe, and art galleries for me.

Brooding is not my nature. I have indulged in it somewhat in these days, since the smart of humiliation when I see his avoidance had smirched me. I shall no longer brood. He may believe what he will of me, I shall not approach him, or even look at him if I can avoid it. I shall just quietly resent his distrustful and cowardly nature and ignore him.

She had him right, thought Eliot, dwelling on the words *humiliation* and *smirched*; he was a coward. He had hurt her, and there seemed no way that he could repair that hurt other than to let her resent him.

She was not some poor damsel who sought a connection from a man of respectable fortune. She had no need of him in that way. The tree incident, as she called it, had allowed a friendship to spring up between them. He might not have teased her so readily that day if it had not been that he had known her already, from the journal pages.

But then he had run away, afraid she would misunderstand him, or want more than he could offer ... it was all cowardice. He might have been her friend at least. And she was right. If he had, Ophelia might have joined them and perhaps Queenie, too, might have become more healthily attached to the wild ones. He had reservations about the other family's upbringing, perhaps — but of all of Naomi's *Royals*, Queenie might benefit most from a touch of the wild in her restricted, timid life. His confusion, his cowardice, his theft of Naomi's inner thoughts, had put paid to all of that.

She *should* resent him. He resented himself. But there were things Eliot Marchmont planned to do with his life, that he had begun to do already, and nothing about this friendship would do other than delay them.

A door opened. A small dark haired figure in a nightgown and bare feet came in.

'Is that not *Naomi's* journal, sir?'

CHAPTER 7

The Punishment

As Eliot Marchmont had looked into the innocent eyes of Berthe, he had known dread.

The ignominious words, '*Do not inform her!*' had escaped his mouth before any more urbane excuse could occur. The only explanation for this was the dreadful shame that had engulfed him after reading the last journal entry. His brain had been temporarily addled and he had betrayed himself completely. He saw the dark eyes turn crafty.

'Then ... what might you give me in exchange, sir?' she asked.

'Mutual trust and respect,' said Eliot, sufficiently recovered to himself to forgo bargaining with a child.

Berthe blinked. 'But you are reading something you should *not*.'

'I am sure *you* have read many things you should not,' Eliot remarked, unimpressed.

'Mama says that to excuse one's actions by the actions of another has no in...integrity. I think that means honour.'

He sighed. 'Your mama is correct. I should not, in fact, have read your sister's journal. I did so carelessly at first, but I should not have continued.'

'No,' chided Berthe, 'you should not. Mama says that to repeat a wrong action is no longer an *accident* but a *sin of commission*, which is a very much more serious crime.'

Eliot finally found himself amused. 'Would you call it a *crime*? I do not believe it to be against the law of the land.'

'This is mere ... mere Soffy ... something. Richard says that all the time when Phoebe is trying to be tricky.'

'Sophistry. I shall not bother you with the derivation of the word, but it refers to making spurious arguments.'

Berthe was silently moving the word "spurious" around her mouth in practice, looking up, but then her gaze returned, as frank and determined as before. 'I think I should tell my sister.' But her eyes held more than mere honesty. She was resuming a bargaining stance.

Eliot breathed heavily. 'You probably *should* tell your sister and I should *not* urge you other.'

'But...?' said Berthe, intuiting more.

'But it would spare me, and I believe your sister Naomi, some embarrassment if you did not mention it.'

Berthe considered. 'I do not understand embarrassment.' She cast her eyes up, 'Did Naomi say things about your family that she would not like you to know?'

'Yes.'

'Did it make you cross with her?'

'Not at all. I agreed with most of it. And reading the journal also let me understand your family a little more.'

'Do you *wish* to? You never speak much to us.'

Eliot thought of not wanting his own family to misunderstand him. Of avoiding Naomi because he should not know what he knew. 'It is complicated.'

'Adults always say that. I find it silly. If you wish to know us, *speak* to us. We are very friendly.'

'I shall.'

Berthe moved forward and took the book from him. 'I shall take this to Naomi. You should not read it again.'

He was chastened by an eight-year-old. But the moment she took the book from him and closed it, Eliot felt bereft.

'I cannot think of anything to ask you for,' considered Berthe, 'And trust, says Mama, must be earned. At least after one has behaved badly. So, as Mama does, I should ask you for something beneficial to the punished one.'

'Excuse me?'

'Well, if Mama thinks I have been careless with other people's things, she forbids a maid to clean my room, and makes me sweep the floor and dust myself. And even once, fetch coals.'

Eliot waited as the message was about to arrive.

'But it is very nice having the room tidy afterwards, and I like the feeling of having done so myself, and so it is punishment that is *beneficial* to me. As well as a reminder to the lazy part of me not to be careless again.'

'I understand.' He began to see how Lady Eleanor's offspring, so wild on the surface, were formed. It seemed a better rearing than his own.

'I cannot seem to think of a good punishment for *you.* Cleaning your room does not fit the crime.' She began to rub one naked foot against the other, and he beckoned her to the fire. She came and gave him a childish grin as thanks, and he laughed. Suddenly, her eyes lit up with a thought. '*I* know! For your punishment, you must speak to one of us, Mama or Richard or Naomi, or Tabitha, or Phoebe, or Stephanie, or me, for at least *five minutes* every day. It should take a week.'

'That might be...' began Eliot.

'*Ten* minutes!' Berthe said, and Eliot suddenly discovered how the child's mother gained obedience.

'Very well!'

'If you do not, I shall consider that you have not learned your lesson, and then I *must* inform Naomi.'

'Very well!' sighed Eliot once more. 'You and your mama are strict.'

'Of course. I shall be even more like Mama when I become a woman.'

Eliot suddenly saw that she would.

Naomi was leaving her bedchamber with Stephanie next morning when Berthe handed her the journal. 'Is this yours? I found it in the library.'

Naomi was not much surprised and reentered her chamber to put the book in the desk drawer. 'Poking your nose in places you should not!' she chided her sister, hitting Berthe's nose with her forefinger.

'You should be grateful to me,' said Berthe obscurely. But Naomi wished for her breakfast and ignored her, running down the last flight of stairs that joined the two Wings, and past a protesting Charles to achieve the meat, Stephanie following her with hair flying.

'Hoydens!' Charles complained, continuing his descent.

Berthe entered behind them, also having overtaken the more stately gait of Charles. He made up the rear, and found that both families already seated.

Eliot Marchmont raised his eyes, but they moved past Naomi's to Berthe, then across the table to Phoebe.

'You have not looked in your usual spirits for some days, Phoebe,' Eliot began, quietly, 'are you well?'

Phoebe and he were sitting at the end of the table, and his low remark was not overheard, but his moving lips and inclined body were noticed by Ophelia at his side, and by Berthe, who waved at him behind Phoebe's back, then took a seat next to her mama.

'Quite well!' said Phoebe dismissively.

'I do not know you well,' Eliot said quietly, 'but that remark seems less direct than usual.'

Phoebe's marvelous dark eyes raised to meet his, and darkened even further.

'Did you arrive sooner than I thought at the riverbank?'

'That *is* direct!' said Eliot, then gave her a candid look in return, 'Yes, I did.'

'I may wish to be more candid, sir, but not before *your* family.' Eliot sighed at her rudeness, but then she added, as though somewhat regretful, 'Let us walk after breakfast.'

It was his own fault, thought Eliot, Berthe had only asked him to converse, but his opening to this wild female had been intrusive, and invited confidence. Certainly not the polite-but-friendly interchange that he had aimed at. In a similar situation, Ophelia, appreciating the concern but with her usual reserve, might have smiled and thanked him for his interest, but told him he need not be concerned. But Phoebe was *not* his sister.

He should have complimented her gown or some such thing, but the girls were back in their dull colours. Phoebe's dress was the grey of slate today, in a sturdier cotton than his sisters might wear. He glanced down the table at his brother Cedric, who was using a journal to avoid conversation, and saw him glance over briefly.

Eliot looked at his plate and replied to her in a lower voice still, 'I'll meet you at the rose arbour in five minutes.'

Phoebe, who had perhaps noted the turn of his head, nodded a little as reply and began to speak to Tabitha, at her side. As he left the breakfast room, with a bow to those still at the table, Berthe pulled on his jacket sleeve, her mouth full of roll as she said, in an accusatory whisper. 'That wasn't ten minutes!'

Her mama, catching this aside, adjured Berthe not to speak with her mouth full, but Eliot had said something in a low voice at the same time and moved off.

What he had said was, 'It will be!'

Phoebe arrived, running a little, dark curls flying around her face, as he stood beside the arbour kicking his heels. They set off together walking, and she began, 'Do I really look unwell?'

'A little. Less lively, at least.'

'Oh.' She walked ahead. She had donned an old cloak over the grey dress, and her wild black curls tumbled into the hood and escaped it too. She filled her lungs with air and then said, 'I expect you wish to give me a lecture on the indiscretion of my behaviour.'

'If I wished to do so, I should use another word than *indiscretion*.'

'Shocking, then!' she said, but a little angrily.

'Perhaps, but I was going to say ... *dangerous*.' He walked on a little, 'I too have balked at societal rules, but I find, as I get older, that they generally have a purpose.'

'You *would* think that!' said Phoebe, surly. 'I am only surprised that someone from your family should admit to flouting rules.'

'I did not say I was brave enough to *flout* them, just *balked* at them.'

Phoebe, whose demeanour had been prickly, probably a little defensive, laughed at this.

'It is I who am *dangerous*, not he. You saw it, evidently.'

'Yes. But I still know where the danger truly lies.'

'You are mistaken. Some things are beyond the normal rules,' she said this passionately, stopping and looking at him fully in the face. 'You would not understand.'

'Then why are you not *happy*, Phoebe?'

'Because his business caused him to leave. Because he is not here! Cannot you *understand* that?'

But it was more than this, he was sure. He looked into her dark flashing eyes, 'And does your *family* understand that?'

She turned and continued to walk, saying merely. 'They *would*, if they knew.'

'You have not told them.' He paused and added. 'I wonder what Richard's reaction would be.'

She turned and grasped his arm. 'You will not tell Richard?' she asked desperately.

'You have not told your family your tale because they may *not* understand.'

'No!' Phoebe said, 'Well Richard, perhaps. Since Papa died he has been so protective of us that he acts first and thinks later. I did not want him to *ruin* anything...' She chugged on, over a muddy patch of ground, not even holding up her skirts. 'You make it sound as though I am *ashamed*, and why should I be?' She moved on a little and Eliot, who could think of nothing to say, remained silent until, 'it is just that it is all so early, so new. It is something mysterious that I want to hold onto by myself a little. For I cannot well explain why an encounter should produce *such ...!*' She grasped at her bosom, turning shining eyes on him.

He was not equipped for this family. He did not wish to know all this, or deal with it, however concerned he was. He cursed Berthe.

She continued. 'I never thought there would be something that I did not instantly share with Naomi and Roseanna. But now, because you saw it, I have *you,* Eliot Marchmont, my judgmental confidante. How strange!'

'I should probably tell your mother—' he heard her gasp, '—but I won't!' He sighed, 'It is no business of mine, and I would not know of it except for an unhappy chance.' He detained her for a little. 'I have no desire to be your confidante, judgmental or otherwise, but if ever there is something in this to give you *concern*, tell me.'

She searched his eyes. 'You do not like Sir Osbert Barclay.'

'I do not know him intimately.' Eliot said dismissively. Then he gave her a cynical look, allowing a brow to fly up. 'But he *is* a friend of *Charles*!'

This made Phoebe laugh aloud. 'You are more wicked than I thought, Eliot Marchmont!'

'Mmmm!' he said, stopping suddenly. 'I have things to attend to. Make your own way back!'

He walked back the way he had come and saw the rest of the wild ones on their walk, on a parallel path, he crossed over and Roseanna said, 'Oh! Eliot, will you join us?'

He did not stop, only saying to Berthe on his way past, 'That was more than ten minutes!'

She giggled and he heard Naomi ask, 'What did he mean?' and Berthe reply, 'Oh, it is just a game!'

The next morning, walking down the stairs, Berthe skipped up to him, 'You could talk to *me* today,' she said brightly.

'I do not want to,' he replied, moving around her. She dodged to his side again, blocking the room.

Roseanna, in a fondly chiding tone, said, 'Oh Berthe, are you being a nuisance?'

'No!' Then, as Eliot continued descending, she called after him, 'It is my turn *one* day!'

After breakfast, during which Berthe gave him darkling looks, Eliot considered talking to Lady Eleanor, but found he could think of nothing to say besides inanities. He had almost decided, after the debacle of Phoebe's open heart yesterday, that inanities were the way forward to fulfill his quota of minutes, but Lady Eleanor, while reserved, had deep eyes and a turn for honesty that frightened him. He looked over at Roseanna, and caught her eye, which led her to look back at him. A politely hopeful look was on her face, ready to engage in any inanity he cared for, he felt, and that scared him more. He dropped his eyes to the table.

Phoebe, opposite him, said amusedly, 'Do you judge the rolls, too?'

He realised that as his mind wandered, his eyes had fixed on the dish of rolls, and he looked up and smiled vaguely in return.

After breakfast, he was surprised to see another small person at his side, but not as small as Berthe. Tabitha looked up at him gravely, taking longer strides to match his.

'Berthe says you mean to be friends with us,' she said seriously.

'Well I ...' Eliot found himself drawling, almost in the manner of his brothers, to turn her off.

'I *knew* it!' Tabitha flushed, as though she had been duped, and turned away.

'Stop!' Eliot said. 'I *do* mean to be friends.' Where had his fund of light conversation gone? Could he not even manage it with a twelve-year-old? He was offering friendship to a very serious child whom, he suspected, might be just as literal as Berthe.

'Really?' said Tabitha. 'Then, can you take me to the village?'

'Now?'

'Can you not?'

'What about one of your sisters?'

'All are busy ...' After just a second of his hesitation, she held a little hand up as though to cast him off. 'Do not trouble yourself.' A proud little thing. Not so terrified of him as she had been when her family had first arrived.

'What do you clutch so tightly?' he asked before she could leave. She held a folio to her chest that was bigger than it.

She said nothing.

'Where do you wish to go in the village?'

'The blacksmith's.'

He waited for more information but the taciturn child did not speak. He jerked his head as he headed for the door.

He drove her in his gig where she sat silently, still clutching the leather folio. He did not press her to speak, feeling a little more like her servant than her relative or friend.

At the blacksmith's, she left the gig quickly and went ahead to approach a beefy man who had just put down his tools in the dim workshop, lit principally by the glow of the forge.

She held out her folio, showing him a sketch at the top of several others. 'Can you make this?'

The man peered, wiped his hands on a rag, and took the sketch to look more clearly. 'What's this?'

Tabitha looked at him, annoyed. 'Well gears, obviously,' she informed him.

'I ain't a foundry!' he said, handing it back.

'Yes. Can you make it?'

'No. I do not have the time, or tools enough, to be playing around wif l'il girls drawings.'

'I can pay you when my brother comes back.' Tabitha said, following his retreating form. 'I am very rich.'

The big man looked at her tweed short cape, a garment which had shocked Eliot too when he saw it, for it seemed ancient. The trouble with Scottish tweed was, it was indestructible. This was evidently a garment from the Scottish ducal castle, but it looked a hundred years old. '*Yes* miss!' he scoffed. He turned from her, picking up a tool to work.

'*Is* there a foundry around here?' she continued, Eliot was regarding this interchange from the threshold of the large opening to the workshop, fascinated by her persistence. 'I did not think so,' the child continued, musing, when she received no reply, 'or Rich would have mentioned it to me.'

The man ignored her, picking up his tools.

Eliot stepped forward and the noise made the blacksmith turn.

'Mr Eliot, sir!' he said, respectfully. Eliot ignored him and placed a hand on Tabitha's shoulder. 'Let us get some lemonade at the inn. You can show me your drawing,' he told her.

Tabitha looked him up and down. 'You wouldn't understand.'

'Probably,' he said, leading her out, 'But show me anyway.'

Over lemonade at the inn, she reluctantly handed him the folio, open at the correct page. 'It is a gear sequence for an engine. I have changed the design of angle of the cogs and I just need a model to see if it helps or hinders the resistance. There is nothing at home that I can use to...'

'At the Towers you mean? Might there have been something in your Scottish home? Is it so different here?'

'Certainly. There were a lot of machine parts *everywhere* at the castle and I could have filed down ... oh, I cannot explain it to you.'

Eliot looked up. 'You simply need a model to test?' he asked. 'Must it be in metal?'

'What are you thinking?' she leaned forward, finally interested in his words.

'Let me take you somewhere.'

An hour and a half later, he and Tabitha reentered the hall at the Towers, Tabitha saying seriously, 'Thank you, Eliot! You were almost like *Richard* today.' It was evident that she could give him no finer compliment.

Roseanna called, 'Oh, Tabitha, we were looking for you, but Berthe told us—' she smiled at Eliot at this point, but Eliot's eye moved to Naomi, who was watching him and her little sister together, frozen.

He attempted a smile, but Naomi turned and moved back up the stairs, saying, 'Come, Tabitha!'

Tabitha was saying, 'but I thought you were coming *downstairs*, Naomi!'

Naomi said nothing, but her determined back showed anger, and Roseanna gave an apologetic curtsy to Eliot, and followed her at a run.

Eliot felt as though a blow had been landed on him. She had looked right through him, just like every time he had seen her recently. It was all his own fault, but it hurt. He was at a loss of what to do.

He never knew how to behave with women. He had even had unexpected consequences with both Phoebe and Tabitha. Nothing was as he planned it. A small hand pulled at his sleeve. It was the terrible child. 'How is my punishment *feeling*?' she inquired.

'*Horrible!*' said Eliot, with venom.

'Oh, *good*!' said Berthe with relish.

He headed for the green salon. 'Do not follow me!' he said, rudely.

Ophelia was there, lounging on his favourite seat. 'Eliot Marchmont, what *is* going on with you?'

CHAPTER 8

More Punishment

Not wishing to give more fodder to the wonderment of his own family at the change of his behaviour, Eliot forbore to start any but civil conversation at dinner that night, or breakfast the next day. But he was aware that his punishment, knife-like as it was, was far from over.

Therefore he followed Lady Eleanor Marchmont to her sitting room in the west wing after breakfast, avoiding his own family's eye. He marvelled a little as he went at the order and care displayed everywhere. Flower arrangements brightened the corridors which were swept, furniture waxed. The rather romantic spiders' webs of his childhood memory were banished.

'Lady Eleanor, might you spare a moment?' Eliot said, as he reached her sitting room door, just after she did.

She turned and smiled and ushered him in. In a second she was seated, and had taken up some work. It seemed to be a large tapestry of medieval date, and she was using some gold thread on it. She looked up at him in greeting, her raised brows her only question.

The room had a friendly fire already lit in the massive old inglenook fireplace, housed by a new, neat grate. The oak wainscoting was polished and warm in colour, the furnishings a mixture of modern and old, with an emphasis, he thought, on comfort.

'You have worked wonders, my lady,' said Eliot honestly, 'I have never seen the place look so well.'

'I think I prefer the old part of the house. My husband was fond of it too. It was used in his grandmother's time, I believe, but he mostly remembers it empty, as somewhere he played.' She looked at him with intelligent eyes. 'I have noticed Berthe following you these days with mischief in her eyes.'

'Yes. I will be frank. She is meting me out a punishment.'

Her humorous brows rose once more. 'And do you deserve it, sir?'

'I am ashamed to say I do.' Eliot admitted. There was a silence. He considered telling this calm lady everything, but he found himself ashamed indeed. 'But do not fear, ma'am, she is your daughter and has given me a punishment befitting the crime.'

'I admit I am intrigued, but I shall not press you, Eliot dear. How can I help you?'

'I am merely visiting your kingdom, Lady Eleanor. I admit that I am more curious than I believed. What do you work on?'

'A tapestry that I found in the attics. It was well wrapped, and I had it cleaned as well as we could, and now I am attempting to replace the parts where the gold thread has worn off. I think it will add to its charm. It depicts some lovers in a garden theme, I think, and is very large, as you see. But I believe it will look well on the corridor wall when I have finished. It is woven of course, but I believe the original gold was sewn in.' She frowned. 'Could they weave with gold In those days? I judge it to be from the seventeenth century, but depicting some centuries before.' As Eliot had no idea how to answer her inquiry, he kept silent. 'Berthe wants a dress like the lady's in the tapestry, but I think not.' She smiled at him. 'Shall I take you on a tour of the wing, for you to see what has been achieved? The girls have gone out, no doubt, so we will disturb no one.'

They moved around the wing together, and Eliot marveled anew. He tried to look surprised at the existence of the muniments room, and at the presence among the ancient papers and artefacts (many broken, but interesting) of the more childish items chosen by Berthe and Tabitha. As Eliot regarded them and complimented Lady Eleanor for her care of family history, she smiled.

'I hear you took Tabitha to the village yesterday, sir. That was kind of you. But apparently the blacksmith was unhelpful. When Richard comes back, we must set up a workshop for them both.'

'Tabitha does seem very serious in her love of *gears,*' he said humorously.

'Oh she is,' smiled the proud mother, a trifle seriously, 'and talented, too, her papa and brother tell me.'

'She impressed a friend of mine. He has agreed to make her a trial design in wood for a new gear design.' He still sounded amused.

'Tabitha knows more than you would believe, Eliot,' she said lightly in the face of his amusement.

'Oh, I believe you madam,' Eliot said, 'only it is just such an usual preoccupation for a young child.'

'I expect you mean girl-child.'

'I should not dare say so, if I did,' said Eliot.

'Well, you have a sense of self-preservation at least. Richard would roast you. He fends off all those who wish to steal Tabitha's self-belief and ingenuity with disparagement of her sex.'

'I can imagine.' He answered her respectfully. Then he added, as though suddenly thinking, 'At any rate, might I suggest a workshop site?'

'Yes?'

'There is an old lodge in the grounds that fell down from disuse, since the boundaries of Tremaine got much larger, and there was no need for a lodge there at all anymore. But there is a large brick stable and carriage block still standing, and it seems to me that with some attention to the roof, it might make workspace.'

'It sounds right. I shall have to take Richard to see it.'

'I expect Cedric would have no objection.'

'Oh I don't think we need bother the earl with such stuff. If I do not make his property *worse*, but only improve it, he would not cavil, would he?'

Cedric, thought Eliot, would cavil at much less, just to assert his dominance. But in the case related to the *other* Marchmont family he was hanging fire. Perhaps because Lady Eleanor's purse seemed deep indeed, and Cedric was not finished dipping into it.

He and her ladyship exchanged knowing glances, and she continued showing him the rooms, including the girls' rooms. Phoebe's contained a pianoforte of diminutive size, a cello, a violin and was strewn with drawings, loose and free sketches of landscapes and faces and figures. 'She does not choose to *paint* as yet, but I believe that she will be talented when she does,' remarked Phoebe's mother. Eliot, somewhat of an artist himself, agreed silently.

Berthe's room looked like it had been searched by robbers, or perhaps Bow Street Runners. Mounds of books and clothes and assorted other things lay around, and her mother gasped. 'She has lost something again!' she sighed. Her bed alone was untouched, with a child's doll set in the centre of it, like a little queen.

Tabitha's room was neat, but piles of books on engineering stood around in towers, tomes whose titles he would have thought challenging for an adult. He opened one at random and felt his head hurt. A pile of sketches of machine parts sat on a lady's desk, set below a mullioned window.

Richard's room was very large, and its accroutrements were very like his own. More books in tall towers, miscellaneous riding and sporting equipment, and it all had a smell of saddle soap.

Stephanie's room looked too much like Richard's to believe it a female apartment. There was, inexplicably, a crossbow under her bed.

Roseanna's room was was neat too, with feminine fashion plates on view in several open journals. They depicted over-trimmed dresses, and Eliot descried the influence of Charles. He hoped her sensible mother would stop her daughter following any such advice.

There was an open jewelery box, with many shining objects, hair ornaments making up the bulk of its contents.

Naomi's room was next. He fought the urge to linger here, for Lady Eleanor still accompanied him. He saw a red Morocco leather journal, almost glowing at him from her desk, saw the handsome quill and inkstand. It was unfortunate that the journal was closed, for he would very much have liked to get a glimpse of her latest entry, even if he could not turn the page. He wished to know the precise cause of her anger at him, which seemed to be growing apace.

He saw her neatness and organisation, despite her often unkempt appearance. Why did these silver backed brushes on her night stand not keep her hair tidier? Why were there fewer hair ornaments than in Roseanna's room?

There were a few wind-up toys there. A clown, a porcelain figurine of a lady in a gown of another era, with a turn key on the bulky platform she stood on.

Lady Eleanor smiled at him as he turned it on. 'A gift from her father.' He was not quite surprised when the figurine turned, but he was amazed when music played. It sounded like an Austrian folk song he had once heard a street musician play.

He had read of such an object as this music-producing mechanism, but never seen or heard such a thing. He understood that beneath the platform that the dancer turned upon, metal combs were being plucked to deliver the sound, but it held him spellbound. Swiss watchmakers had invented such a marvel. He could only imagine its rarity, not to mention its cost.

Perhaps this was Naomi's way of enjoying mechanisms, a more fanciful one than her sister Tabitha's.

The rather sad song was winding down as he left the room.

Lady Eleanor said, as they walked the corridor. 'Have you found what you were looking for, Eliot?'

'What I am looking for, my lady?'

'Your reason for visiting me.'

'Well,' he said, not wishing to tell this lady an untruth, 'my visit today exceeded my expectations, Lady Eleanor.'

'So happy!' she said, in a dry, perfunctory tone that acknowledged his avoidance of her question.

He bowed and took his leave of her.

Later that afternoon, he found himself reporting to the awful child. 'Your mother,' he said to her grave, inquiring eye.

'I shall *check*,' she warned.

He found her dreadful and amusing, both. He gave her an awful look.

'Hah! You have only Stephanie, Naomi and me left,' she said, 'I am looking forward to talking to you, I have a *great* deal to say.'

He did not doubt it. He dreaded either conversation, and he saw that she was relishing his despair.

'I think you will leave Naomi til last. So is it me tomorrow?' He frowned at her, and she skipped away happily, a footman opening the salon door for her.

'Oh *good!*' he heard her say, happily, 'it's *you*, your lordship!'

He could only wonder at the dread this would inspire in his usually imperturbable brother. The child had *some* uses. As the door closed behind her, he wished

Naomi were in the room so that she could later recall the joys of the encounter.

At this moment she arrived with Phoebe and Stephanie on either side, with Roseanna and his sister Queenie coming in behind. He was surprised, but then he remembered — it must be the continuation of "the most ridiculous friendship in the world", as Naomi had called it.

Naomi had been smiling and talking to her sister as she entered, but as her gaze found his, she froze and became stone, moving past him, Phoebe still chattering. He had nodded, but she ignored him. The familiar stone fell into his heart. My fault, he reminded himself, completely my own fault.

He understood her drawing back as he had himself, but he did not really understand the violence of her anger. She took pains, at dinner for example, to conceal her thoughts from all but her family. Only when pricked by some attempt by the Royals to insult one of her own did she use her sharp wit. But her anger to him these last days was very obvious — why?

But he supposed, like some of his own behaviour recently, she could not help it.

Before dinner that night (a meal Eliot was considering avoiding, such was his confusion about his present situation and the tension it produced) the red-haired sister of Naomi came into the green salon where he was hiding. She came in rather boldly and stood in the middle of the carpet several feet from him, gazing at him with her clear green eyes. The gaze appeared to say 'Get on with it!'

'Stephanie. Can I help you?'

'That little monster!' was her reply, disgusted.

'Berthe?'

'She said you wanted to see me.'

Eliot sighed. 'Yes, well. That is correct.'

She eyed him intelligently, and suspiciously. 'Whatever for?'

Eliot's mind drew a blank. Whatever indeed?

'I mean...' she said, those green eyes strangely stark in her pale face, the lashes that rimmed them invisible from here. Her brows were dark, but not her lashes. Strange he thought, she alone among that family was not dark. She was probably some throwback to a Celtic princess. It was a colouring he had only seen in the Irish and Scottish, and it came with a light sprinkling of freckles on her rather upturned nose, '...you have not even looked my way before. None of your family has, or only the Crown Prince, who shuddered at my hair colour.'

Eliot attempted a smile. 'Well, as you can observe, Charles has no taste.'

She smiled a little at this.

He thought about her presence or lack of it at the meals they shared. 'But you did not want any of us to speak to you, I think.'

A sudden flush, shocking on the pale skin, burned her face and neck. She looked furious and embarrassed at once. 'Why would I?'

'When we are all so unpleasant?' he asked, brows raised.

She pursed her lips. The flush still burned. He thought she was aware of it and ashamed. 'Why did you send for me? Or was it a prank of Berthe's?'

'Not precisely. I have been given a ... task from your sister. I must speak to all of you for ten minutes each. But I did not expect you today.'

'I see.' The flush was receding a little.

'Do you have the temper suggested by your hair?'

'Papa always said that that idea was superstitious nonsense.'

'I agree.'

'But it *has* made me angry, being here.'

'It would,' Eliot sympathised. 'It makes me angry, too.'

'But you are a man, and not a child.'

'Yes, and that is why I am often from here. But sometimes I need to return. They are my family. Added to which, it is expensive to rent rooms.'

'Ah! That is why you are called The Black Sheep. Queenie told Roseanna. It is because you do not like to spend money like your family.'

'I *do* spend money, but not as they do.'

'I see. You might be like Tabitha when she is older. If she spends money, I think it will be on a foundry.'

'That's it!' said Eliot. 'What would you spend money on? If you were older?'

'Horses. No, one magnificent horse. The best horse in England.'

'Ah! A laudable ambition. I hope you achieve it.'

'Well, Mama and Richard will probably help me do that. What do you spend *your* money on?'

'That is a secret. Yes, I know it is not fair to say so when you were frank with me.'

'I expect you are not used to being frank, but it is very unfair and *cheating*, I think.'

Eliot regarded her. His whole moral character was undergoing terrible introspection in the presence of his distant cousins. She was, of course, correct. He narrowed his eyes. 'How good are you at keeping secrets?'

'I am a steel trap.'

'I shall tell you then.' He ushered her forward and whispered in her ear.

At this moment Berthe came in. Behind her, crossing the hall, with her hand out as though to restrain Berthe from entering, was Naomi. He was caught in the ridiculous pose of bending over to whisper into the red curls of her sister. Naomi's eyes widened and she turned away, with a very bad impression of cold indifference.

The punishment had chafed at him that night. Even talking to Stephanie, whom he had previously hardly noticed, had led to him telling his secret to her for no more reason than a sense of fairness. The directness of that family seemed to leave him without defence. So next, Naomi or Berthe?

Talking to Berthe seemed full of hidden pitfalls, for who knew what she would ask about or from him? And she had a way of getting what she wanted.

Trying to begin a conversation with Naomi seemed nigh-on-impossible, in her present humour at least, he feared he would grovel and betray the reason that he was undergoing this torment in the first place. As his depressed steps walked to the breakfast table, he saw Berthe look up at him expectantly, almost wagging her tail. He frowned her down, but looking at Naomi's stone-face, he supposed he might have to talk to Berthe after all. Ten minutes. How hard could it be?

But a commotion in the hall saved him. 'Richard!' said Tabitha, getting up abruptly and knocking over a fork in the process, 'Richard is home!'

'Well, madam, constrain your child!' said Agatha, the countess. But she was talking to the wind. All six of the female members of the wild family were already in the hall. Table linen and plates discarded.

Lady Eleanor continued to eat, eventually encountering the countess' dreadful frown. 'The children are all very fond of Richard.'

But it was the earl who drawled, 'It is unnecessary to tell us so,' and he looked up in disgust as Richard entered in a throng of sisters, being pounded by questions about horses and his journey.

Tabitha was attempting to tell him about the trip to the blacksmiths and finished by saying, '... but he said there was no foundry.'

'Told you so,' remarked Richard, as usual favouring the interjections of the two youngest.

Berthe said, 'I must speak to you, Richie-Rich, for I have the most stupendous secret to tell you!'

Her brother touched her hair, as Eliot drew attention to himself by saying, '*Be-erthe!*'

Berthe looked over at Eliot, saying, 'Not the secret behind the secret, just the secret over that!'

Eliot groaned, trying to make something of it, and found both the Royals and the wild family regarding him.

Richard Marchmont, disengaging from his sisters to be seated at table said, 'Thank you for the hotel recommendation, Eliot. It suited me admirably.'

This began the Charles moans about staying in unfashionable accommodation again, while Cedric drawled, 'I hardly think it matters what hotel Mr Richard Marchmont stays at. He has already said he does not mean to be part of the fashionable world.'

The earl's jealous approval of this decision was so obvious that Naomi remarked, 'Oh, but he must, however! Richard will attend us females in town, of course.'

Cedric's eyes glittered.

'*Really?*' sighed Richard. But it was resigned, not rebellious.

'Indeed you must,' said Naomi, then more significantly, at Cedric, 'And I hardly think that a gentleman of my brother's appearance and fortune can escape notice in town, do you?'

Cedric's eye hardened, but it was Charles who said with a titter, 'Wearing *that* coat, he might.'

'Then,' said Lady Eleanor's stalwart voice, 'we shall have to force a tailor upon him.'

'Mama!' Richard complained, looking at Charles, aghast.

'Mr Eliot Marchmont's tailor might be a better fit for you, dearest!'

'Oh yes,' said Naomi into Charles disgusted face, 'gentlemen like Eliot and Richard have no need to adopt the excesses of fashion.'

'You are right,' said Phoebe, 'Rich and Eliot are both so handsome that any decoration would be excessive, I feel.'

Naomi blushed at this. Was it that she had given away her opinion on his appearance, or something else? After his illicit reading of the journal it came as no surprise to him, of course, should he now look shocked to be called handsome?

The breakfast table rang with Richard's account of the horses he had brought and the teams that would soon arrive. Eliot watched amused, as his own family looked on, astounded. So many horses and carriages were being apportioned that they were in awe.

'I have all but one of the sporting carriages stabled in London, as well as some of the horses. The two traveling coaches you desired I brought, along with their teams and some postilions, so we should be able to get around more easily on longer trips, including to London. And the rest of the mounts will arrive today, and we should be able to ride all together this afternoon.' He smiled at Berthe at his side. 'And I have a special gift for you, little one.'

'What is it?'

'A little trap pulled by a Shetland Pony. It is time you learned to drive...' At Berthe's squeal he admonished, '... but only in the paddock for the moment.'

'Oh *Rich!*' sighed Berthe, 'can I go to see it now?'

'Well, the pony is in the stable. You may go and name him if you wish.'

In a second she was gone.

As the wild ones donned capes and pelisses, Eliot approached Richard. 'They are all very pleased to see you,' he remarked.

'It is the horses they are pleased about,' Richard shrugged. 'Usually we ride as a family, you know.'

'Yes.' Eliot replied. 'Would it be an imposition if I came and saw the horses with you?'

Again he shrugged, his face neutral.

But as Eliot moved off, this time beside the man in the midst of the wild throng, he realised he had somewhat longed for this — being part of the mob, not standing to one side. He talked a little to Naomi's brother, with a real desire to get to know him. The girls, who were striving to get Richard's attention, unable to wait to see the horses, but demanding information as they went, brushed against Eliot again and again. It was jarring at first, then quite wonderful. Only Naomi kept to the edge of the group and did not approach. He was, he realised, spoiling her happiness. Nevertheless, Berthe was noticing his efforts at conversation with Richard, and that her brother had once sworn at Eliot as he was knocked into his elbow by Phoebe. Richard had said, in apology it seemed, *'Girls!'*

Perhaps Richard wanted a little more fellow-feeling against the feminine influence in his life.

Once in the newly refurbished stables, the conversation was easier. Most of the single riding horses were here already, as well as two handsome teams for the carriages, one team of blacks, another of chestnuts. The girls cooed over the horses allotted to them, and Eliot remarked that the chosen mounts were very strong for ladies.

'My sisters,' remarked Richard in a dry voice, 'are all excellent riders.'

The only pony was for Berthe, it seemed, but it was much taller than the Shetland pony she was petting at the moment. Even Tabitha was to ride a tall mare, Richard informed him, scratching the nose of the black, 'Berthe could ride a horse this tall already, but she is *too* brave and not careful enough as yet. She will prove herself on the pony.'

Berthe, overhearing, frowned.

Eliot, seeing something in this, approached the head groom. 'Belcher, make sure all of the boys know, *never* saddle anything but the pony for the youngest Miss Marchmont.'

Richard laughed at this, 'You have become more intimately acquainted with Berthe, I see, Eliot!'

As they all left, the girls to continue a walk, Naomi laughing, free of his restrictive presence, thought Eliot sadly. Richard held back Tabitha for what looked like a serious talk.

Eliot, joining them, heard, 'Can we start the patent with no model?'

'Eliot helped me to have a wooden model made. The man seemed competent. We go to the village together tomorrow to get it. If it looks as I think it will, write to Uncle Gavin to begin.'

'We should have a proper model made. I can visit a foundry near London.'

'But we should be quick.'

'The other design will come out first, in any event.'

'Fortunately, it was my early drawing that was stolen. I have made an adjustment. If it works, we have only to write to the engine owners to tell them to await the improved design.'

She was *twelve*, Eliot thought.

Richard nodded his assent. 'Perhaps Uncle Gavin can get ours through faster and we need not worry.'

'But they will believe us after our last patent's success?' The child was a little anxious.

'They ought to.'

'Your last patent?' Eliot found himself asking Tabitha. 'It was your papa's?'

'It was mine,' said Tabitha calmly. 'I am listed as T.A. Marchmont. I do not suppose the gentleman at the patent office think that I am Tabitha Anne.'

'Then, when you said to the blacksmith that you are rich, you meant ...?'

'From my first patent. Papa began it, and licensed it for me and Uncle Gavin has put my funds in trust, but Richard franks my expenses. I keep a strict tally, I assure you, so that when my trust matures I shall pay him back.'

Richard's eyes met Eliot's briefly, a slight challenge there. 'As an honest business woman should.'

Tabitha ran off to find her sisters, and Richard said to him, 'we have both inherited Papa's love of engines, and I design myself, but Tabitha is the first sibling to be patented. I have ideas for grand designs, for machines that accomplish things that people do at the moment. But Tabitha's real talent, and one that Papa said should be encouraged, it to see the detail in existing engines, and find how to improve them. Her last gear changed an engine in cloth manufacture, improving it, without the expense for the manufacturers to buy new machines. Uncle Gavin understood the process, and sold the gear design for a great deal of money, a fifth of the price of the whole machine in fact.'

'For a gear sequence?'

'It meant an increase in production, and avoided the necessity of buying a new engine, keeping the companies in line with competitors' newer machines.' Richard looked at Eliot's amazement. 'Tabitha's latest gear design, for a ship engine, was stolen by a rival engineer. It was my fault. I did not guard my baggage well enough. But I have now found out in London that a patent based on that design is pending.'

'Rogues!' said Eliot. 'You will punish them of course.'

'If Tabitha's newest addition works, the punishment will be in the failure of the attempt to sell their patent.' He looked ahead, and Eliot found him intense. 'But someday there may be more direct punishment. I have a long memory.' He shrugged again, 'But Papa has always told me that one must focus on the job in hand. And Tabitha is twelve. Even if this attempt is not successful, many more will be. Getting a taste of failure is something necessary in life. Papa said that it acts as an impetus to do better. When I told Tabitha that her design was stolen, she sat down to improve it immediately.'

'Your family is remarkable. I wish that I had had a father such as yours.'

'Your own father...'

'I do not wish to compare, merely to appreciate your father's wisdom. Mine ... well, mine though not engaged in the *grubby* world of trade, was rather more attached to Mammon than you father seems to have been. You may see his pattern in Cedric.'

'The earl? Oh, I see.' Richard walked ahead, pulling fingers through his unruly black curls. He gave Eliot a sideways glance. 'It is strange that we, who talk so little, have confided today. I suppose it was because you were kind to Tabitha earlier.'

Eliot found himself slightly smirched by Richard's approval. 'That may be why you spoke to me. *I* was kind only because of a punishment that Berthe has bestowed on me.'

Richard's brows rose. 'Berthe?' like his mother he also asked, 'And do you deserve your punishment?'

'It does,' Eliot replied wryly, 'fit the crime.'

Richard regarded him narrowly, but eventually said, as they reached the house, 'If you pay the price so readily, I must suppose that she is blackmailing you. It is Berthe's specialty.'

'So I have discovered. But I do not repine.'

They had entered the hall as they spoke, and Richard, about to turn away had a last remark. 'I suppose you, too, despise our family involvement in the grubby world of *trade?*'

It was a question, and Eliot, after some hesitation, said in a lowered tone, 'Not at all. Unbeknown to my family I, too, am engaged in trade.'

Richard laughed, heading to the west wing, 'You must tell me about that some time.'

Eliot, regarding Richard's relaxed gait as he climbed the stairs, said, 'I will!' and as he said so he realised what a relief it might be to tell this intelligent younger man the scope of his present gamble.

There had been the respite of Richard's appearance, but Eliot knew that he had to face the last two of the family. He dreaded both, but in the end he settled on Berthe next. When he looked covertly at Naomi over dinner that evening, he could not yet find courage to talk to her.

One could see all the girls at their most natural this evening, as they excitedly pelted Richard with questions and future plans. Naomi thus looked incredibly pretty, her amused smile and her arch look on display at Richard's responses, he teasing them all about the difficulty of finding suitable mounts for the girl's perceived riding imperfections. Thus Richard himself was more voluble and Eliot saw both of his brothers gaze at him at different times. Eliot was interested if Cedric and Charles, like himself, was wondering what it was to be surrounded by so much affection.

Perhaps his sisters Ophelia and Queenie looked on, too. Would they wonder at *having* such an affectionate brother themselves? Goodness knows that neither he, Charles nor Cedric fit the bill. He caught Roseanna's eye on Richard. She admired him, obviously, but she was frightened of his casual affection. At one point, he touched the silent Tabitha's head, just as a fond support of spirits which obviously were constrained when the two families were together.

'The table is so noisy!' The countess said in a complaining tone. 'Is it too much to expect that we eat in peace?'

Lady Eleanor said, 'I agree, countess,' she stopped Naomi's chatter with a hand on her arm. 'I do not suppose the earl's family wishes to hear quite so much about our horses,' she gave a look to Berthe whose mouth was open in dispute. '*Or carriages*, Berthe. We may talk of these excitements in our sitting room later.'

'That seems more appropriate. If you continue to favour dining together, Lady Eleanor,' said Cedric after silence reigned, 'it would be polite of your family to remember my sensitivity to rattles, which I share with my *Celestial Treasure*.'

'What is a rattle?' asked Berthe.

'Something,' said Charles with acerbity, 'that makes a great deal of noise.' He added, *'Like you!'*

'Oh,' Berthe turned and reminded Cedric helpfully, 'but I remember it was the *countess'* voice that gave you a headache before. That must be *very* inconvenient since you live together.' She smiled, her open eyes guileless. This was the unbeatable power of the awful child. Eliot was suffering from it himself. Berthe turned to Charles, whom she seemed to treat as a person the same age as herself. Mentally, Eliot reflected, she may not have been wrong. 'And at least *I* don't make as much noise as *you* when I *eat*, Crown Prince!'

'You *horrible—!*' but Charles suddenly remembered the violence of Richard, Eliot thought, and stopped himself. This was unnecessary, Eliot felt. Richard was eating his dinner without interest. 'Sticks and stones...' Richard did not care much what people *said* to his sisters (although Eliot imagined there would be *some* line there), just what they *did*. But at any rate Charles changed the subject. 'We have had a delivery from the silk merchants today. We must begin to see to your clothes for the Season, ladies. Roseanna, would you care to join us tomorrow for a look at what I have chosen for Queenie?'

Roseanna said she would, with quiet enthusiasm, and Eliot gazed towards Naomi. She sent her eyes to heaven. However, she caught Eliot's eye, and ate in silence once more, her face closed off. Thus he was able to look at her once more, at least.

What was adorable was that Naomi's stone face was really so expressive. The muscles might be immobile, but a quick glimpse at those large luminous eyes betrayed her. He clearly saw the hurt pride, and more. He clearly saw that she was wounded, but still vulnerable to some offer of friendship and affection from him, perhaps. Naomi's pen could be acid, but her soul was not. It was younger, he believed, than Tabitha's or even Berthe's. Her eyes could never quite close themselves off, even in her anger — just as Cedric's never let anything in, even in his assumption of affection. Naomi shone.

'Berthe,' he said quietly, 'shall we go for a walk tomorrow morning?'

'Is it my turn?' Berthe whispered back, excited.

'If you like,' he said, indifferently.

CHAPTER 9

Berthe and Tabitha

As Berthe and Eliot began to leave the next day, Tabitha came up from behind. 'I need you to take me to the village to check on my model,' she ordered.

'What about the others?'

'Busy with horses and such,' replied Tabitha.

'But this is *my* day!' whined Berthe, pulling at Eliot's sleeve.

'What do you mean?' asked Tabitha looking from one to the other.

'Never mind!' said Berthe crossly. 'I shall not tell you. Only that Eliot owes me *ten whole minutes*.'

'He can give you that in the carriage to the village.'

'You will *hear* us,' Berthe said, still whining a little, 'and I have something *particular* to say to him.'

Tabitha considered, in her quiet, adult way then said, 'If we took a landau and you both sat on the box, I doubt I could hear anything from behind.'

Tabitha, reflected Eliot, was not of a prying disposition, unlike her younger sister. But Berthe seemed to know so, too, therefore she merely said, 'You must give me a favour later, mind. Oh, very well, then.'

They did as Tabitha suggested, and Berthe turned to him.

'Well, Eliot, how did you find the punishment?'

'It was very interesting.'

'But I fear it is the kind of punishment to *continue,*' said Berthe with some glee.

'What do you mean?'

'Well, Tabitha thinks you will just obey her if she needs you, and I think Richard likes you now, so very likely he will continue to talk to you.'

'That is not precisely *punishment*.'

'But I am *very* pleased with myself, because it is *just* like the punishment mama gives. In my case, I like to make things tidy now. Even when I upset my room, I like to set it right before I sleep. And for you, Phoebe has begun to tease you a lot, and will probably not let off. You went for *one* walk and now I do not suppose you can go back to being distant with her.'

Eliot sighed. 'You are quite correct.'

'Or with Mama, too.'

'Ah, that is different. Your mother is kind to everyone.'

'She is not kind to the earl, I don't think. She never punishes me if I have made the *earl* upset. You are not really friends with Roseanna yet, but *she* is very nice, you know!'

'I do not know how to be friends with Roseanna, I fear. It is similar with my sister Queenie. She is so *obliging*, which is so very far from my own nature that I feel separate from her.' Eliot could not believe he was talking this way to an eight-year-old child. He looked down at her and her disconcertingly candid stare looked back at him.

Then she grinned an evil grin. 'But you still have the *biggest* one to do.' Berthe's glee was harder to swallow this time. '*Naomi*.'

'Why is Naomi the hardest?' said Tabitha from the seat behind. As Berthe and Eliot jumped at the interjection, she added, 'Oh ... I was mistaken, Eliot. I can hear your whole conversation from here.'

'Well, I shall *never* reveal your secret, Eliot, never fear,' said Berthe enjoying her sense of mystery. 'After all, once you speak to Naomi for ten minutes, you will have received your whole punishment.'

Eliot, to whom a sigh was becoming second nature, issued one again. He turned his head to Tabitha for a second. 'Berthe saw me read Naomi's journal, and set me a punishment.'

'Read her *journal*? You *should* not have done so, Eliot. That was not gentlemanly. We should tell Naomi.'

'You should, and I would face my humiliation well, but I think it might hurt *Naomi*, who does not at all deserve it.'

'Why would it hurt her? The spying?'

'Well, Tabitha, would you like everyone to know all *your* inner thoughts? I began to read Naomi's journal to get to know all of you. It was not quite proper, but you were not quite *real people* to me at first.'

'Like the Royals with us?'

'Probably. So I sent my conscience to sleep and told myself it was not an intrusion. Well, no more of an intrusion than a strange family appearing in my home.'

'*How* do you send your conscience to sleep?' inquired Berthe, interested. 'Whenever I do something I ought not, I sting myself all day until I tell Mama...'

'You *frequently* do things you ought not ... and it never seems to bother you in the least,' said her sister.

'No, I sometimes do things *others* think I ought not. But I seldom do anything *I* think I ought not,' said Berthe crossly.

Tabitha turned to Eliot, who had stopped the landau in a broad piece of road, dismissing Berthe, it seemed. 'I suppose I see that our family were not quite *people* to you yet. But it is still *wrong*, Eliot...' Tabitha had some of the dignity of her mother as she said so.

It made Eliot smile. 'I know. And I am still trying to justify my behaviour, and that is not like me.'

'Grown ups think around corners,' Berthe said, in conclusion.

'But then,' explained Eliot, 'Naomi described her thoughts on us all in the journal, she calls us The Royals, because of Ophelia's names for us all. But also she remarks upon what she knows about all of you, and I realised reading the journal became something akin to listening behind a keyhole before I knew it.'

'Like your butler Godwin!' said Berthe.

Eliot was not surprised to realise that the child had noticed the butler's proclivities. '*Exactly!*' he said with distaste at himself.

'Well,' said Tabitha, brows down, 'I still think Naomi should know.'

'You must decide, Tabitha,' said Eliot. 'But first I will just finish my punishment like a man and talk to Naomi tomorrow.'

'You had much better tell her what you did, Eliot!' said Tabitha sternly.

'Perhaps that is why I have left it for last. Perhaps that is *just* what I fear I shall do.'

'There is another secret behind this,' mused Tabitha. 'What is it?'

'You would have to read Naomi's journal to find out,' said Eliot with grim humour.

'Pooh! *I* only want to think of gears. Let us visit Mr Quigley and see how he does with my model. If he is finished, I can show it to Rich this afternoon.'

'Is today's punishment at an end, Berthe?' said Eliot, feeling exhausted.

'I do not know if I have had my full ten minutes. I was going to tell you my surprising secret, but I think we shall all just admire Tabitha's model on the journey back. Then I am willing to say you have passed today's punishment.'

'My sister Ophelia is wondering what I have to say to you all.'

'I expect she is just jealous, as I am when Richard spends too much time with Tabitha. You should talk to her more to please her.'

Eliot listening, was stunned to realise that the terrible child was probably correct.

The day of days had arrived. He could put it off no longer. But the woman he wished to talk to, she of the easy smile and humorous eye, was no longer the Naomi who graced their meal tables. Along with Phoebe, she was somewhat withdrawn, at moments when her family were not demanding her attention.

Eliot also worried a little about Phoebe. Something more must have occurred with Barclay than he had thought. It seemed her heart was affected. But Eliot, noticing this in passing, was focused on the journal's author. He tried not to look at Naomi, he had tried hard not to since the incident under the tree. However he had found that he had a new ability. A half second glance at Naomi, unnoticed by anyone else, and she was etched into his mind. He could judge her mood, her looks.

The other time he was permitted to look at her was when her family was talking and someone said something amusing, causing hilarity. All the Royals glanced over then, so it was safe for him to do so too. But when he did, he found that there was some movement — some gesture or turn of her head, or flush of her cheek, that showed that she was conscious of him and listening less to the chatter of her family.

The family were able to talk freely at breakfast because Cedric was not generally present.

Charles desired to rise later, but the demands of his stomach would not let him, and he generally came downstairs in his night attire: frilled, long nightshirt covered by a richly coloured brocade gown worn over it. However voluminous the nightshirt, this raiment was not quite respectable enough for Eliot's taste, for when Charles sat, outlines of his form were quite visible. His ankles above brocade slippers were often on display, his navel was visible beneath the cotton if he sat on the gown ill, and it stretched over his stomach.

Eliot had adjured his brother to dress before breakfast, since there were now ladies *who were not his sisters* in the house. But Charles, uninterested, simply refused, for often he took to bed again after eating a prodigious amount at the breakfast table, and only reemerged from his chamber preened and primped some time in the after noon.

Charles engaged in none of the country pursuits. He rode, but only when necessary, and he did not drive alone, but took a coachman or groom. He did not use a gun (loud, dirty and annoying things) he did not fish (how dreadful to get one's feet wet). Charles was at Tremaine to show off to the village and the neighbours how noble he was. And he was preparing for his next London Season, where he could be guaranteed to be in the first of the arrivals and the last of the departures. On one occasion he had tried to stay in London, but apart from the company being so small, it had been a year when smallpox gripped the capital, and Charles had flown back to Tremaine, afraid.

Cedric, too, had been afraid, and had restricted Charles to his room for two weeks until he was sure there was no sign of infection. He had only been able to keep him there by having Cook send a great deal of food.

But the Wild ones talked, and though Charles affected a headache and often directed superior looks to the other family, he was too engaged in his important task of eating to make serious complaint about the noise. So he simply kept up occasional conversation with Ophelia and Queenie, ignored the remarks of the awful child, who seemed fascinated with him, and disparaged the cut of Eliot's coat or waistcoat. When the countess deigned to come to breakfast, the Wild ones were more subdued and gave her little to complain of. But still she managed it.

'I cannot imagine, Lady Eleanor, why you do not instruct Phoebe and Stephanie to put up their hair. They are hardly *children,* though you seem to treat them so,' Agatha sniffed.

Eliot had heard from Charles that the countess was most put out to discover the carriages, of the newest design, being housed in a building once derelict on the estate. However, being forbidden by the earl to bring up such matters with the presumptuous duke's daughter, she had to take recourse to other complaints. Eliot decided that Agatha was truly stupid. She had not won such an encounter since the Wild family's arrival.

'Can you not?' said Lady Eleanor faintly, with polite disinterest.

Ophelia, to Eliot's surprise, waded in. 'I think my sister asks only what the Polite world will. I am interested in the answer myself.'

This was said with a more open look, less critical tone and Lady Eleanor returned her candid look with the same slight histrionic attitude, '*Are* you?' It sounded as though Mrs Marchmont was much interested in Ophelia's interest, and might give an answer, but then she smiled and turned towards the horrible child. 'Shall you try the pony and trap today, my Berthe?'

Ophelia, caught by a manner as insolent as her own, and an opponent on whom her tricks of candour did not work, coughed a laugh.

Eliot glanced at Naomi, and felt that as she smiled at her porridge plate, that she was composing the journal entry for this incident in her head. She looked up and caught his gaze on her and the look she gave him was fire and ice combined. It set him back in his seat. But her eyes dropped once more, a flush on her cheek.

In a few minutes they rose to leave and Eliot followed, 'Miss ...' he began as she passed his chair.

Phoebe's voice called to him, 'Eliot, might I talk to you?'

Naomi looked over her shoulder at this and walked off briskly; Eliot looked down at her lovely, dark-haired sister. Ophelia rose too and as he glanced over at her, her brows were raised sardonically.

'Not here!' hissed Phoebe, to make matters worse.

'What is this...?' expostulated Charles.

Eliot led Phoebe to the green salon and looked down at her, a trifle frustrated since he had mustered the courage to talk to her sister today, and now was delayed.

'I won't bite, Eliot. Only I wanted to ask ... do you know Barclay's direction?'

'No.'

'Then, I must suppose your brother does.'

'I suppose so. So why do you not ask *him*?'

'I do not wish to give rise to ... oh, you *know* why, Eliot! Stop being such a prig.'

'You do not wish this ... *connection* with Sir Osbert to spread further.'

'Precisely.'

'If it is something this underhand, Phoebe, do you think it appropriate? I think your mother is someone it is safe to confide in. If you are sure you are about to do the right thing, why do you keep it from her?'

'Underhand?' Phoebe sounded furious and incredulous both. 'No Eliot, merely private. I wish to protect my privacy...'

'No, Phoebe. I think you wish to protect *his*. I do not think you are sure of him...'

'You are *wrong!*' Phoebe said, furious. 'Would I have offered my kiss to someone who did not tell me ... you are mistaken Eliot.' She tossed her black curls.

'Do not write to him. It only leaves you open to misunderstanding. And worse.'

'I shall do as I see fit, and not as a stuff-shirt such as—'

'I?' Eliot looked down at her. '*Someone* must curb your willfulness before you do yourself and your whole family harm.'

'Is this how one of your sisters became so afraid to break the rules, and the other so unfeeling? It will not work with me, Eliot. Consult your beliefs in your own affairs, not in mine.'

'Very well, I will pass the matter to Richard, and he may discuss it with you.'

'You *promised!* You said that you had seen it only by chance. How can you change?'

'I promised then, but that was before you were about to commit a new folly. One that might impact on Roseanna, Naomi, Stephanie and even the younger girls.'

'You know Rich will likely *kill* Barclay, before I can explain a thing.'

'Then you must choose for yourself, Phoebe.

She turned from opening the door 'I *hate* you Eliot Marchmont!' she screamed as she banged it shut.

Through the door, in the brief moment when Phoebe had thrown it open, Eliot saw Naomi on the stairs, while Ophelia was crossing the hall, dressed for a drive.

Eliot opened the door in a hurry to find Naomi had descended and gone to Phoebe's side, Ophelia having detained her. His sister was saying, 'While I agree with the sentiment at times, Phoebe, what on earth has The Black Sheep done to make you say so?'

Phoebe dashed an angry tear from her eye and said, 'Your brother is interfering and annoying!'

'*Eliot? Interfering?* He has never before been so. He is annoying, but generally because he is so boring and *dis*interested in anything the family might do.'

'He seems to have *taken an interest* in my sister, however,' spat out Naomi. 'Enough to distress her very much!' she put an arm around her sister's waist. 'Come Phoebe!'

'Naomi!' Eliot called. 'Can you spare me a moment to speak to me?'

'Me? Why ever should I wish to do so?' She turned away coldly.

Watching the sisters leave, Ophelia remarked, to the hall in general, 'Now, I thought Naomi the one member of that family to take things lightly,' she tittered, 'What a bore!'

Eliot clenched a fist. 'Stop being a witch, Ophelia.'

'Then tell me all, dear brother,' said Ophelia avidly, following him into the green salon.

'What do you care?' Eliot said, with an assumption of indifference.

'I asked you before what is going on, and you refused to tell me. You know I can scent gossip. Even if I do not *care*, it does not mean I am not inquisitive.' She looked at him. 'Has the new Marchmont family finally melted your cold heart?' She raised a brow. 'I thought it was between the pretty but vapid Roseanna and the beautiful, passionate Phoebe, but now the third candidate arises. Which has stolen your heart?'

'Stop amusing yourself at my expense.'

'But what could make Phoebe hate you?' she laughed, 'I can barely stay awake in your presence it is so distant, what can have made a young girl display such a passionate feeling as *hate*?'

'Merely that I interfere with her freedom,' said Eliot dismissively, 'and she is not used to it.'

'So is it protective action, or perhaps *jealousy* that afflicts you? *Do* tell, brother dear.' She had thrown herself into a chair and twirled an ankle as she added, 'You have never cared to interfere with my freedom, *whatever* I have chosen to do.' It was said sardonically, but Eliot became aware of some hurt beneath. It was true, for the most part, he was a bad brother. She added, 'But then, Phoebe is very beautiful!'

Eliot ignored the last sneer, and said, addressing her penultimate remark, 'I should have done more, Ophelia, for you and for Queenie. But there are things ...' he stopped. He was not ready to explain himself.

Godwin came in with a missive from London. 'It was brought by fast courier Mr Eliot.' He said, with a significant tone. Eliot seeing the butler's eyes on the sealed note, was amazed that the seal was not broken already. Godwin lingered.

'Should I leave you to your business, Eliot?' Ophelia seemed embarrassed that her feelings of hurt had somehow been exposed to her brother, and she was unable to continue her sardonic tone.

'*Godwin* should leave,' said Eliot, holding the express in trembling fingers. 'Ophelia, stay, I pray you!'

The butler left with bad grace, and Ophelia looked surprised, at Eliot's trembling hands. Her cool brother Eliot was shaking.

'*Eliot...?*' she breathed.

He broke the seal and read the missive, then suddenly looking up, beamed at her.

'Whatever...?' she asked.

'*Ophelia!* It is the *gamble* ... it has paid off!' He was grinning in a way that Ophelia had not seen in many years. He held his arms open and walked towards her. She backed off.

'What is this...?' she said, stunned, looking at his open arms askance. 'You have been living with the Other Family too long!' She became more serious. 'Your *gamble*? I had wanted to ask you why, when you at least are independent of Cedric, would you do such a thing as gamble half your fortune? It made no sense.'

'For you and Queenie, of course!' said Eliot, too pleased for restraint, 'and it is almost done, Ophelia!'

He came towards her again, and she pulled him down onto a sofa and said, 'Tell me all!'

He did. He told her of his investment in shipping, his fear of losing the bet, but his hope for a growth of his fortune enough to secure his sister's safety, too.

'Is this why you have not spent... Why you are wearing such an *ordinary*...!' She was trembling, and Eliot knew that the last sardonic remark was to keep her from more emotional displays.

'I needed to have sufficient funds to invest, so that the return would be as big as today. *Now* you may both be dowered at least, substantially, or the money held for you in trust if you do not marry.'

'You did not trust Cedric's words about choosing partners for us wisely, did you?'

'Cedric will dictate a marriage favourable to himself, if I were to let him. You should each be at least free to choose.' He frowned at her. 'I am not there yet, Ophelia. I want to buy a house and have enough put by for your Season's finery, too. I need just one more lucky voyage... I am awaiting just such another...'

'But if the ship goes down, you will lose all again, like Charles at the Faro bank.'

'I do not have an estate to profit by even. I cannot repair Marchmont Hall, for it still belongs to Cedric and as such...!'

'But I tried to believe that with the earldom he had enough ...!' said Ophelia, distressed. 'Has he really destroyed all?'

This was not something to be disclosed to his sister, he was not here to add more criticism to Cedric. 'The Tremaine estate is free of mortgage and will remain so legally. But ...!

'We do not know what other follies he might commit. *I* know. But things seem to have changed...! Ah! Lady Eleanor! But why *should* she aid Cedric?'

'Family reasons.'

'Is it that Richard Marchmont is Cedric's second heir, after Charles?'

'It is a trifle more complicated than that, and I am not at liberty to say. But it seems that her ladyship's purse and her disposition both give her some power to halt some of Cedric's behaviour.'

'Not for long, I fear!' Ophelia's cynicism returned. Then her voice changed to a more sincere one, 'But Eliot, you have been thinking all this time about Queenie and me ... what about *you*? Do you not want to start up a home for yourself, for a wife and children...?'

'Once my sisters are settled, of course.'

Ophelia, to Eliot's shocked dismay, wailed. 'Oh Eliot! I thought you did not care for us at all, while all this time you have been saving and planning, all for Queenie and for me.'

'It is just ... as you once said, how does one know when all this lifestyle will disappear? Cedric, Charles, and even Dorian might drag us all into ruin before we know it. The threat will continue. They cannot sell the estate, but what use will it be if the servants be unpaid and the land not worked? Or if there are horrendous debts of honour that drag the family name through the mud?' He shook his head.

Ophelia held his hand impulsively. 'You have thought of all of this? I too. I nearly married March last year to save myself and Queenie. But I happened to see another side of him ... and I found I could not.'

Eliot nodded. 'I should have done everything in my power to stop you making such a bargain as The Earl of March. Rakes seldom make good husbands. But Ophelia, if our brothers know I have money, then they will undoubtedly batten on if their funds run out. I wish them to know nothing of my business. Tell Queenie if you must, to allay her worry. But tell her only that there is a secret bequest that grants you a dowry, but that it must not be disclosed to your brothers.'

Ophelia threw herself on her brother's chest, finally letting the arms she had resisted earlier surround her. 'No, I will tell her the *truth* Eliot. For it means so much more to me to know that you *care* than that I am now independent. And it will to Queenie, too.'

Eliot, unable to respond to his sophisticated sister's tears, patted her back in an awkward fashion.

'But why must you risk *more*, Eliot?'

'I have just received ten times and more on my investment. But I will consider it only five times my investment. That is how I shall think of it, and so must you. Then it shall matter little that I gamble the rest on the next boat out. My Fortune was £2000 in all. I invested £1000, and now I have £10,000 courtesy of my gamble. I have laid out Grandmama's legacy on another ship already, but that I do not yet think of. But these profits I shall think of it as only £5000, not ten. From this, you shall each have £2000 as dowry, or as your independence.'

'£2000? It is not credible!'

'Yes it is. I will take the remaining £1000 and restore my original fortune. It is enough to keep us, but not in style. I need to buy an estate large enough to provide an income, and that is why I will put £5000 into the next ship. I could buy a small estate instead, but I wish my sisters to live elegantly, but not by being indebted. One more investment return and I shall be able to purchase land enough to give us an elegant income.'

'And if it sinks?'

'Then I can make the £1000 gamble once more.'

'You will become like the other brothers. That last bet might ruin your security.'

'Not quite. It will only mean that you two will have to work harder at becoming married sooner. I can live frugally quite happily, but my sisters are more expensive creatures.'

'I will be no burden on you, Eliot. I promise!' They sat thus for a while until Ophelia rose, wiped her eyes of her joyful tears, and went to speak to her sister.

Eliot was still writing instructions to his lawyer as to the disposal of his funds when a red-eyed Queenie entered the room.

'Eliot dear!' she said, eyes spilling over.

He got up from behind the desk and came to take her hands 'Now Queenie, there is no need to cry.'

He led her to the sofa which was probably still wet with Ophelia's tears.

'I do not know how much ... I had no idea ...!' She gulped. 'I think you have been afraid that Cedric and Charles have been unkind or ungenerous to me ...'

'Indeed, no Queenie. It is just that I have been concerned a little at the uncertainty produced by losses at the gaming tables...'

'Oh,' said Queenie seriously, 'but Charles has explained to me that luck *always* turns around.'

Too trusting, the elder of his sisters. Ophelia was much older than Queenie in her soul. Eliot did not want to disabuse her innocence. 'Perhaps, but I am your boring, sober brother, and I do not choose that you live in uncertainty.'

Her eyes watered. 'Oh, Eliot! *How* can I thank you..?'

'Two things, Ness. First, keep a guard on your unruly tongue. If my brothers know I have funds, I shall be bothered indeed.'

'I *promise.* I hereby forget that I know of your funds.'

'Anyway, I have only just restored myself. I am no richer than yesterday. My new fortune is gambled again soon.' He raised an ironic eyebrow. 'It seems that I am more like my brothers than I believed.' They both laughed at this absurdity. Then he touched her rouged cheek briefly. 'And your dowry shall concern no one but your future suitor, Ness.'

'We shall not speak of it in Town or even to Cedric?' she nodded. He saw some thoughts go through her head. It was certainly true that if the *Beau Monde* knew of such a dowry, the number of his sister's suitors might increase.

'I think...' said Eliot gently, '...that to do so might encourage the *wrong sort* of suitor, do not you, Ness?'

'I shall be guided by you, Eliot dear. I did not know you had my interests so close to your heart. You are correct.'

'And that goes for the *second* thing you may do for me, Ness.' Queenie fixed her eyes on her brother trustingly, listening for his condition and clasping his hands. 'You must marry *only* a man that you admire and love, Ness. Not just a man to oblige the family.'

For some reason Ness was convulsed with tears at this, and Eliot suddenly thought of her disappointment in her first Season. He did not know what to do, so he stayed silent.

Eventually she pulled herself together enough to look up at him seriously and say with watery determination, 'I *shall*, Eliot. I ought to ask for Cedric's opinion, as he was once my guardian before I came of age. But instead, I shall trust *you*, Eliot, and only marry if *you* approve my choice.'

Eliot felt this as a burden rather than a privilege, but it was better than Ness being afraid again. 'Very well, Ness. But I shall judge harshly, mind. He must deserve you!' She laughed as though this was absurd, his poor sister, and then she flushed. 'I only want you to be happy, Ness.'

'Oh, *dear* Eliot! My very dear Eliot. I promise you, even if I do not marry, I *shall* be happy in the future.' She smiled at him, looking at the long missive he was writing. 'But I will leave you to your business, my dear.' She stood, and became rather stiff again as she did so. 'I still wish there was something I could do in return.'

'I expect there are many things, Ness.' His eyebrows rose as something occurred to him. 'First, could you return in twenty minutes and drive this letter to the mail stop at the inn?'

Queenie looked willing, but raised her brows in inquiry.

'Godwin knows about the express today,' Eliot explained, 'and I suppose he will wish to *pry* into any fast response from me. He may even ...!' he left the thought unfinished. 'If you could send off the letter on a pretext of a hunt for ribbons in the village, Ness, then ...!'

'He will not tell Cedric. Or even attempt to read it. He will not think it so important.' She looked a little bleak. 'Once, long ago, I fear Godwin *did* read a letter of mine and show it to Cedric.'

'Very well. Anyway, he will not guess you carry it for me today.'

'That will make me *very* happy.' She smiled, and Eliot understood that this was the first real beaming smile he had seen from Queenie for a long time.

After Queenie's return to collect the letter, Eliot sat at his fireside warm and content, contemplating the flames. His contentment was curtailed however, when a dark-haired child entered and sat herself opposite him, jumping a little to reach the seat.

'Naomi says she will *never* speak to you at all, Eliot. So, since you have failed to complete your punishment, and upset Phoebe *also*, *I* must decide what to do next.'

She kicked her legs gaily and Eliot regarded her with a vicious frown. *Terrible child!*

CHAPTER 10

Eliot the Disrupter

Naomi, furious with Eliot after Phoebe's outburst, and even more agitated that her open, passionate sister would not tell her what the dispute with Eliot was about, eventually pleaded fatigue to tell her only confidante about her situation. She, who could usually tell her family anything, was reduced to cope with her feelings on paper only. She reached for her quill and began to write, hearing the noisy movement of her family in the corridor, heading out for another ride on their new mounts.

What did he mean by it, the impertinent Mr Eliot Marchmont? He wishes to speak with me? A person he has been ignoring these last days, a person whose eye he avoids, even. All this time he has spoken to others, to the children, to Richard, to Phoebe ... especially to Phoebe. What happened between them today? I have asked her and she will not say. Just as I am not discussing things with my family, so too is Phoebe, the most open and closest of my sisters, locking me out of her thoughts.

If we stay here any longer perhaps the Curse of the Royals might fall upon us, making us a family full of secrets and false displays of manners and everything that oppresses instead of expresses love and trust. But I cannot say that Ophelia's indifference, Queenie's reticence, the countess' disagreeableness, the Crown Prince's puffed up conceit, the earl's evil sarcasm (that occasionally hits a mark), could have bothered us. Such behaviours were tiresome, but amusing to me and most of the others. Phoebe scratched back, Mama used her force of character, Richard ignores them, Roseanna is universally pleasing, Stephanie is largely like Richard, and I looked at them as fodder for my sharp pen. No, the real reason for all this discord, the real evil before our family is none other than the brother who seemed the least dreadful of the prideful Royals, Eliot Marchmont!

From an early admiration of his face and form, I am now beginning to loath the man. I was right in my early assessment of his being cold and aloof, and all of this I could tolerate and even understand. Who would enjoy a rowdy crowd of relatives invading one's home? He had a right, perhaps, to his extreme reserve. Had it stayed thus, my family would remain intact at least, but no!

Eliot Marchmont stepped forward to us, the rough family, starting with the day under the tree with me. I may have begun it, but I now see that he ought to have maintained his distance, if that had been his way to deal with us. But all at once he wishes to show himself to me as amusing and charming, as a person of humour and wit, and his reserved dropped. Then he laughed with me at dinner, before completely retreating once more. It shamed me. It made me feel as though he thought me in pursuit of him. But now, as events unfold, I shall put the blame to rest where it should. If he wished to keep his distance, then he should have done so. And to treat me so afterwards is the act of a coward and a person who shirks blame. I despise such a person.

While I doubted myself, he has repeatedly shown himself to me again and again. Kindness to my younger sisters made me soften, but after further coldness towards me, it seemed like another slap, underlying the dreadful thought that I am the one who is to be discarded — because I am the person who cleaved to him.

He asked questions of Roseanna, very polite and friendly, then he takes Phoebe aside and appears very intimate indeed. Does he incline to her? Even if he does, a gentleman would not show such difference in treatment to two sisters. He should be able to put off the one with friendliness and leave some space for the later intimacy of in-laws.

What am I saying? But there is no escaping that the connection between Phoebe and Eliot is intimate indeed. Has he offered her such openness and then the rejection that he offered me? Is that his way of flirting, perhaps? I know little of men, and neither does Phoebe. But if Eliot treated her so, Phoebe is not me. He will live to regret it. She won't permit such falseness, such duplicity. I wish to brush it under the carpet, to protect my own dignity, but Phoebe is not the same. She cares nothing for conventional dignity, only for her own truth, which is superior dignity, in my opinion. She will rail at him if he cuts off her affection, and I admire her for it. I just fume and write these pages.

But worse than the rest of his family's evil intentions to us, is Eliot Marchmont's come and go of affection. Now he talks to Richard, to Stephanie, to the children, and gains their trust. And this has the potential to separate us. I do not choose to tell others the reason for my disaffection with him, it sounds petty and its subtleties will be lost in the telling. Is this what guards Phoebe's tongue too? I always thought us too different to develop inclinations towards the same person. She admired Sir Osbert Barclay, for example, much more than I did.

But perhaps being exposed to a person of beauty and such charm (when he wills) as Eliot Marchmont, after a fairly restricted pool of eligible gentlemen, it was inevitable. Not that I have considered him in any way more than a potential friend, and that is what has hurt so much. I am a victim of HIS imagination, not my own. Perhaps it is the same with Phoebe? But her hatred so expressed argues not.

I want to talk to Mama about all this. She could help us. But now, with new secrets, I feel at a distance from Phoebe and I have no right to expose that she too has secrets with Eliot Marchmont. I smiled suddenly, remembering the way I used to bring up secrets with Mama, when I was much younger. 'If someone was careless and broke an or-

nament, Mama, what might she do if she didn't want to make her parents disappointed in her?' Now, that sounds like Berthe to me, and I suppose I must have been a similar age when I asked this question. Mama had looked at me gravely, but darling Papa, passing through, had given a crack of laughter which mother's eyes admonished him for. Dear Papa! Perhaps if he were here I could ask him something about how gentleman behave. It is useless to ask Richard. He has no idea about anything beyond engines.

I just laughed again, imagining how I should have begun the conversation. 'If a gentleman is unfriendly, then very friendly, and then cold again to a female, how should she behave?' and Papa would give his crack of laughter, piercing my attempt at anonymity.

The journal page became stained with tears, and some ink ran, but it was still legible.

Having written this, having finally seen the danger, I will not let Eliot Marchmont drive us apart. Perhaps I should speak to him, quite as directly as though I were Phoebe, but with something of Mama's dignity. I will tell him that I have no interest in him and that his behaviour to me is thus insulting. I shall not coat the words in honey. I wished to conceal that I minded, or even noticed, his withdrawal, but to save our family from this paralysing reserve I shall be frank. I will not indulge in a Royal game, led by the nose by such as he. I will talk to him, and then talk to him again and again in public. I shall be myself and not be influenced by him at all. It may mean that the Royals will suspect me as a shameless woman out to ensnare their handsome brother, but when did I begin to care about what such a family as they think of me? He may respond to my talk or not after I have had our interview. I shall not at all mind it. At least I will stop suffocating.

I trust Phoebe will continue as she wishes. She is a brave and redoubtable girl. But I, too, shall make sure I tell Eliot Marchmont what I think of him.

Naomi wrote on some pages, about Tabitha's amazing model, about their new horses, about Mama's possible plans.

Mama will be open about most things. You simply have to ask her the correct questions. Mama is reserved in some ways, but she explained to me, while I was still a child, that adults had responsibilities that need not burden their children. Children had quite enough to do growing up properly (increasing their intelligence, responsibility, joy, kindness) and in discovering the world.) That, had explained Mama, was the work of a child.

Now Mama is planning our Season in London. I have seen that she is having correspondence with old friends, receiving recommendations and so on. She even consulted Charles Marchmont as to the most fashionable milliners and dressmakers in Town, beginning correspondence with same. She is bringing out three girls, after all, and Mama does nothing by half. Even the younger girls will have to be clothed rather differently in Town, though they will not be socialising at the Season's events. She has told me that all of us must come out of mourning, and the children will wear colour once more. I did not ask why Stephanie is not being introduced to society also. I considered that it may be better for her to come out with us all, but she is reluctant, and I do not wonder at it. Also, as Mama hinted, Stephanie is as independent as Phoebe, and it may be easier for Mama to have only one daughter to keep an eye out for in public, one tongue to curb.

Phoebe does what she must in the moment, without a thought of consequences. Stephanie has the same passion, but thinks rather more and achieves her purpose before she asks permission. Stephanie chose a stallion that I think Richard meant for himself, for example, by jumping upon it and riding off. Watching her, it certainly meant that no one could claim the horse was outwith her control. So Storm, the mottled grey, became hers. Stephanie does things before anyone guesses her intention. As Mama says, it might be better not to wonder what she will be up to in London ballrooms quite yet.

She will, however, be in London. But I am sure Mama will have a plan for her.

Before dinner, Naomi found Eliot in the green salon and as he stood, she sat without permission — rather more stiffly than usual. Her hair had been tidied. She was wearing the violet muslin, rather than her more sober clothes, and Eliot eyed her worriedly. And then he looked to the mantle.

'How may I help you ... eh, Naomi?'

'I am here to tell you, Eliot, that I consider your behaviour in the last days *disgusting*.'

'Towards you? I ... I ...!'

She raised an ironical eye. 'Your tongue is tripped by all your impertinent suppositions, and now cannot even finish a sentence.'

Eliot was rebuked, but a little angry, too. '*What* behaviour do you refer to, precisely?'

Naomi shook at his flagrant flip of the power, but squared her shoulders. 'You spoke to me under the tree that day—'

'I was pulled down—' he said brows raised.

'You might have resisted, seeing our difference in strength—'

'I was being polite!'

'And you *continued* to be polite and even *charming*—'

'I had no desire to charm, perhaps you are too susceptible—'

'You did *not* seek to be amusing, you claim?' she challenged him.

Her eyes were so beautiful that it was hard to keep from looking into them. He flicked an eye to the mantle once more.

'I cannot help being amusing,' he said nonchalant, 'no more than can you.'

The boast and praise both took her breath away for a second, but then she said, 'but after that same evening at dinner, you acted as though you did not know me—'

Eliot, feeling that he was giving genuine distress, said softly, 'There were reasons for that Naomi ... I did not mean to offend you—'

'Your reasons are *perfectly* plain to me and why I sought this interview.' She was trying for haughtiness, but she was adorably confused.

'You had much better *not*, Naomi—!' he warned, worrying for her.

'I shall *suffocate* if I do not say so. And my whole family will be *destroyed* by you!'

'Destroyed ... by me?' he asked, genuinely confused.

'Phoebe and I already have secrets because of you...!'

'No, not me...!'

'And it is spreading to the children. You are the more dangerous because you seem pleasant enough. At least we see the threat of your siblings!'

Eliot looked down at a figure quite as passionate as her sister Phoebe, and he was entranced and afraid at once. He must not allow her to go too far, for her own sake as well as his ... she would be humiliated by a lack of a decent response from him, and despite his good news today, he was not quite in the position to tell her ...! He knew that she might spurn him even if he spoke, but he would have taken his chance now, if only he were free to.

She looked up at him sardonically, suddenly sitting back at her ease, adopting a posture more usual to his sister Ophelia. 'You are more conceited than your brothers, even.'

'More conceited than *Charles*?' he said giving her an openly astonished look.

Her lips twitched. As he saw it, he realised he had wanted to amuse her, even *now* when he should, in fact, stop her from speaking openly.

'Yes.' She said soundly. 'For you think that any young lady who speaks to you is *pursuing*—!' No, thought Eliot, looking down at her rather sadly, only *you* because I have read your journal. But she had interrupted herself as he looked toward the mantle. 'Why do you keep regarding the clock?'

'Ten minutes!' he said and sighed. 'I am sorry to have to leave you, Miss Marchmont, but I have something to do.'

He turned on his heel and left, Naomi too surprised to do more than stay seated.

Eliot met Tabitha in the hall. 'Where is the horrible child?' he asked her.

'Berthe is in her room.'

'She has not yet spoken to your mother?'

'I do not think ...!'

Berthe tripped down the stairs and Eliot blocked her path. She tried to get around him, but he scooped her up, saying, 'I need a word with you!'

Richard, descending the stairs, said nonchalantly, 'Did she break something?'

'Not at all!' said Eliot, taking Berthe to the library, opposite the green salon where he had left the angry, no doubt confused, Naomi. He set Berthe on a chair.

'Ten minutes, just achieved. Have you told your mother yet?'

'I have not. You do not mean you managed to speak to Naomi?'

'She came to *me* — to chastise me.'

'Whatever for?'

'It is none of your business!'

'Did she find out about your crime?'

'No, and my crime is now expunged by my labour.'

'Ex-punged?'

'Wiped out.'

'Ah! Then I shall not tell. Congratulations, Eliot! I did not think you would complete the punishment, and that would have meant that God wanted me to tell. But I must say, two of my sisters rebuked you today. You must be not as nice as I thought you.'

'Very likely,' he said, moving off. She caught up with him and took his hand, skipping to keep up with his long stride. He pulled his hand away, but she grasped it again and it didn't seem to be worth the fight. They entered the dining room hand in hand, to hear her mother say, 'Where is Berthe? She came down before me, I am sure.'

'Eliot wanted a word with her...' said Richard, vaguely.

'You talked to that child of your *own volition*, Eliot?' said Charles, seeing their entrance. 'That is not to be recommended.'

'Why, sir?' asked Berthe. 'And why is your nose so red?'

Charles, who had imbibed since lunchtime, sent her a horrible look.

'Did Eliot finish?' asked Tabitha, as Berthe sat beside her.

'Finish what, dear girl?' said Queenie, leaning forward.

Eliot interrupted. 'Oh, just a game I played with the girls.'

'Do tell us of it, Eliot,' said Naomi clearly, 'my family have no secrets.'

Richard laughed. 'When did *that* begin?'

Naomi frowned at him. Since when did her brother protect The Black Sheep?

'May I join the game, dear?' asked Queenie, smiling.

The earl looked up at this. Queenie putting herself forward? 'Let us,' he intoned, 'address ourselves to the fish, and stop this yelling across the table, *I pray you.*' This last was said in failing accents that made Queenie flush.

'Quite right, my dear! We must restore the tone of our dinner table,' approved the countess.

'Always a support, My Benign Goddess!' said Cedric in his faint, mocking tone.

The countess twitched at the acidic appellation, Queenie collapsed like a pricked bladder, and the table was quiet once more for a while. After a minute, Berthe lent over and said in a stage whisper, 'This game is finished, Queenie, but I will think of another for you *soon.*'

Queenie smiled briefly, with a quick look up the table at the earl.

'Oh, childish games!' said Charles with a sniff. 'Trust me sister, there is danger in playing with such a child.'

'Pray what do you mean by *such a child*, Charles?' asked the quiet voice of Berthe's mama.

'It may,' interrupted the countess haughtily, 'be better to adopt a more formal style of dining, Lady Eleanor. Let us not speak *across* the table, so that your children might begin to learn company manners.'

This ultimately segregated the families from one another, since Eliot, Charles, Ophelia and Queenie were at one side of the table, with the Wild family (as he had begun to call them internally) opposite, the table flanked bottom and top by the earl and countess. It was a unbalanced arrangement, eight ranged at one side and only four at the other, but it had existed from the first of them living here and had more or less continued except at the more informal breakfasts.

There was a pause where Eliot felt that Lady Eleanor might best the countess as usual, but he was disappointed, for she merely said, 'Certainly! My children, confine your conversation to your siblings on either side of you this evening.'

The next day Eliot, riding back from the village, saw the Wild Marchmonts together as usual on a walk which appeared to have broken into a run. His path lay by the narrow brook, an offshoot of the river that traversed the estate, and they were walking on a much higher path, bounded by trees, so that he could see only glimpses of their unruliness among the woodland and hear only the loudest of calls. Berthe ran ahead as always, and stood at the top of a steep bank that swept down to the other side of the brook. Eliot halted his mount to look. Berthe, with a quick look over her shoulder, crouched suddenly and made herself into a ball to roll down the hill in a shockingly dangerous manner. Eliot held his breath. A cry went up, and Stephanie burst forward, red curls flying, bonnet hanging by its strings around her neck, and followed the rolling motion of her sister only a second later. Phoebe and Naomi were next to appear, calling out, then, with a quick grin at each other they too threw themselves down in unison. Richard and Roseanna arrived, and Roseanna called something to them, before hitching her skirts and trying to walk down. Before the steepness of the hill caused her to reach terminal velocity and lose her balance, Richard caught her — but he was rear-ended by Tabitha, also trying the descent on her feet, and they were tipped forward all, with Eliot still unable to catch his breath at the sight. Perhaps four seconds had passed.

As heads began to lift and bodies to untangle, Eliot watched and heard Tabitha scream 'You are all *stupid*!' which, since her own brown gown was around her waist, displaying her petticoat, and the hood of her short cape was twisted and was obscuring one eye, seemed peculiarly humorous. It did not shock Eliot to see that a wave of anxiety-fueled laughter shook them all, sending Phoebe and Naomi onto their backs again, laughing at the blue sky.

Stephanie was at the bridge, touching the end post and saying, 'I won!'

As Eliot rode over the bridge, Berthe called, '*I* would have won!' And she crawled to the bridge desolate, touching the same stone and raising her eyes to her sister. 'But I bashed my head.'

As Eliot arrived, the others were standing and brushing themselves off, still laughing. 'Are you quite alright, ladies?' he said pleasantly, his eye resting on Naomi, who ignored him. 'That seemed a little dangerous.'

'Not *ladies* but *hoydens*, you mean,' said Richard.

'Berthe wanted to cheat in the race to the bridge by risking her life,' said Naomi, 'so we could not but follow her.'

Richard had swept up Berthe in his arms, examining her head. 'Just a bump!' he said, carelessly. 'And you deserve it. Never do so again.'

This seemed redundant as he had followed suit, but Eliot was silent. Richard swung Berthe up towards him on his horse. 'Take her back, Eliot!'

Eliot smiled at Richard's authoritative tone, for he was several years younger. He grasped his burden, however and said, 'I shall deliver her to your mother,' then seated the child before him.

He smiled down at the rest of them, who were beginning to resume their walk, encouraged by Naomi. 'There is a twig in your hair!' he said helpfully as he rode past her on the narrow track.

'Thank you!' she said, but with rancour.

As they rode forward Berthe said huskily, 'Do not tell Mama, Eliot!'

'Why not?'

'I did not tell on *you.*'

'*It was dangerous, Berthe.*'

'Not really, or Richard would not have followed.'

'You did not see, you horrible child, but Richard only followed to help Roseanna, who attempted to come down on her feet.'

'Well, that *was* dangerous. I was much more careful.'

She was frustrating. 'And yet your head is hurt,' he admonished.

'*Do* not be cross, Eliot,' Berthe said, in a little-girl voice that he found suspicious. She laid her head against his chest and closed her eyes.

Since her grip on his driving coat slackened, he held her tiny form more tightly. He looked down at the dark curls ruefully.

She had bested him once more.

Since Berthe had been relegated to her bed, Eliot settled in the library fairly sure of peace to read his book. But it was not to be. Richard came in, throwing himself down on a chair opposite to give Eliot a brief account of his new hunter. He took up a journal rather aimlessly and sat while Eliot read. He stood after a half-hour and said, 'Thank you. Since the death of my father I miss the company of men.'

'Oh there are men enough in this house!' said Eliot sardonically. 'You should drop by Charles' dressing room so that he can give you a hint on the cut of your coat.'

'The company of my sisters seems suddenly more appealing.' He gave a twisted smile and left, and Eliot reflected that indeed Richard's company had not been burdensome. As with his brother Dorian (when he gave up his London facade for a while) they seemed to enter silence together with ease.

He settled down again, this time being interrupted by Godwin, hand delivering his replies from London. These Eliot gave a quick eye to, then tossed aside carelessly as though uninterested in their content, and the butler left disappointed.

He took them up again when he was finally alone. One was from his London agent, telling of a terrible shipping loss that had ruined one of his clients (no loss of life, thankfully, but loss of the entire cargo), and at the same time confirming his newest investment: a sailing he had tentatively looked in to was now a full commitment, as he had instructed. It did not seem *entirely* reassuring, but the man had gained his trust by being blunt with him from the first. The agent also wrote of the Trust documents for his sisters, worded as he wished, which had been begun with his lawyer, and that it might be necessary for him to visit London soon to sign some papers in this regard.

Naomi's face swum before Eliot. He wondered if he could, even if his last gamble did not pay out, be able to speak to her honestly? She was funny and warm and as unrestrained as all her family. He remembered her descent down the bank with Phoebe, her laughing at the sky. Could he perhaps just stay at the Towers and have them make their life here? To keep her near her family, he could. But he needed, at the very least, a home of his own to have to offer her, so that they know themselves secure from Cedric's profligacy. He still felt he had nothing to give to her until then.

Next Season ... he suddenly imagined her finely dressed, exercising her wit free of Tremaine Towers, leading her own court of gentlemen adherents. He thought of some of the wittier members of the *Ton*, who might appreciate her gifts. By the time his ship came in, even if successfully, Naomi Marchmont might be taken.

Her opinion of his appearance had always seemed to him founded on lack of experience. He did not, he believed, especially stand out amongst his contemporaries. He had received feminine attention, it was true, but so did many men. No, in Town she might see that she was exaggerated in her praise, and find some others she admired just as much.

He wished for her happiness, but he wished to *be* that happiness, if only she did not choose another meantime. He was quite sure, sure since the day beneath the tree, sure perhaps when he had first read her journal, sure he wished her to be his. He remembered considering that Roseanna and Phoebe were more beautiful, but he could not recall why now. When you saw the entirety of Naomi, there could only be one choice for him. She was lovely, inside and out. She was free and yet not willful, she was beauty without artifice, she was true to those she loved, kind to those beneath her, funny and very brave.

He was even glad that his rakish brother Dorian was from home, in case he cut him out in her admiration. He had heard a lady in town say Dorian had a heavenly face and a heart from hell. But it was Dorian's angelic beauty that he wished to keep from Naomi — she who had an admiration for such things.

CHAPTER 11

The Bite

'Ah!' said Charles, reading a letter over breakfast, 'Barclay writes that he will visit this evening, and bring a friend of ours, he says.'

Eliot's eye strayed to Phoebe, who had emitted a sound. She smiled broadly, then seeing Tabitha's eye on her, she indicated that she should pass the chocolate.

'How delightful!' said Lady Tremaine with dignified smugness, 'I wonder he does not name the friend.'

'He plays games, as usual,' said Ophelia, unpleasantly.

Phoebe gave her a searing look, which his sister missed entirely. She played with her food a little, and then left the table, hardly able, Eliot felt, to contain herself.

Ophelia gave him a look, an eyebrow raised, but he ignored it. He would not discuss Phoebe's business with his sister, even if she mistook his interest for jealousy. He glanced at Naomi, who looked flushed.

Eliot picked up the missive Godwin had laid beside his plate. 'Oh, it will be a full table, countess. If it does not discompose you, my two college friends arrive this afternoon, also.'

'Not at all! The country is rather thin of good company, we shall be a happy table this evening.' This was said in her customary flat voice and it curled Naomi's lip, Eliot noticed.

The earl, unexpectedly arriving for breakfast, begged to be informed of the root of her happiness. When the arrival of guests was explained to him he sighed deeply, accepting a coffee from Godwin. 'How pleasant for you, My Fount of All Merriment,' he drawled. 'I admit that *I* find the dinner table *sufficiently* noisy these days.' His hand gestured to the wild side of the table.

'Not now we keep to company manners, my dear. You must remember I have set a new tone for those not broached in etiquette.'

'My Touchstone of Sincerity! How could I forget it? You are always so ... ah ... diligent.' His eyes swept over her disdainfully. 'That cap ... I suppose it cost a great deal?'

The countess flushed. 'It offends you, my dear?'

'I should not go so far as to say so. It is just ... it is the kind of thing that prevents me coming down to breakfast.'

Queenie gasped, and Naomi said, '*Disgusting!*'

The whole company looked over at her, and she raised her eyes innocently, gazing around. 'Do you not find the new rolls so? Cook ought to change the recipe, I think.'

Ophelia gave a crack of laughter.

'If you do not like the fare, Naomi, you may leave the table!' It was said, Eliot thought, to protect her husband, but it merely made the recipient smile.

'*Quite* finished, Lady Tremaine. Enjoy your breakfast! You must tell me where you bought your cap later. It is utterly *ravishing*! I might purchase such a one for Mama.'

The salon where the two families generally assembled before dinner was looking much smaller tonight. As Naomi and Phoebe entered last, since Phoebe had paid rather more attention to her toilette than usual, the countess was introducing the families to four new faces.

'Lady Eleanor Marchmont and her family who are staying with us at present. Roseanna, Naomi, Phoebe, Stephanie, Tabitha and Berthe.' This was rattled off as quickly as possible. 'This is our neighbour, Miss Emily Fairweather,' indicating a tall, well dressed young lady in a sprigged muslin gown quite as elegant as Ophelia's, 'and Eliot's friends, Mr Giles Hornby,' indicating a slim bespeckled man, with a straight shock of blonde hair only just tamed for the evening, 'and Francis Sedgewick.' Sir Francis was a handsome man, in a rather sharper coat than his friend Eliot's.

'Your mother cannot join us this evening, Miss Fairweather?' wondered Charles in his most vague voice.

'I had her mother's permission to bring your neighbour here tonight,' said Sir Osbert Barclay taking Miss Fairweather's arm with an ironic smile, 'to introduce her to my friends as my affianced bride.'

In the half second of silence at this before the trickle of congratulations, Phoebe Marchmont threw down the fan she had been carrying, violently. It hit a side table and dislodged a Dresden figure, which smashed on the floor. The room looked over, in slight surprise, but saw a raging virago before them. For Phoebe's eyes burned hot, gazing directly at Barclay. Then she laughed derisively.

Barclay blanched. Not everyone, Eliot supposed, had understood or even noticed the drama. The betrothed, for example, was taking the compliments of Queenie and Roseanna and did not quite notice. Phoebe walked forward after a second, her look of disdain not cool but red hot. Barclay sought a way out. He kissed his betrothed's fingers and said, 'Excuse me!' faintly and went, cravenly, to the door. He touched Eliot's arm on the way past whispering, 'Marchmont! *Control her!*' and then he was gone.

Eliot turned to find Phoebe, for her own sake, not Barclay's, but he saw that she had left by the garden doors. He touched Naomi, 'I'll go!' he said. Her lovely eyes gave him thanks, but something more confused.

He did not find her, and it was some minutes before he could locate Barclay, too. Eliot had reentered the house by a side door, and he saw the baronet cross the floor and speak to Godwin. Barclay looked relieved — probably the butler had made mention of Phoebe's absence from the salon. The baronet was headed back when he heard a voice call him from behind. Phoebe

Marchmont's voice. Eliot gasped, starting forward, but Barclay pulled her into an adjoining corridor and Phoebe Marchmont turned to him fearlessly.

Eliot stopped dead. He could see and hear the scene clearly from his vantage point, and he was ready to step in. But perhaps it was better to let the meeting occur *here* rather than in the salon.

'You seem upset, Miss Marchmont,' Barclay began, trying for a sincere, but offhand tone.

Phoebe reached for his hand, and he, thinking she had softened, put his out to console her. She jerked it to her mouth and bit on the pad above his thumb viciously. Barclay yelped and tried to pull away, but her teeth did not dislodge for two seconds.

He pulled himself away at last, saying, 'Are you *mad*?'

'You used this hand to brand me, sir! Go back and wear *my* brand before your betrothed.'

Barclay raised his hand, furious and more, then turned and left.

Eliot stepped forward. Phoebe was breathing hard and had flattened herself against the corridor wall as though her legs might give way. But her gaze was elated as she looked at him. He was afraid that the fragility beneath might overtake her at any time, however. 'Let me escort you back to the salon, Phoebe,' he said indifferently, to subdue any emotion.

She laid her hand on Eliot's extended arm, breathing more easily.

As the butler opened the salon door for them, they heard Miss Fairweather say, 'Why do you pull at your sleeve, my dear?'

'Oh it is the wild child, Berthe!' Then he muttered something under his breath which made the lady laugh.

'Are you saying it is *I* who bit you? I was here.' Berthe appeared from under the piano behind them, with a book. 'It was prob'ly Phoebe. She bites.'

Phoebe came in on the arm of Eliot, and her smile let the astounded company know it is true.

'But *why—?*' began Miss Fairweather.

'Do not finish that question lest you get an answer you do not like, my dear Miss Fairweather,' recommended Ophelia.

Their young guest looked confused, then regarded Phoebe Marchmont in horror.

The countess was flushed. The earl said merely in a faint voice, 'Ructions. The ructions of ill-breeding, I'm afraid.'

'I am very glad my son is from the house today, for I do not hold with violence,' said Lady Eleanor placidly. She looked directly at Sir Osbert Barclay and added, 'On the *whole*.' She turned to her daughter, 'Are you quite alright, dear Phoebe?'

'*Bitingly so*, Mama.'

'Good! I am desolated to tell you, my lord and lady, that my family will take a quiet supper alone this evening. I do hope you enjoy your meal.' And rising in the stately manner that Eliot's sister-in-law the countess could never quite emulate, she moved from the room, followed obediently by her children.

The room, thought Eliot, had returned to its normal, spacious dimensions. Indeed, even with four more guests, it looked sadly empty.

When the ladies left the gentlemen to their port and brandy, Eliot moved to sit beside Barclay. Though Cedric, Charles, Giles and Francis all glanced at the bite mark on the guest's hand, no one mentioned it. The brand, as Phoebe had called it, looked angry.

Since Charles was at Barclay's other side, Eliot said under his breath, 'I have no interest in how you explain Phoebe's action to Miss Fairweather, Barclay. But make her understand, as I make you understand now, that any discussion of this among her family or friends will go ill for her and yourself.'

'Damn you, Marchmont! The girl's a fiend.'

'And you are a rake and a deceiver. Something I shall speak to Miss Fairweather's parents about, if you say a word concerning Miss Marchmont.'

'An interest there yourself?' sneered the baronet.

'Not at all. I am warning you that you might fall foul of her family.'

Again Barclay sneered. 'From *you*?'

'Yes. But also from the earl.'

The baronet scoffed, looking at the earl's demeanour, which could hardly be more casual. 'I do not think Lord Tremaine is particularly concerned to speak for a hoyden.'

'You think so? Cedric is concerned with little it is true. Except his purse.'

'How could the reputation of such relations as that family affect the earl's purse?'

'They are relations, Barclay, but not at all poor. Lady Eleanor might be one of the richest women in England, and as you saw tonight she is protective of her own. Her son is protective in a more direct manner. He throttled Cedric for merely putting a hand on the smallest child. I hate to think what he might do to you.'

The last Barclay was not concerned with. He considered himself a match for any man. But the previous remark had made him pale. 'They are rich? But they are dressed as bumpkins ...'

'*Extraordinarily* rich. You put your wager on the wrong horse, Barclay. Your swift engagement to a lady of modest fortune suggests the urgence of your circumstances. But Miss Phoebe Marchmont would have been a purse of never-ending gold.' Eliot found he could sneer quite as well as his brothers. 'It is a relief you did not know.' Eliot left the table, gesturing with his head to his two friends to follow him.

In the library, after a strangely awkward dinner, with only Charles and Barclay attempting to make easy conversation that fell into the embarrassed silence, Sedgewick said, 'Did that ravishing beauty *really* bite Barclay?'

'Mmm!' agreed Eliot, swigging his brandy.

'Don't she care what the world thinks of her?' said the baronet. 'I mean, Giles and I will be mum, of course, but she could not know that.'

'She scorns deception.'

'She looked beautiful, with her eyes burning. What had Barclay done to deserve it?' Giles Hornby wondered.

'I suppose we can imagine,' uttered Sedgewick cynically. '*The dog.* Under the roof of her family!'

'He is a dog,' sighed Eliot, 'but probably not quite as bad as tonight might have made you imagine. Rather, he played a game he thought he could win, and found *she* would not play along.'

'He flirted and she took it seriously?' asked the baronet with a raised brow.

'I should rather say he led her on and she would not pretend, for the sake of her reputation and the proprieties, that he had not.'

'Brave, but foolhardy.' Giles Hornby said, adjusting his spectacles.

'That about expresses her,' agreed Eliot, smiling.

'You sound like you admire her yourself,' Sedgewick remarked.

'I admire her entire family. They are all exceptional, as you will find as you stay here.'

'Never saw such a bevy of beauties. Your own sisters, too. What a collection,' said the baronet.

'I suppose.'

'Not quite in the usual way,' continued Sedgewick, 'with the Phoebe girl and her red-haired sister still wearing their hair down. I ventured to mention to the younger one that she looked charming, and she looked right through me.'

'Oh Stephanie! She is not interested in gentlemen.'

'Which do you favour?' Sedgewick asked with an ironic leer.

'Eliot the monk?' scoffed Hornby. 'Do you not know him?'

'He has never said he admires *anyone* before, and now it is a whole family.'

'I admire their brother Richard, too, Francis,' said Eliot, 'but alas he was from home this evening. It was probably as well. He does not mind words ... but if he suspected a substantive insult to his sister he would not have stood still.'

'Our age?' asked the baronet, interestedly.

'A little younger, but he seems more mature as he has been master of his family for two years since his father died. As much as anyone *can* be master of those girls.'

'The mother was a character, too!' Remarked the baronet. 'I admired her retreat.'

'She is! Only child of a Scottish duke.'

'Ah! She has that aura.'

'It seems that life at Tremaine Towers has become more interesting,' said Giles Hornby in his usual placid tone. 'You have not stayed so long before.'

'You *could* say that. It is no longer dull. Even the children ...!'

'You pay attention to the *children*, even?' said Sedgewick.

'They are not the sort of children one can easily ignore.'

'Noisy, demanding?'

'Not *that* precisely. Just *unusual*.' Francis cocked an eyebrow, and Eliot added, 'Do you know that Tabitha, the elder child of twelve years, designs gears for cotton mills?'

'The *child* does?' said Hornby, at last surprised.

'Mmm!'

'I see what you mean. *Interesting...*'

'What about the other?' asked Sedgewick.

Eliot raised his glass, the three fingers not clutching it splayed in warning. 'You should not risk yourself in getting to know Berthe. You might not get out with your skin intact.'

'Is she a biter, too?'

'Very probably. But it is your brain and spirit she bites. She has completely eviscerated Charles.'

'Charles? He can fend off all sorts of sophisticated attack, surely?'

'He can. But that is *precisely* what leaves him defenceless against honesty.'

Sir Francis evidently thought of the drawling earl, the haughty countess, Charles the fop, the divinely flirtatious Ophelia, the contorted Queenie, and the rake Dorian and said, 'No, honesty has probably been missing from these walls for years.'

'It must be like a gold strike for you to come across it, Eliot!' agreed Hornby.

'Perhaps.'

To see a beloved one in distress is a dreadful thing. Roseanna and I went to Phoebe's room this evening and found her crying passionately, part in despair and part in rage. We hugged her, our eyes meeting over the heaving back, Roseanna's eyes swimming in sympathy. My sympathy for Phoebe's state was real, but there was an element in me that stood back. The grief we had felt at the loss of Papa was more real than this. Though I did not know what had happened between Barclay and my sister, I knew that her loss was the loss of an illusion, not a man of worth.

Mama had just left. She would have supplied physical comfort, I supposed, but few words. It had been enough that she had shown by her demeanour tonight whom she trusted, and her disgust of further pretense. To be at that dinner this evening with Phoebe, Barclay and his betrothed all at the table would have been the worse kind of falsehood, but one that many parents would force upon their child for the sake of appearances. It makes me proud that my mama is not one such. It makes all of us, I think, confident in our own way.

'Did you really bite Sir Osbert, dearest?' asked Roseanna, gently but incredulously.

'Yes!'

'Then he must have deserved it,' I said with certainty.

'Oh, Naomi! I wished to speak of it to you before ... but I wanted to keep it for myself for just another while.'

'You met with Barclay on your own?' I inquired.

Roseanna gasped.

'It was not quite like that ... When he visited last, I happened upon him while I walked to catch up with you all...!'

'Of course you <u>would</u> not agree to meet a gentleman separately, my dear,' said Roseanna consoling. I was not so sure what Phoebe might do on impulse, but I held my tongue.

'What did he say to you ... what did he do...?'

'I do not want to talk of it, Naomi, it is over now. But lying here I have thought, and I was not wrong, whatever he may have pretended tonight ...! He made me think, he deliberately made me think...!'

'Of course he did!' I said, making no room for any self-doubt that might arise. Phoebe's instincts were pure. 'You know, I noticed before that Ophelia Marchmont did not like him, and she has known him longer.'

'But Queenie ...!' protested Roseanna, then closed her mouth, realising that the dissenting voice was not helpful.

'I would rather take Ophelia as a knowing one than her sister,' I remarked.

'I hate him!' Phoebe said into a pillow.

'And so you should, for the moment at least. Soon he will be an irrelevance. Mama has warned us of what awaits us in London. We should not be too wary, but we should act as each other's confidante.' I decided on full frankness, so I chided her a little. 'I have been so miserable, Phoebe, that you have not spoken to me when I knew you were worried. I thought perhaps that Eliot Marchmont had committed some ...!'

'No! It is just that Eliot saw me with Barclay, and my behaviour ...!'

'Oh, so that is what you were speaking to him of?'

'Yes! But he promised not to tell anyone.'

'Well, discretion is certainly a virtue,' said Roseanna, nervously, 'but perhaps Eliot should have mentioned it to Richard or Mama. He must know more than us of the world, after all.'

'He was understanding, but then he went back on his word when I asked for Barclay's address.'

'You wished to correspond with the baronet?' said Roseanna, shocked.

'Do not sound so, my well-behaved sister!' said Phoebe shaking her arm, 'I believed that he ... promised ...!'

'Yes, yes. And that was why you fought with Eliot. He was sensible and would not let you ...' Roseanna said.

Phoebe rolled over. A new humiliation occurred to her. 'Oh, thank goodness! What if I had written?'

She pulled the cover over her head and wailed again.

'You should thank Eliot to have spared you that at least,' said Roseanna.

I did not agree with her, but to my surprise, Phoebe did.

'You are right, Rosie, I will thank him tomorrow. He has seen everything, after all, it cannot be any more humiliating.'

We left her to an exhausted sleep after a while. But I resolved to go to her bed later. There was the affronted Phoebe, of course, but I also saw a desperate hurt. In my present condition, I could understand it. Eliot had not said sweet words, as the wicked baronet had to Phoebe, giving me to hope for a romantic understanding. But I seemed to feel the loss of his friendship just as much.

The way his 'I'll go!' had comforted me that day. His reassurance to me alone. It seemed my due, the due of our connection. The understanding forged under the tree was not romantic, but his withdraw-

al from friendship hurt me, perhaps as much as Phoebe is now hurt, though I should not say so. Or only on these pages might I wallow in such a thought.

But Eliot is not a flirt after all, at least not with Phoebe. Just as I began to think he was my illusion, as Sir Osbert was Phoebe's, he becomes real again. Someone who kept my sister's confidence, but who would not let her do more to harm herself.

Would we grow cynical and harder like Ophelia after we went to London? Or would we be trusting and hurt again? I begin to see a fashionable coat as a suspicious item.

Sir Francis Sedgewick has a very fashionable coat. We should avoid him at all costs.

CHAPTER 12

The Beginning of Friendship

The entire Wild family was missing at breakfast next morning.

Present was Charles in his nightshirt, Eliot and his two friends, Lady Tremaine, also in *deshabiller,* and both of the Royal sisters.

Cedric arrived and looked askance at Eliot flanked by Queenie and Ophelia, being given smiles by both. Ophelia normally showed only cynicism, and the earl raised a pained brow at the sight.

'What,' demanded the countess of her husband, 'can be done about the behaviour of those people that live with us? I do not feel I can support violence in my own home, my dear!'

'Should you not ask the cause of the violence before you speak, my lady?' asked Eliot, taking a sip of his chocolate.

'I do not care to know!' declared her ladyship, turning to Eliot so quickly that the lace on her cap quivered. 'That guests in our home are assaulted is quite sufficient.'

'Indeed!' said Charles.

'I know you would think so, brother dear,' sighed Ophelia. 'I imagine that Barclay got his just deserts.'

'How can you say so?' said Charles, attending to his hair, 'The other family are missing this morning for shame, I imagine.'

'I hardly think so. What has a young lady to be ashamed of in defending herself from over familiarity?' said Eliot.

'Oh,' protested Queenie, 'Sir Osbert would *not*!'

'I think he might!' said his more cynical sister.

'Not at all!' said the countess, as though disposing of it.

'I witnessed it!' Eliot said, eating some beef. 'Not last night, but on the baronet's earlier visit, he laid his hand on Phoebe. It seems probable he led her to believe...!'

'And then came *back* here?'said Charles, incredulous, 'Barclay is not such a fool!'

'Why not?' said Ophelia in cynical tone, 'He thought he might carry it off and remain your friend, Charles. I believe the fashionable maiden's response to such behaviour is to keep one's face and then later go into a decline.' Ophelia chortled. 'He chose the wrong Marchmont. Perhaps Queenie might have obliged him, and even I would have preserved my countenance and sought my revenge later.'

'I do not believe Sir Osbert Barclay would have insulted any lady of this house,' said the countess, firmly.

'Then you are wrong,' said Ophelia more quietly.

'Ophelia!' called Queenie, distressed.

'Charles witnessed the end of it. It was at the Cowper's ball.'

'You told me it was nothing but a misunderstanding,' protested the dandy.

'Yes,' said Ophelia, 'I said what was expected of me, to keep my dignity.' She gave a half smile and said, 'I admit I prefer Phoebe's method.'

'Do you hear, my lord? That family's contagion affects your own!' cried the countess, entirely dismissive of the insult to Ophelia. 'We must dislodge them.'

'Since when, My Gentle Divinity, do you seek to question my decisions? Your most precious quality, Daughter of Athena, has always been your womanly obedience. Do you,' he played with the stem of a glass and gave a sharp glance to his wife that belied his faintly deprecating tone, 'seek to have *opinions of your own*?'

The countess turned white at this, 'My dearest...! I should not have spoken.'

Eliot watching, wondered at the level of Agatha's fear. She dearly wished for his brother's affection, he knew, even as experience should have disabused her of this hope. But sometimes he wondered if there was more to be afraid of in Cedric than his tongue.

'It seems,' said Ophelia, 'that Lady Eleanor's purse is not yet closed.'

'Poor Phoebe! I was sad last night, but she must have been so ...!' Queenie had been looking at her plate, but turned to Eliot, 'You think he led her on, Eliot, dear?'

'Nonsense!' cried Charles. 'She imagined all herself, no doubt, and then acted like an animal. Goodness! A London season is full of the disappointments of young ladies. Are those other Marchmont girls going to *bite* their way through the *Beau Monde*?'

'Well, you have not flinched when I confessed his insult to me, Charles. Therefore I wish Phoebe Marchmont was here so that she might bite you, too.'

'I find your tongue remarkably unrestrained this morning, Ophelia. Do you forget whence your bounty arises?' the earl said faintly, but as a warning, 'I prefer it when the breakfast table is silent. I cannot deal with fractiousness in the morning.'

The earl returned to his breakfast and was surprised when Ophelia muttered, 'And *you*, Cedric!'

'O — *phel*—ia!' cried the countess, shocked.

Queenie choked.

As Eliot passed through the hall, he saw a cluster of wild Marchmonts returning from the stables.

'Naomi,' he called.

He saw her stiffen, but not answer or turn to him, but he grasped her wrist as she passed and she allowed herself to follow him.

'If you were anyone else, Richard would have dealt with you for manhandling me.' She remarked, standing stiff in the middle of the library.

'He knows I mean you no ill.'

'What do you wish of me, Eliot?'

'Only to tell me how Phoebe is.'

'She says you know the reason for her distress.'

'I do. But I think Barclay is the most distressed. He is probably having to explain to Miss Fairweather the reason for Phoebe's behaviour.'

'Oh, that will be no problem for him. She was so pleased with herself to be engaged, and will wish to believe whatever he says, including that my sister is a dangerous lunatic.' This was said in the ironic voice he was familiar with in the journal and he smiled. She looked up at his eyes suddenly, 'Oh sir, do you think she will set that about?'

'I took precautions. Barclay will see that she does not. I would imagine that he will tell her that to recount the incident would tarnish *his* reputation. That however mad Phoebe may be, any talk of it will rebound on *him*. He may even tell her that I said so.'

'Thank you Eliot,' she said with difficulty, her eyes open for once. 'I shall take my leave.'

He reached out and took her hand leading her to a sofa, saying, 'There is something else I wish to say to you, Naomi.'

She sat, but took back her hand, covering it on her lap with the other, as though it might fly away.

'There are some misunderstandings between us—' he began.

'I do not think so,' she said coldly.

'Yes! Misunderstandings caused by my own behaviour.'

She looked at him, still silent, cold.

'We began to be friends and then I pulled away.'

'Yes.'

'You must have wondered why. Perhaps you thought it was something to do with what I thought of you—'

'You had the impertinence to think I might pursue you!'

'No, no! *That* is the misunderstanding.'

'Then what? You talked to everyone else in my family...'

'Naomi! I want to say ... or actually, I have not wanted to say, except that I did not expect I would have given you such distress ...'

'Me? Distressed?'she gave an unconvincing laugh.

'Yes, a lovely, vibrant girl is going against her nature by being cold and stiff just to teach my "presumption", as you called it last time, a lesson.' He looked at her even as she looked down, willing her to lift her lovely eyes. 'Have you not asked yourself, Naomi, *why* when we smiled so easily that first day we talked, that I would avoid you and talk to the other members of your family so easily?'

'I did wonder, and I told you my conclusion.'

'That I thought you would pursue me, Naomi? No. It is that I feared, I was *terrified*, that *I* would pursue *you*!'

Her eyes flew to his, a storm of emotions therein. '*You* pursue *me*?'

'I should not have said so much. I wished to be your friend, but even after that evening at dinner I could see the pitfalls. It is so easy between us that being your friend alone seemed doomed.' She blushed. 'Not on your part, but on mine!'

'And you did not wish to ... who said I would want—?'

'I know, I know, Naomi. It is that if I were to grow closer to you ... oh, I sound like a bounder. I *would* have pursued you if I talked to you any longer. I could feel it.' He did not see that her face was flushed and her breath quickened as he said this, so confused was he at his own lack of erudition. 'And then I would have either given you hope of more, or else given you the discomfort of rejecting me.' He finally looked at her. 'I am not so vain as to believe that it might be the former.'

'But we had only talked for a day ... how could you speculate so far ahead without at least becoming friends?'

'I cannot tell you why ... or I will not. Only that I did. But it is because of my circumstances ... I cannot speak of them to you, Naomi. But I cannot see you hurt by the thought that I believed you forward, or full of a girl's fancy. I did not. What I feared was not *your* fancy, but my own.'

'Your circumstances...?' she said.

'I believe a man should be independent in front of ... if he wishes ...' Eliot realised that this conversation was precipitate. He had no more right to speak than before. He felt himself covered in confusion. 'I only said as much because perhaps ... my circumstances might soon change, though it is by no means certain. That being the case it might be too early to ... besides being previous ... but I did not wish you to be angry, or perhaps hurt by ...' He had never, in his life, been such a blithering, babbling idiot. He finally held his tongue. He had begun this thinking that he knew what he wished to say, but it appeared not.

There was silence in the room. The clock ticked. The embers displaced in the fire. Distantly, they could hear Berthe, and perhaps Stephanie, laughing. Two minutes later, Naomi said, 'Eliot. I ... it seems to me that perhaps, without worrying too much what will arise in the future, we might begin to be friends now.'

He breathed a long sigh. 'I would like that. But—!'

'No buts. Your family think ahead too much, it seems to me. About appearances, or consequences. My family are simply pleasant to those who are pleasant to us and some of us are *not* so pleasant when others injure us.'

'As Barclay knows!' Eliot laughed.

She exchanged her look with him, that laughing, delicious look of conspiratorial collusion.

'Friends, Naomi!' Eliot said, leaning forward and taking her hands.

She pulled them away. 'Friends, I hope. But perhaps not the kind of friends that hold hands.' She smiled at him, a little wickedly.

'Yes, ma'am!' he said docilely. 'I am glad Phoebe is a little better.'

'It is difficult when one's illusion dies. It is what I believed happened to us ... I expected friendship and ...!'

'I am an oaf!'

'Yes!'

'A *presumptuous* oaf to boot!'

'Indeed,' she laughed at him. 'Don't worry, Eliot! I shall treat you as I do Richard henceforth.'

'So I may use your leg as a pillow when I read by the fire, as I saw him do with you that first evening?' Even as he jested, he could see the territory they were entering so quickly. This was a flirtatious remark, he was too happy to deny it.

'Do not make me regret my decision, Eliot Marchmont,' she warned.

'Yes, dear friend.'

'Eliot!'

'What is it, Naomi?' he asked, innocently.

'Never mind! Do not overstep the mark or I shall set Phoebe on you.'

'I am shaken at the thought.'

'Or Stephanie. You have yet to see Stephanie unleashed. You may yet regret becoming friends with our family.'

'I am already. I must tell you that my recent spate of friendly conversation with your family is due to a punishment of Berthe's.'

'I thought there might be something. But why—?'

'That, I will not tell you. But I have fulfilled my purpose now. Any future conversations with your family will be purely volitional.'

'I am pleased to hear it. I will discover the truth of it all from Berthe.'

'Do not!' he said too quickly. 'At least ... as my friend, Naomi, I beg that boon.'

'Secrets lead to unpleasantness and misunderstanding. Just think of us ... I have practically *hated* you these last days.'

'Have you?' he said sadly, 'I hoped it was not so.'

'Well, I *tried* to hate you!' she conceded. 'But secrets lead to no good.'

'This secret I promise I will tell you one day, Naomi. But please, not quite yet.' He was a coward, but he wished them to be closer once more before he risked her inevitable wrath.

She regarded his pleading eyes. 'You look like a cocker spaniel,' she remarked. 'Very well, I shall not probe quite yet. But tell me soon, Eliot. Patience is not a virtue of mine.'

'I thought I was patient. But I could not wait to speak today, though it may have been ...'

'Desist! It is nothing to be friends, after all. We need not think too much about it.' She smiled at him, a shyer smile than he had seen her use, and her very shyness warmed him.

All of this, he thought, was fraught with danger for both of them. He must not flirt more, he must keep the tone of a friend for both their sakes, but even then ...!' He could not think of it, would not. Naomi was correct. He had thought too far ahead ... what friendship begins with a fear of its ending? It is only other kinds of connection that one should worry about... Let them be *friends* for now. His life felt so much richer at the very thought. Queenie had wished him to think of his own happiness. It would begin, he thought, with the friendship of a lovely girl. They might permit themselves that much. Naomi had a great deal of intimacy in her life, but he had only hers. She would recover from the loss of his, he believed, if that day should come, but he may not. But for his sisters, at least, he had a duty to live on.

He was thinking ahead again, and his friend Naomi had forbidden him to do so. He would stop. It would be dinner time soon enough, and then he might see her again, and warm his heart anew.

In the salon before dinner Eliot moved close to where Naomi was twirling a tassel on the curtain cord between her fingers apparently fascinated by what she could see in the twilight outside. Even by candlelight he could see that she blushed, but though there were a number of people present, they were too occupied to notice.

His friends Hornby and Sedgewick were the most to be pitied, since the elders of his family were betraying a stiffness for the Wild family to understand their disapprobation. At least the earl, countess and Charles were being stiff, Queenie's apparent stiffness was simply embarrassment, as Eliot knew. Ophelia was amused, and watched the show. The Wilds, as rebuttal, were being a little louder than usual in response, capturing the outsiders in their conversation. Richard made sure to be near Phoebe, though he appeared negligent. But all this posturing had made it easier for Eliot to approach Naomi without being observed.

She flushed as she became aware of him and said softly, 'Eliot, I have thought of one question I would like to ask my friend.'

'Anything!' he said rashly.

'Your *circumstances,*' she asked, hesitantly, 'They do not include a female attachment? I only ask as a—!'

'No. No attachments,' he answered in a low, serious voice.

'I only—' her voice was a trifle uncertain, embarrassed.

'It is a question *any* friend might ask,' he said, as casually as he could.

She turned to him and gave a grateful look, then quickly looked away. She drifted off to join the others.

I am surrounded by loving family who do, in all their own ways, understand me. So why is it so precious to me to have a new friend like Eliot? Our eyes reach for each others at any absurdities over the breakfast or dinner tables, and I have concluded that there must be a part of me not quite understood by my family. A tiny part perhaps, but it is something that Eliot sees and Eliot shares. Tiny bubbles of joy burst in my chest when we share these moments. When Roseanna and Queenie had a conversation with Charles which became almost a competition to see which could utter the most apologies per minute, Eliot and I shared the absurdity with a look. I realised that we were laughing at both of our families at once, which smote me with remorse. When I came upon Eliot by chance on my walk later, we sat together on a bank and I told him so. It was the steep bank that Berthe and the rest of us had rolled down, and Eliot had the temerity to chide me — not as a hoyden, but as a person who did not look to her own safety enough. It made me giggle to be instructed by him and we ended by laughing — he at himself and his bootless attempt to rein me in. We did not say so, just knew it.

It seems to me that Eliot knows what I think before I tell him. And in such a short period, I feel as though I have been acquainted with him since birth. I know him. He took my hand when I rose from the bank and I think perhaps we held on too long when

I was righted. His hand warmed me, and I did not pull away in time, and nor did he. But it warmed not just my hand, but somehow my whole being — at first it was comforting and then (I seem to have lost the words to describe it) it made me tremble. All of this in perhaps three seconds before he pulled away with a jerk.

On the way back he looked at the path ahead, distracted. I could feel that he might pull away again, so I made him laugh about Queenie and Roseanna and the apology contest. I almost said that I understood why Queenie, with such a family, would be so lacking in self-esteem, but that I could never sufficiently explain how Roseanna has the same fear of displeasing. None of the rest of us do. But I do not wish to talk too much with him about The Royals, it is to invite him to be disloyal. That we are already doing so with Queenie and Roseanna is quite enough.

Anyway, I exhausted myself to be amusing but in the friendliest way, in case he was thinking too much about the three seconds. Perhaps that is not why he was becoming withdrawn at all, perhaps I am the one who is too conscious, but I saw his look as he pulled away from me, and in those deep set eyes I saw many, many things. Many possible things. Certainly a sudden self-consciousness, perhaps embarrassment, perhaps regret (but for the end of the touch or that it happened at all I am not quite sure), perhaps something else: some heat emanated from him — was it anger? Or is there something else?

I am evidently, as I read this back, refining too much upon a moment. Too much on his words in the library: "What I feared was not your fancy, but my own." And "I would have pursued you if I talked to you any longer. I could feel it" Those words I have promised myself, these two nights, that I would not think of more. We are friends, that is our truth, and tonight at dinner he did not withdraw from me again, as I feared he would.

Things begin to change around the table as well: since the bite Ophelia and Phoebe exchange the odd remark, and I can see there might be the beginning of friendship there, too. Also, and I do not quite know why I believe this, but I see that the earl, who normally tries to ignore the world at the table, is a little put out by his sisters whenever they address Eliot. There does seem to be more warmth in the conversations with Ophelia, the sister my friend appears closer to. Before their exchanges were fewer and usually ironic, but now she occasionally smiles at her brother, or passes him a dish a footman failed to.

Queenie, too, talks more with him, and sometimes blushes when she has said yet again, "What do you think, Eliot dear?" Eliot's eye seems to warn her of some danger and she desists for a while.

Even the countess noticed, though. 'Has my brother-in-law suddenly become your god, Queenie dear? You seem to consult him overmuch.'

And indeed, in the case of her dress, I can think of no man less useful or interested, unless it be Richard. Ophelia distracts her sister by words or touch when she begins, and Queenie is obediently quiet. All three seem somehow split off from the earl, the countess, and even Charles, these days.

Eliot lay in bed staring at the dim view of shapes and shadows, who all coalesced into one figure, Naomi. No matter what words he said to himself, he could not get her to leave. He felt himself smiling again and again as he thought of the scene by the window where she asked about *female attachments* in such a shy manner. The Naomi in his head was never shy, she was wickedly insightful, sharp of tongue to those who abused her, angry when she felt he had mistreated her, a lovely, laughing, natural beauty when with her family. Full of teasing and play, sometimes thoughtful and considerate, always affectionate and loving with The Wilds. She was confident, too, like all the siblings bar Roseanna. So for Naomi to be hesitant and shy had been almost too sweet to see, a sight he would treasure, like the delicate flush that mounted from her collar bone. He might have teased her longer to prolong this secret joy of his in watching her confusion, but it had been too important a question. It had kept her worried, and he could not abide that.

She was such a darling. She came to breakfast the next day with the short wavy frontage of her hair, the part he always wished to tidy a little for her, looking somewhat different. When he regarded the difference closely, it seemed that someone had used a curling iron on it, then thought better of it and pulled out the curls. He believed he understood this too, he had spent more time than ever in his life choosing his waistcoat and adjusting his cravat that same morning. When he caught sight of himself in the looking glass, he had suddenly thought of marble statues and he, too, had flushed, and deliberately pulled at his cravat, sending it into disarray, and pulled the ends through a waistcoat button in an effort to seem casual.

They were attempting to be natural with each other, and for the most part they managed it. He believed that she, like himself, did not wish to make their new friendship a thing of note amongst their families, and this was made a trifle easier by the children, and Phoebe and Richard too, all addressing remarks to him occasionally. In fact, only Naomi did not. But they shared smiling eyes when they found something funny, or merely ridiculous. Some pontification of Charles, perhaps, or some pointed remark by Lady Tremaine at Naomi's mama, always calmly and efficiently dealt with by Lady Eleanor.

On a walk, one where they *accidentally* met beside their tree, Naomi confessed she felt sorry for the countess, constantly beginning a battle she would never win. Lady Eleanor let a great deal pass, and this would sometimes make the countess follow a false scent of weakness to attempt a win. But everyone else with insight knew she was being let off, and eventually even the earl would tire of it and order his wife to desist.

Eliot's intimacy with The Wild family was of course noticed, causing Cedric to murmur in his faint, deriding tone as they left the salon, for the dinner table, 'Defected, Eliot?'

'As well be on the winning side, Cedric,' replied Eliot, to annoy him.

'Ah, so your pockets are to let and you found the bill paying too vulgar for your elevated conscience, so you seek your fortune in a more roundabout fashion. I commend you, brother.'

'I confess you are too deep for me, my lord. *How* do I seek my fortune?'

'Charles informed me that you have walked alone with Miss Phoebe Marchmont,' Cedric laughed unpleasantly, 'too much of a spitfire for me, but everyone to his taste.'

'Better a spitfire than a milksap, I think.' This remark was somewhat beneath himself as it could be referring to his sister-in-law's devotional obedience to her husband.

The hooded eyes looked more disdainful than usual, 'Even if you succeed, you will be at the mercy of her mother's purse strings. Not a flexible woman, Lady Eleanor.'

'You must have applied again, and been rejected I fear,' Eliot said, his laugh also unpleasant. 'Is it not beneath your noble dignity to carry a beggar's bowl, however?'

He did not usually give himself the trouble of baiting Cedric, but the earl's suspicions were so vulgar, especially at this time when a delicate friendship was forming between himself and another Marchmont sister.

Thinking of his dear friend made Eliot happy — and he would not have it despoiled by the earl. Over the tea after dinner, he sat between Ophelia and Queenie. His intelligent younger sister whispered. 'What is transpiring with you and Naomi?'

He looked at her surprised, and Queenie, who had not heard, said, 'What are you talking of?'

'My friendship with Naomi,' said Eliot in a low voice.

'Oh but you are friendly with *all* the other family, are you not, Eliot dear? I myself find Roseanna the sweetest person, but I have not yet ventured to know the others so much. I find the child rather terrifying.'

Eliot imagined Berthe remarking with her usual bluntness on Queenie's eyebrows, and thought she was right to be afraid.

'The child is wonderfully honest, I find,' said Ophelia, with her customary drawl. 'But one keeps out of her sight line in case. Charles's remarks draws her attention, so she offers him helpful opinions. It is very droll.'

But Queenie was fixated on Eliot's first remark and a crease crossed her brow. 'So you are special friends with *Naomi?* I do not see you converse much. How did you come to think so, Ophelia?'

'Precisely because they do *not* converse, but only share amusement with an intimate look sometimes.' Ophelia informed her sister, all three conversing in a low tone.

'Oh, could you be ... oh, *Eliot* ...' Queenie's eyes were gazing up at him in rapture and when Eliot saw Charles' head turn his way, he nipped her. She was shocked, then giggled. It was the kind of play they did not usually indulge in.

'I do not want Charles to remark on anything Queenie! We are merely friends. Perhaps her humour is similar to mine. But I have become friends with all of the other family in a different way. They are an unusual bunch.'

'The badly dressed rich,' remarked Ophelia. 'Dangerous.'

Eliot raised his brows. 'Naomi is very fond of you, Ophelia, she finds you amusing, even if you are "shiny" as Berthe calls us.' He heard it as an appeal to her, and for once she did not turn it off with sarcasm.

'I like the look in her eye and her dexterous tongue, too. I have simply been guarding myself against intimacy with strangers.'

'That family are much less interested in guarding against strangers than us.'

'How is Phoebe?' Ophelia suddenly asked.

'She is well, I think. Or better.'

'Oh, was there some disappointment with Sir Osbert? I, too, have felt a slight inclination towards him. Who could not?' she sighed. 'But evidently he could not deny his heart.'

'Could not deny Miss Fairweather's five hundred a year, more like,' said Ophelia raising one brow. 'He could not guess that Phoebe with her shabby dress could be worth *much* more.'

'Oh *no*, Ophelia!' it cannot be so. 'Is that what poor Phoebe believes of Sir Osbert? Perhaps I should talk to her on the topic...'

'*No!*' said Eliot and Ophelia simultaneously, then laughed.

This brought the attention of the room to them, Charles saying. 'You look cosy, you three. What do you speak of?'

'Oh merely some town gossip, Charles.'

'I did not know Eliot knew any gossip,' remarked Lady Tremaine acidly.

'I do not,' said Eliot placidly. 'I am being instructed by sisters.'

Berthe, in the process of being sent to bed, said, 'You speak a great deal more to your sisters now, Eliot! I *told* you you should.'

The earl, countess and Charles gave the child unpleasant looks, Queenie's eyes opened wide, and Ophelia curled her lip, 'Thank you child, I am very grateful. Or he might have *ignored* me for the rest of my life.'

'I wondered at the new intimacy,' remarked Charles. 'It seems you only needed instruction from an eight-year-old to become a better brother.'

'Sometimes,' said Berthe looking up at Charles with her open, serious look, 'your mouth turns down when you say nice things and makes you look not happy at all.'

'Come Berthe,' said Roseanna anxiously. 'I will take you to bed. Say *bonne nuit* to the company.' As Berthe did so, Roseanna added compassionately, 'She is just a child Charles, dear, you must not mind her!'

As Charles had been attempting to pass on this remark by ignoring it, Roseanna's compassion was ill-timed as usual.

'Anyway, I *cannot* think what you three have found to speak of all evening,' remarked the countess in a pet, 'as though you keep secrets.'

'It seems your wife objects to me talking to my sisters, Cedric.'

The earl looked up from some reverie he had affected and said, 'My Sole Object of Delight is often a trifle from the mark in her comments, but in this case, she may for once have put her finger on a mystery,' he narrowed his eyes. 'Our sisters *do* favour you recently, Eliot. I wonder what you have done to deserve it?'

His brother's venture close to his secret left Eliot bereft for a second and his saviour came in an unexpected form. 'Well, King, don't you think they might have become jealous since Eliot has begun to speak to *my* sisters, too?' Tabitha's quiet voice added. 'If Richard talked to *your* sisters more often, I should likely be so.'

Richard patted her head with a casual hand. '*Sisters!*' he muttered indulgently. Naomi laughed.

The countess was discomfited by the discussion across family lines, and salved herself by saying unpleasantly to Tabitha, 'I did not think you, too, were pert, Tabitha!'

Tabitha receded at this unpleasantness and Eliot rose. 'Do you go to bed now, Tabitha? Let me take you and make my sisters jealous!' He held out a hand and she came to him easily, surprising her mama. Lady Eleanor looked at Eliot, as though reassessing him.

'Are there no maids to escort her?' said the countess sarcastically, 'no wonder the child has no manners, if she is treated like an infant.'

Phoebe growled, but Naomi held her arm and looked at her ironically, jerking her head towards Tabitha, who was merely pulling on Eliot's hand. The child had no need of rescue, she seemed reassured by Eliot's hand. Phoebe subsided, encountering a look from her mama, too. Richard, after a glance at Eliot, had been uninterested in the interchange, reading a book that he had brought into dinner and left on a side table.

'I want to show you my drawing, Eliot. *Come now*!'

'It is as I said,' remarked the countess to her husband.

Queenie ventured nervously, for the sake of the child's humiliation, 'Goodnight Tabitha!'

The girl turned and smiled back at her. Eliot just saw the accusing look the countess sent his sister's bravery.

Tabitha could be heard asking, quite in the manner of her younger sister, 'Do I really have no manners, Eliot?'

'Not many,' said Eliot dryly.

Naomi thought she heard the serious Tabitha give a rare giggle at this.

He walked off with the child, the best riposte to his sister-in-law. Richard gave him a nod. The rest of the Wilds followed more slowly, Lady Eleanor leaving the battlefield at her own leisure, not the countess'.

CHAPTER 13

Les Rendezvous

Naomi entered the breakfast room early to ask a footman for a roll as usual, before the others came down. Only Eliot was there, evidently having an early cup of coffee.

'Stephanie and I are the earliest risers,' she blurted, somewhat embarrassed by their solitariness. Apart, that is, from a footman who stood ready to pour some coffee or chocolate.

'Oh yes? I, too, am an early riser,' Eliot said, with his feigned casualness.

'I expect,' Naomi said in a rather lowered voice, 'that Stephanie will take out her horse at dawn, but I will only ride once everyone comes down, usually around seven.'

'Your sister seems to be of an active disposition.'

'And competitive!' laughed Naomi. 'I would worry if she were a gentleman. She would be one of those sorts of men who are constantly challenging their friends to horse races or driving along impossible courses, or beating them all at archery and fencing and pistol shooting!'

'She does *not* fence or shoot, does she?'

'No, for mama feels she is not to be trusted with a foil as yet, never mind firearms. But I would wager that she would be as good as any shot in a very little time, though perhaps not very careful, if her archery prowess is a judge. I think Richard has permitted her to hunt rabbits with a shotgun, for she once had a bruise on her shoulder that I saw. She excels at sports. She is magnificent with the arrow, can run and climb faster even than Berthe, and can do anything on a horse. She takes on the highest hedges. It is quite terrifying.'

'I wonder that your mother does not forbid that.'

'No. Mama has warned her that she is responsible for her own safety. She just will not risk the safety of *others* by handing her a foil or a gun!'

'Your mother's method of parental care is unusual.'

'It adjusts to every child, I think.'

'While Stephanie rides, perhaps we could walk a little,' Eliot ventured.

'Well, if the weather is not inclement,' said Naomi airily. But she smiled at him, that teasing smile that warmed and tortured him at once.

Ophelia came to Queenie's room that evening to find her readying herself for bed, her maid taking out the pins, but leaving the snaking little plaits in her hair intact, to be raised the next day if they survived her night cap. Besides this there was a razor on the *tirroir*, but Ophelia gestured the maid away.

Oh dear, Ophelia thought, it was time to intervene. 'You must not let your maid shave your brows, Queenie.'

'But Charles and the countess tell me that my own are far too thick and disfiguring to be seen in public.'

'They are very similar to Phoebe Marchmont's. Do you think her disfigured?'

'No, no,' protested Queenie. 'She is very beautiful!'

'There is a large family resemblance between you two, I find.'

Queenie blushed. 'Nonsense!'

It was hopeless, Ophelia thought. 'Grow your brows again. You have time before the Season. You may grow them, and then revert to the razor if you dislike it a great deal.'

'But it would seem insulting to the efforts of dear Charles and Agatha. Besides looking ill while they grow.'

'You spoke up before Agatha well this evening, my dear.' Ophelia smiled. 'It must be in the knowledge that our future is independent.'

'I should hate to believe that my respect for my brother and sister-in-law is *dependent* on my dowry! It is just that those words to poor little Tabitha seemed unjust.' She looked up at Ophelia. 'Did you see her tremble? She is not as accustomed to unpleasantness...'

'... As we are?' Ophelia said. 'At last you consent to see Agatha in her true light.'

'She can be a little difficult in her manner, but she has much to try her, I feel.

'You mean the King? Yes, Cedric is much worse, I'll grant you.'

'Ophelia!'

'You know he has an unpleasant mouth, Ness,' Ophelia said, with candour.

Queenie looked uncomfortable. 'Well, yes. And I sometimes feel that however much Agatha respects our brother, it may not be a *felicitous* union.'

'Really?' said Ophelia, as though shocked. She laughed.

'Do *not*, Ophelia,' begged Queenie, her dark eyes shining with compassion. 'Only think how unpleasant it would be if the partner you love becomes distant? Or if the one you chose for life when young and inexperienced, is someone you cannot feel affection for after marriage!'

'Do you speak of Cedric latterly? Let us not be mealy-mouthed Ness. I do not remember the beginning of the union between Cedric and Agatha, but I will wager Cedric felt no such inclination even at the beginning. It seems evident that he married her for her inheritance, which he has long since disposed of, I'm sure.'

'Do not say so.' Queenie was distressed.

Ophelia eyed her older sister with exasperation. 'I *do*. And that since he has made his bed, he must sleep in it. But since Agatha is sincerely hoping for scraps of affection, even after knowing him these long years, it does give the tale a touch of tragedy. But she is *much* too unpleasant for me to truly sympathise with.'

'Ophelia!' protested Queenie, but it lacked force. There was a new candour that had struck up between the sisters, and Queenie sensed she must seek to match

it. Compassion and good manners were ingrained in her, but she had no notion that her clever sister was truly ill-intentioned. Ophelia was less ironic in tone with her, and she must therefore consider her honest feelings.

'Ness! We have been given the chance at a truer life now. Let us not have these half-truths between us. You and I know the character of the great earl and countess. You are kinder than I in justifying every action, but if you compare it to Eliot's honest treatment of us, you must see the difference. If we later live with our third brother, you will no longer tremble every day in fear of a sharp remark, or an insult.'

'Oh, no, dear Eliot is never unkind! But I think that Cedric may suffer from dyspepsia, you know. It likely makes him more fractious.'

'What should I do with you, Ness?' Ophelia touched her sister's hair gently. 'You are too kind!'

'As are you, my dear! I know you say that for my own good! But perhaps you, too are a little sharp in your judgment.'

'Yes, my dear! And if you know I speak for your own good, grow your brows and have a less fussy coiffure. Your hair is quite beautiful enough.'

'You cannot know what it takes a *plain* woman to be fashionable, my pretty sister!' Queenie protested.

'You are *not* plain,' protested Ophelia, almost defeated.

'You are too affectionate to think so, my dear,' Queenie patted her sister's hand, 'but Agatha and Charles have more detachment to better advise me.'

Ophelia sighed heavily, then squared her shoulders. 'I am removing the razor, sister. For now, you will obey *me,* for I am much more fashionable than Charles or Agatha!'

Queenie too sighed, but seemed to accept her fate.

Every night now, Eliot went to sleep reliving his days with Naomi. Their morning walks had not been discovered he was sure, or only by Stephanie, who was uninterested and obtuse, both. Sometimes too, he would *happen* to be nearby their family expeditions, and sometimes Naomi would wander off alone — as any one of them might, on projects of their own, to pick up objects to sketch later, or to find somewhere to read undisturbed. However, parted from the sight of her family, Eliot and Naomi might thus *unexpectedly* encounter each other, and spend a half hour's friendship time together. Always, he wished these intervals were longer, and he felt from a look over her shoulder, or a tardiness in leaving after she announced her intent to do so, that Naomi felt the same.

His "wagers" on the sea voyages, as he phrased them in his head, which he had previously placed with a peaceful heart, became something of an obsession with him now. When he felt his thoughts turn to what he could not control, he stifled it well, but now a positive result meant that he could say what he wished to say to her. He had entered into these investments after much research, choosing ships he knew a great deal about. The success rate for investors, the reputation of his business partners, the character of the ship's captain and the soundness of the vessel were all known to him by his own eyes and investigation, not on another's word. He was satisfied, on each occasion, to have given himself the best chance for success. However, after placing his bet, he must consider the investment money gone. It was, he had concluded, ridiculous to think one can battle against such elements as weather, piracy and the mighty power of the sea. So it was a case of casting his rock and not holding onto the result. But for Naomi he was taking more interest in the result. Investments such as this paid fabulously well, but lost too, and it was generally richer men than he who placed that wager. But now, it might change his whole life. The money meant little to him, but it might give him the right to love.

As though he did not already.

I do not remember when I have ever looked at myself critically in the looking glass as I have just now. A glance perhaps most days to see that the coil on my head is not put up crooked. Today I look more carefully. The front portion of my hair, which is cut to behind my ears, is wavy and untidy, even when combed. I tried to curl it the day that Eliot and I had our truthful conversation, and though I was not at all skilled with the tongs, it did not look ill, precisely. However, it did not quite look like me, and so I pulled at the curls that day to release them. It seemed to me not the time to look as though I cared too much for my appearance.

I am uneven of temper these days. Sometimes ridiculously joyful for no apparent reason, sometimes cast down because Eliot has come down last for dinner. It is not as though I can even greet him when he comes in, indeed I do not. Our new friendship is delicate, and now I somewhat understand why Phoebe failed to tell us of her connection to Barclay. It is because it is confusing and private to be buffeted by these sudden spurts of feeling that seem to have little to do with actual events around one. Or only tangentially connected. I feel slightly out of my own control. Everything before was simple and natural. I indeed watch my capricious tongue amongst the Royals for the most part, but this, as Mama says, is simply good manners.

I feel now, a little less than natural. We are, of course, being aware of other's eyes and avoiding them. This seemed an easy thing to agree to, but it is requiring so much energy that I am frequently exhausted after dinner. Not to lift my eyes towards him, not to turn his way, not to join a conversation that he is part of, not to smile when he is amusing or sardonic, resisting all of it is like resisting a current in a fast river. I have to strain every muscle to arrest my drift towards him. And after dinner there is the strange dissatisfaction that sinks my spirits, so that when my family gather in our sitting room in the west wing, they remark on it. Then I must pretend to lift myself, and only wait for dawn when I can see him on my own.

These morning walks with him before I ride are a salve. It is not that we cross any boundaries between a man and a woman in behaviour or speech, it is just that we can be us, Eliot and Naomi, the friends that we wish to be. Talking and laughing and relaxed. Except when either of us looks too long at the other, and gets caught. And then there is a consciousness between us that I do not have the wit to describe. Only that it is awkward, confusing, but somehow delicious, too. If we did not have these walks, however, I do not think I could survive the pretence of the day.

But today's use of the looking glass, while it was to check whether I really look on the verge of madness, was also caused by a glance at Eliot this evening. He was standing in the , further lit by the firelight playing over the surface of his face. I saw with clarity once more, how very beautiful he is. And so I came back to my chamber and looked at myself in the looking glass with attention. It is perhaps better that the light is soft, and not too harsh with the truth.

I see my hair, which is dark brown and wavy, not the dark and luscious curls of my sisters. I see blue eyes, rather large, which look back at me in a kind of sad candour. A nose that is straight, a mouth that is usual, a face shape smaller than the others, somewhat overtaken by the size of my eyes, rather as baby kittens, before they grow into their face. I think I do look strange. I tried to smile at myself in the mirror and it looked awkward. But suddenly I thought of how Phoebe would laugh at me for my attention to myself, and it made me smile again, this time more genuinely. My face looked rather better then, but I am not as pretty as Roseanna, or as wildly beautiful as Phoebe. I have always liked that my face is bland, all the better to conceal my wickedness from the world, and keep it for these pages. But now I wish I were more beautiful, with Phoebe's gorgeous curls, or Roseanna's pretty mouth, so that I may be a better match (as a friend) to Eliot's perfection.

I lie to myself frequently now, I find. This is something I despise. I pretend not to remember Eliot's words that day, or what they might imply. I pretend that all of the above is less than I know it to be. If this carries on, he really will be the bane of my life, the man who destroys the core of me. The honesty of my heart. I need this one attribute to write, and to live in a genuine way upon the earth. I will pray not to lose myself in all of this, I will pray not to become false to the world merely to protect one thing. Is this how one becomes the earl, or the countess, or Charles, or even the terrified Queenie? Does it start with one almost necessary falsehood and infect all of one's life? I heard a sermon on that once. It was overlong, and I fell asleep in church, but the salient points stuck with me. The beginning of sin.

Might I tell Phoebe some of this? But I think that the easiness Eliot and she have somehow found together may be broken. Roseanna would whisk it into a romantic confection that is far from the truth. Stephanie is too young to understand. Mama would, but I feel that she may afterwards be disappointed in Eliot, might not quite understand the "circumstances" that hold him back from ... more — since even I do not. I wished to tell him that I am wealthy in my own right. All of us girls are. Mama has talked of it to Richard, and he to me, a little. All of us have a thousand guineas a year for life. Papa chose to leave it to us girls as an annuity, in the charge of Uncle Gavin. Mama has agreed that settlements will be her business, but the annuities will be dispensed to us girls personally, even after we marry, for Uncle Gavin has this right, granted by papa, and encased in some old Scottish law that Uncle Gavin found. This is an unusual arrangement to say the least, but Papa trusted his girls, he said, rather more than the greater number of gentlemen of his acquaintance. He trusted we would marry wisely, but we must never, he said, be fettered. Only the vast profits from his machine designs and licenses from all over the world, could have allowed the phenomenal sum needed to grant us all such a wealthy independence.

But obviously I cannot say so to Eliot, to Eliot of the tender concern and feelings. And then again, of what interest might it be to a friend only? I lie again. Even on these pages.

I am not even in spirits, I find it hard to concentrate sometimes, then find a new of meaning to each material and emotional thing, causing a depth of joy I have never known. I think, that with prayer for my integrity, I wish to remain in this state, since the alternative would be unbearable.

It is only six hours until I see him again.

CHAPTER 14

The Spread of Amity

A troupe of maids were coming up the back stairs to the west wing, and Richard Marchmont stood back as they passed him in the corridor, some bearing a pile of bedding and some sundry looking effects. He counted nine of them in all, and they went up the attic stairs, bearing their burdens. They were not his mother's maids, even Richard could see, since they did not wear the uniform she had insisted on, but sundry work dresses and aprons.

The troupe of maids, like a line of ducks heading to a pond, penetrated Richard's usual disinterest and he asked his mother, who was just leaving her room, 'What is happening?'

'Oh, the workmen on the roof found holes further along and will be stripping it off and fixing it in the next few days,' said his mother distantly.

'And?'

'And the section is just under the maid's attic. I suggested to Godwin that they should be housed in *our* attics for the present.'

'Berthe told me that there is a battle raging between the two sets of maids at the servants' dinner hour.'

'Trust her to know,' said Lady Eleanor. 'But she is correct.'

'You organised this to facilitate peace?' said Richard.

'Now how might I have organised holes in the roof?' said his mother reasonably as they went down to breakfast. 'Let us say, I see it as an opportunity.'

'Does the countess know?'

'What need is there for her to know? A change in maid's accommodation is beneath her notice.'

Richard laughed shortly. 'Mama ... what precisely are we *doing* here?'

His mother's eyes glittered. 'Like the matter of the maid's accommodation, it is beneath your notice, my son.'

'Perhaps it is *time* I noticed, Mama.'

'Oh, if you think so, Richard. I might share all my concerns with you. The girls' wardrobe for the Season, for example. Our accommodation, the payment of bills, the problems of your father's legacy, the management of our estates in Scotland and England and Ireland, liaising with workmen, tenants, dressmakers, lawyers, estate managers—'

'No, no Mama! I have the machines to look after. That is quite enough for me. I leave the rest to you. I ask no further questions on household matters.'

'I thought not!' said his mother.

But there was something in this conversation that had Richard seek out Eliot. He was in the library answering correspondence, but Richard gained his attention by throwing himself into a chair and humming. Eliot said sardonically, 'What do *you* want?'

'A man's advice.'

'Oh, the earl would be delighted, I am sure!'

'I said I wanted a *man's* advice.'

Eliot laughed shortly. 'I'm flattered. What is it?'

Richard related the substance of the conversation with his mother. 'But I thought ... though I have no wish to learn such stuff as yet, perhaps it is time for me to take more responsibility, do you think?'

The handsome young man looked unusually concerned and sought his eyes. Eliot, touched, kept his face still as he replied. 'It seems that you, too, are dealing with business that enriches your family ... is that not so?'

'Yes, and I'm infernally busy, but I thought I perhaps should not ignore my responsibilities for the estate at least.'

'I expect your mother has borne these for a long time, and would be loath to have you wrest them from her. Did she not do so for your father also?'

'I do not know, I expect so. He was fully involved in his inventions.'

'Then, as far as assuming extra responsibilities, I think your mother is saying to you ... *not yet*!' Richard looked relieved, but still a little guilty, so Eliot added, 'If you like, you may learn a little now, to lighten her load at a later date. But it is not as though you are a lounger. You are already doing much for your family. And I have never seen a woman more capable than your mama. What is more, she relishes it.'

With a grateful nod, Richard left, his usual detachment in place.

Eliot was beginning to learn more about gears than he wished, and Berthe, a trifle put out by Tabitha taking his time, plagued him to help her make a kite. Since he had never attempted such a thing, he refused, but undaunted, she arrived in the library with string and paper and twigs she had taken from the garden as well as flour paste that she had asked a kitchen maid to make for her. Objects dropped around her.

Queenie, passing in the hall, saw her enter Eliot's sanctuary and made to follow to offer assistance. She stopped suddenly, remembering Ophelia's idea about a special friendship and she asked Godwin if he knew where Miss Naomi was.

Godwin, surprised at this interest in a member of the *other* family, said, 'I believe she came in wet from the garden and she has gone to change her clothes, Miss Clytemnestra.'

Queenie went upstairs to find her and soon both of them entered the library to find a mess on Eliot's desk and two harassed individuals, who appeared to be quarrelling, looking over the jumble.

'You are no help *at all*, Eliot,' said Berthe. 'You are a big *stupid!*'

Queenie covered her mouth to hide her laugh.

'He may be,' said Naomi, 'but you must not say so, my Berthe. Especially not to a gentleman who is aiding you.'

Berthe, who appeared to have a smear of flour paste on her nose and in her hair, said. 'I beg your pardon Eliot.' She seemed to reflect, 'But Naomi thinks you a big stupid, too.'

'Berthe!' said Queenie, laughing, 'Eliot has not made a kite before, but he is not stupid, which is a very unkind and impolite thing to say in any case,' Her quick hands organised the supplies, as she spoke, 'You must forgive him since there are things *you* do not know either. You would not like it if Eliot called you stupid because you could not read in Greek, would you?'

'But...!' protested Berthe.

'Let us rather make the kite.'

'There are too many on this side of the desk, Naomi,' Queenie said, apparently casually, 'You should help Eliot measure and cut the paper, and Berthe and I will trim and cut the twigs and bind them together.'

Naomi blushed, but covered it quickly by saying, 'I am in awe, Queenie,' said Naomi. 'You know how to make a kite?'

Queenie's eyes misted over. 'A friend taught me, long ago.' She smiled suddenly. 'Berthe, fetch the measure in my work basket, will you? And the larger scissors.'

Berthe went out and Queenie watched as the two at the desk stood closer than strictly necessary, flattening the rumpled tissue paper. Naomi, who Queenie had always thought of as being cut from the same cloth as her sister Ophelia, reserved and rather ironic, with a sharp tongue when necessary, appeared adorably confused when Eliot's arm crossed hers to better lay out the paper. She saw her brother pause, feeling some awareness, and she could swear that a light flush overtook him. Her detached, manly brother!

'There should be two layers, I think,' Queenie said and they looked up, as though astonished that there was another in the room. Queenie smiled inside, but kept her face as composed as she could. While they were laying down another sheet, Queenie felt a stab of guilt. Was it the security that Eliot had given her and Ophelia that had stolen his ability to seek Naomi's hand? *How* she hoped for Eliot's latest wager to come in. Indeed, quite apart from the home that he had promised for his sisters, but only for his own sake, Queenie truly *ached* for his ship to come in safe and sound.

Despite Berthe's enthusiasm and Queenie's deft fingers, all four were laughing in a half hour, somehow covered in paint (Berthe had decided to paint the kite with a lion rampant that looked more like a hedgehog) and flour paste, and holding a sadly disintegrating kite.

'But my *kite!*' Berthe complained amongst the laughter.

Queenie said, 'I think that we have now mastered the kite *plan* and will learn from our mistakes. Berthe, we will take the twigs and bind them more firmly tomorrow. Let Naomi and Eliot cut some new paper now, and you shall paint it *straight* after breakfast. We will leave it to dry, instead of trying to secure damp paper to the twigs, then we will all meet again in the afternoon to finish it completely.'

'Ask a maid to make your bath, Berthe,' said Naomi, pulling on one glued curl. 'You look like an artist's apprentice. Or perhaps a carpenter's.'

'I'll be dirty again before dinner!' complained Berthe.

'Nevertheless!' said Naomi briskly, sounding like her mama.

All this agreed, Berthe skipped away. Queenie, with a sad lack of decorum, closed the door on Naomi and Eliot, engaged in the *very* important task of cutting two new sheets of tissue paper. Queenie foresaw that this business might take many, many minutes.

She was surprised that her conscience smote her not at all. She had seen Naomi Marchmont as a full person today. The interaction and teasing between her and Berthe, and somehow Eliot, too, had shown Queenie a relaxed and charming girl, a little wicked, perhaps in her teasing. 'I do believe you have sausages for fingers, Berthe!' she had said to her sister when she had managed to put a digit through wet paper that they had just attached to the cross of twigs. But Berthe, sure of her love as Queenie had never been of anyone's, had just put her paint stained hand on Naomi's face, making her laugh.

When Queenie, by rote, protested for her, Berthe put a finger tip to Queenie's nose, leaving a paint fingerprint there. This must be *play*, Queenie thought, relishing it. She felt herself to be the organising force in this scenario, perhaps the governess overseeing the play of children. Queenie had thought often, before the earl-ship, that Cedric's situation might require her to go to work as a governess indeed. She had spent time with her friend's children, and had liked it. She had wanted very much to succeed in Town, but no match had resulted after four Seasons. If she had had children, she thought after this afternoon's amusement, she might have done well as a mother. But in this, she had some things to learn from Naomi, and the relaxed affection of her family.

But in any case, Queenie had thought, beyond her first romantic inspiration to push the two together, that whatever happened in the library, even especially if Eliot were to feel he had compromised Naomi in some way, it should be *encouraged*. She shocked herself by this conclusion, but if Eliot's boat did not come in, then his obstinate pride might need a push towards what was patently right for him. Queenie was ashamed of her desire to desert The Towers at any rate. It was just that the vision conjured by Ophelia of a freer life, (infinitely less stressful than running the waves of the earl and countess' uncertain humours) had been quite delicious.

'Oh, Ophelia!' Queenie gushed, finding her sister in the blue salon. 'It is *so* romantic...!'

Ophelia's eyes gave a warning, but not before the countess said, in a suspicious tone, 'What, pray, is *so romantic*?'

Ophelia, about to turn this off, was surprised that Queenie found her voice swiftly.

'The newest novel, Agatha!' she said, quickly.

'I did not think you addicted to such stuff,' said the countess derisively, but with less suspicion.

'She is not, usually' said Ophelia, 'but this volume had such a deal of moralising that I felt it to be more to Queenie's taste than mine. I *quite* gave it up.'

'Ah!' said Agatha, done with the subject. Queenie looked her apology at Ophelia, who simply reproved her with humorous eyes.

Eliot's fingers on the scissors made two mistakes before Naomi, laughing, said 'Desist!'

'Desist? Is that not something a lady says when a gentlemen tries to...!'

His tongue had run away with him, and she said. 'There! It is done! We must weight down the paper with books at the edges ready for Berthe to paint tomorrow. I'm afraid your desk will be quite unusable until the kite is completed.'

He did as she asked, his delaying tactics depleted, and she turned and smiled, 'I must go and change once more. I should have stopped and had us all don aprons. How did you escape with hardly a blemish?' She began to turn away.

'Naomi, stay a while.'

She hesitated. Her feet did not wish to leave at all, and so she cravenly gave in and joined him on the small sofa when he patted the seat.

'Why have I never made a kite before?' he mused, relaxing back in his seat.

'I believe it is more incredible that I have not, since your family are a little...' she blushed.

He turned his lolling head towards her.'It is not like you to be less than frank. You wished to say ... stiff... mirthless! Not the sort to play with kites.'

'You have no idea how very far from frank I am since I came to Tremaine Towers. I curb my wicked tongue and even more wicked thoughts admirably, I assure you.'

'I know!' And then he thought, I have given myself away.

'How could you?'

'Among other things,' he said, scrupulously, 'By your devilish eyes.' "Other things" had saved him from lying to her. He did not wish to directly lie to Naomi.

'Nonsense! I keep their expression bland at all times.'

He laughed aloud. 'Not at *all!*'

'What a silly conversation.' She said, picking at her glue stained fingers. He was, as he had been all day, a little too close. 'How sullied is my face?'

'Dreadfully! Almost as bad as Berthe!' he said solemnly. His eyes moved over her face as he said so, and it almost felt like a caress.

'And you without a mark!' she said. Her eyes searched his face and she stopped. 'But wait, I believe you did not have *blue hair* before this,' she put her hand up to a the stained lock at the side of his head, and then feeling conscious, met Eliot's wonderful eyes. Time stopped, her hand was still raised, she tried to look away but his gaze had pinned hers down violently. He looked suddenly like a hungry wolf, but in a second those eyes were yearning and vulnerable, achingly reaching for her.

'Naomi!' he said and moved his face towards her, never losing her eyes until the last moment, when his gaze dropped to her lips.

Her chin tilted towards him, 'Oh!' she gasped, and it seemed to break the spell.

Eliot stood abruptly. 'You should wash before the countess sees you, unless you wish for a lecture on decorous behaviour.'

She tried to match his lightness. 'Well, when it comes to decorum, *you* need the lesson more than I...'

This fell like a lead balloon into the room, since it brought the near kiss in front of them once more. Naomi almost slapped her own mouth.

'I am sorry, Naomi, I...' Eliot began.

But she stopped him, knowing that their delicate accord might break at any moment. 'You should wash yourself, Eliot. I will see you at dinner.'

He looked after her. She had left breezily, but he felt like a cad. If he heard of such behaviour as he had just indulged in described to him by another, he would think the gentleman did not deserve the name. She was not eighteen, but twenty, but Naomi was nevertheless inexperienced in the world. She was an innocent, and he had almost stolen a kiss. And he knew it would not have been a gentle kiss. He wanted to chase after her, and beg her to be his own. But things had not changed. He had no right to seek a bride while he could not even provide her a home. Or at least a home worthy of her.

What *she* might bring to *him* by marriage was besides the point. He would not stoop to receive settlements from Lady Eleanor, and his wife's income, large or small, would be for her own use exclusively. It was for a man to provide for her other needs, as he wished to provide for his sisters, too. Not to be Cedric was his life's desire, and he had almost succeeded — but seducing a young girl put him on a par with Barclay. Perhaps he should seek out Phoebe to bite him and relieve his guilty feelings.

As it happened Eliot crossed Phoebe's path when he visited a tenant on the estate. A portion of his roof had fallen in during a recent storm, and the man hoped for the earl's boon in making repairs. It was clearly the earl's responsibility, as all estate property was his, but Eliot knew his brother, if challenged, would agree to repairs that he would delay indefinitely since it was money spent with no advantage to himself. Not doing so was to the earl and the estate's disadvantage, but Cedric had never been a long-term thinker.

Lady Eleanor was riding too, and she stopped, greeting Eliot. He had not had the privileged of seeing Naomi's mama on horseback before, and he was impressed. A tall thoroughbred bay held her and she wore a close fitting blue riding dress with a sweeping velvet skirt, perhaps not quite in the first fashion of military attire, but striking nonetheless. She looked past him to the house and lastly the tenant.

'There is some spare timber yonder,' she pointed in the direction of the trees that held the defunct gatehouse amidst them, 'from some construction work being undertook for me. Find the foreman, Smith, and tell him I sent you.' As the farmer looked blank. 'Lady Eleanor Marchmont.'

'Be you she who married little master Marchmont, my lady? My father talked of him often.' Against Cedric's desire, then, word had already spread around the estate.

'Yes, I had that privilege.' Her eyes glazed a little, softening their business-like expression. But quickly she was practical again. 'You may take some straw to thatch too, if there is any to spare.'

'Yes m'lady.' He chortled. 'Old Nobby at the gatehouse *told* me he seen a young gentleman the very spit of the young master riding the estate, and I never believed it'.

'My son,' said Lady Eleanor shortly.

'The *true earl*?' gasped the farmer.

'If you wish to repay me for the timber, you shall not set that about. The succession was legally decided and is not in dispute.'

'Eh? Oh, yes m'lady. I ain't a rattlepate, don't think it, ma'am.'

But Eliot, riding off with Lady Eleanor, doubted this resolution would survive a visit to the inn taproom.

'Do you mind the gossip?'

'It is rather for the earl to mind, and so I regret it. But when I decided to come here, it seemed inevitable that some old retainers might recognise Richard. He looks precisely like his father at the same age.'

'The age he left the estate?'

'Near enough.' She looked askance at him and continued as their horses trotted beside each other, 'you have developed an interest in my family, Eliot, after the shock of our first meeting.'

He avoided a direct answer, merely saying, 'It certainly was a shock and a family scene I had neither witnessed or experienced before.' He glanced at her with a raised brow, 'can you imagine Charles or Cedric on the floor clutching a sister each?'

She gave a grim smile. 'Perhaps not. But you, Eliot?'

'After my initial disapproval,' he admitted, smiling at her, 'I began to see your family as an enchantment.'

'Enchantment?'

'Not any individual, but as a whole. Their love and care for each other. The casual warmth and playfulness. You have raised a fine unit, an enchanted one, full of individuals who are, for the most part, their own selves.'

'For the most part, Eliot?'

'Roseanna.' He answered briefly.

'Yes, Roseanna, my most obedient and caring daughter. How I wish she was *less* obedient.'

'Not a sentiment one hears many mothers utter,' Eliot remarked.

'She drew her strength from her papa, and when he left us, it seemed that while we all suffered, Roseanna was the most at sea.' Lady Eleanor laughed a little. 'I shall tell you a secret, Eliot. I am quite adept at dealing with rebellious children, but dealing with an obedient one has sometimes felt beyond me. She agrees with everything I say, but seems to miss the point completely.'

'Like Queenie, she is too blinded by her desire to do good to heed her own desires at all.'

'Precisely!' She looked at him again, and he felt her penetrating gaze. 'I always saw that you were handsome and intelligent, Eliot. And with the grace to favour my children.'

'Prompted not by grace, as you know Lady Eleanor, but blackmail.'

'But you have already paid the demanded price, and are still patiently regarding drawings of gears. Or making kites.'

This last had him flush a little, much to his own irritation. It brought Naomi to him.

'In fact, Eliot, it seemed to me that I might grant you any boon you should ask of me, my boy.' Eliot's flush became a blush at this. Could Lady Eleanor really descry the boon he truly wished for? 'Except for one obstacle that it is hard for me to overcome.' Eliot held his breath as her glance, now a touch disdainful, swept his. 'With my personality, I cannot *abide* a ditherer.'

She stuck her heels in and rode off while Eliot brought his cob to a halt. Lady Eleanor knew all. They had been so careful had they not? Yet Ophelia had guessed, and told Queenie, and now Naomi's mother knew.

His lack of action disgusted her ladyship, as it did himself. If Phoebe found out she would undoubtedly bite.

By heaven's intent, Phoebe came out before him on a side path. 'Will you take me up, Eliot?' she said, as though relieved. 'I have twisted an ankle.'

'Of course!' he said, preparing to dismount.

'No need for that! I have one good leg.' Phoebe said. 'Just give me your hand and your stirrup and pull me up before you, or we will miss dinner.'

He did so, feeling strange to have a female sit before him, so close, but by the time she had criticised his riding twice, he felt more at ease, threatening to let her down to hobble home alone. He met Richard at the main entrance, and said, 'Take your dashed sister, will you Richard? She has squirmed the whole way.'

Phoebe jumped down into her brother's arms shouting 'Rich!' as he caught her. 'Take me to my room will you? I fell over a root.'

'Idiot,' remarked Richard, catching her up in his arms. 'You are dashed heavy, you know.'

'Thanks, Eliot!' Phoebe called over Richard's shoulder. 'Rich, you must give him pointers on horseback.'

'You ungrateful girl,' called Eliot as Richard bore her away. 'If you are not careful I'll bite you!'

Phoebe's eyes gave a panicked look at Eliot. Oh yes, Richard did not know of the bite. If he did, Osbert Barclay might be dead already.

Naomi caught Eliot in the hall before he entered the salon prior to dinner. 'Eliot, you must not say *bite* before Richard! Mama has even the children silenced before him.'

'I know, it was a witticism, but I thought better of it.'

'Indeed, if your family mentions it, Eliot, I hate to think *what* Rich might do.'

'It seems to be a forgotten topic, does it not?' Eliot consoled. 'Do not fear,'

'Mmm,' she said, but he felt she gained confidence from his words.

Phoebe and Stephanie (who supported her elder with more verve than necessary, Eliot felt) came up behind them.

'Oh Eliot, do not mention...' began Phoebe.

'I know, I know! I apologise, Phoebe. Naomi reminded me.' He added sardonically, 'I shall not mention the word unless you criticise my excellent horsemanship again.'

'To be criticised is the opportunity to *improve*, Eliot dear,' remarked Naomi sweetly.

'What say you, Stephanie?' appealed Eliot to the redhead. 'You are a horsewoman ... is there aught wrong with my seat?'

'Well, I haven't *noticed* anything... but then you have never interested me!' said Stephanie, more concerned with jerking Phoebe forward.

'Honestly Stephanie, I asked for aid,' Phoebe complained, 'not to be *dragged...!*'

Eliot and Naomi smiled at this, then wiped their expressions as they entered the salon.

When the wounded one entered the countess said acridly, regarding her, 'If you are *injured* Phoebe, you need not have come downstairs. Something might have been sent to your room.'

Why Agatha's offers of concern always seemed poisonous, Eliot could not say. He glanced at Phoebe's mother who seemed, as usual, to be deaf to the countess' unpleasant tone.

It was Naomi who spoke, saying smoothly, 'That is *kind*, but Phoebe feared you would miss her, countess.'

Charles laughed shortly at this, and Eliot saw that the countess looked very closely at Naomi then. *Phoebe* seemed to be the most rebellious Marchmont girl, and Naomi had seemed, for the most part, detached. However, there had been occasions when her tongue...!

'Indeed,' the countess replied with icy politeness.

Queenie, to counter the countess' ice said brightly, 'Are you much injured, my dear Phoebe?'

'Pooh!' answered Stephanie for her sister in her rather blunt tone. 'We all tumble regularly and recover just as swiftly. She will be fine tomorrow morning. Climbing trees, I expect.'

'You think of *yourself*, Stephanie dearest,' said Naomi.

'And I. *I* climbed higher than *anyone*,' chimed Berthe.

'Yes, but *I* had to rescue you, for you could not get down again,' said Stephanie stoutly.

'Only *once*,' protested Berthe, 'and I was only *seven* then.'

'You are young ladies now, Stephanie and Phoebe, at least! I do not wish to hear tales of your hoydenish behaviour, or to have to excuse it before my visitors.'

'Very well, Lady Tremaine,' said Phoebe in a suspiciously docile voice, Eliot considered. 'I shall henceforth only climb trees that are not in sight of the road.'

Ah, right again, thought Eliot amused. Phoebe eyes sparkled with naughtiness, but her face stayed prim. Agatha came off worse, as usual. If her complaints to The Wilds were not so ridiculous, he might have been sympathetic at the lack of obedience shown to a countess in her own home, but as it was, he could only be amused. The Wilds, after all, never attacked first. He glanced and saw that the elder of his two sisters, alarmed by any threat of combat, moved forward to the sofa where Phoebe had been seated by Stephanie, stepping between the locked gaze of Phoebe and the countess.

'Raise your ankle do, Phoebe,' said Queenie, and Agatha glared at her, 'I have a salve in my room that I shall have sent to you. It is most efficacious.' Poor Queenie's voice was trembling at her own daring, and Eliot felt again the necessity to remove her from this environment.

'We shall not spoil our evening by discussing the injury of a young lady who has brought her suffering upon herself,' intoned the countess. She inclined her head to the earl. 'Am I not correct, my lord?'

Her carrying voice lifted her husband's weary head. 'Your sagacity is everywhere applauded, my Beacon of Righteousness, so I expect whatever I failed to hear is fitting as always.'

'She only walked and fell over a root as anyone might,' said Naomi. 'I have yet to hear that *walking* is hoydenish behaviour.'

'Then why was she unaccompanied?' hissed the countess. 'Did she l*ie in wait* for Eliot?'

Berthe stepped forward, 'countess, Roseanna says one can get *wrinkles* when one frowns.'

'For *Eliot?*' hooted Phoebe. 'I admit to being a hoyden, my lady, but I would never *lie in wait* for a gentleman who rides so ill.'

Eliot threw a cushion at her that landed on Richard. He knocked it off without glancing at his attacker and continued to read, but grasped Phoebe's swollen ankle and put it on his lap, stroking it absently, turning a page with his nose.

'Well!' said the countess, her cheeks crimson, 'what behavior! And from you, too, Eliot.'

Charles looked at the ankle stroking with distaste. 'You cannot behave this way in company, ye know. I don't know what people might think of you, and it all rebounds on *us*.'

'But we are not in company, are we Charles?' said the definite Scottish voice of the duke's daughter. 'We are entirely *en famille*.'

The earl's plaintive tone raised at this, 'The trouble being that *votre famille, madame, est tres different, dans les affaires de les convenances, que mien.*'

'*Evidement!*' remarked Lady Eleanor, with the same faint scorn.

The countess arose, but Queenie interposed, 'I hope,' she said, a trifle nervously, with an assumption of bright unconcern, 'that there might be a soufflé tonight. I saw a number of eggs being broken in the kitchen.'

'Oh *good*!' said Berthe sincerely.

'You were in the *kitchen*?' seethed the countess at her sister-in-law.

'We both were,' said Ophelia offhandedly, 'to take off our muddy boots in the boot-room beyond, when a delicious smell lured us in.'

'Is one,' asked Berthe, 'a *hoyden* if one visits the kitchen? I am very much a hoyden then, for cook feeds me each day.'

'*Nothing* your family does has the power to surprise me any more,' sniffed the countess.

'That seems like a challenge I am sure we might meet, my lady!' said Naomi.

'Well, I *say*!' said Charles.

'*Enough* Naomi,' said Lady Eleanor. Naomi subsided with a sardonic smile.

There was a brief silence where everyone hoped for the announcement to dinner, and then Berthe, who had made her way back to the countess from her rear, leaned over and said in her ear, 'I recommend being a hoyden, countess, for there are some cakes in the kitchen that *never* seem to make it to the table and they are *delicious*.'

The countess had bent thirty degrees to the side to avoid Berthe's confidence, and the child's mouth near her ear.

Ophelia, rarely entering into such disputes, pulled on Berthe's arm and said, 'They don't arrive because *you* eat them, hoyden.'

Berthe grinned without discernible shame.

Tabitha looked a little more reserved than usual, thought Eliot, no doubt because of Agatha's attack those days ago. Her detachment was a defence for her — but the child was, beneath it, less resilient than Berthe, whom the chides and insults of his family seemed to bounce off in crazy directions, usually hurting bystanders.

As dinner was announced, the earl spoke, a hand to his head. 'The tone of the before dinner gathering is a trifle too *lively* for my disposition. I pray you all remember my *nerves,*' he whined faintly, as though the effort was too much for him. 'Godwin will set up the Chinese room for you, Lady Eleanor, for your family to gather before future dinners.'

His tone brooked no argument, Lady Eleanor nodded and the countess left the salon for the dinner table on her husband's arm, giving a superior look to the woman from the west wing as she did so.

CHAPTER 15

Eliot's Disappointment

I was called before mother like a schoolgirl, which was made more absurd by the presence of Berthe by my side. We clasped our hands behind our backs and looked suitably penitent.

'First you, Berthe. I have already told you that you should not make personal remarks.'

'I do not understand, Mama.' And as my mother's eyes narrowed, the little one added, '<u>really.</u>'

'No remarks <u>at all</u> about other people's appearance or character, do you understand now?'

'Yes, Mama. But I do not do so anymore.'

'Really? When you spoke to the countess about wrinkles?

'But Mama, I was not mentioning <u>her</u> wrinkles. I was only warning her, as Roseanna does to Phoebe.'

I almost laughed aloud again. Berthe, though Mama could control her with only a look, was not the best specimen for her brand of discipline. One had to know why one was punished, believed Mama, but Berthe's arguments were never insolent, only honest. Even for Mama, it is difficult to deal with that brand of honesty. She looked to me for solace for a moment, then began on me.

'And you, Naomi...!' she began, and I broke in.

'I know Mama, you have told me to still my wit, and you must have noticed that I do not say ninety-nine of the hundred things that I could when the countess att—' I looked at Berthe. It was not appropriate to call the countess's criticism attack before the innocent child, 'When the countess is a trifle unpleasant.'

'We are guests in the home of the earl and countess, and thus we shall be pleasant at all times. I thought it beneath you to respond, Naomi. You will make her an apology. She is not a woman equipped to match your tongue.'

'Yes, Mama.'

I thought about the unpleasant task of giving an insincere apology to the countess. I said so to Berthe as we left Mama's study. 'Oh that is easy,' said my little sister airily, 'just think of something that you really are sorry about, and apologise for that.'

I narrowed my eyes, thinking of several apologetic deviations of my little sister in the past that had seemed innocent, and now appeared deliberate. Berthe had hidden depths it seemed.

When I met Eliot on my walk, I told him Berthe's advice, and he laughed, 'The little rogue!'

'No, but she is correct. I do not wish to lie, so you must help me think of something that I genuinely want to apologise to the countess for, it is difficult.'

'Well, it is certainly true that your family has upended poor Agatha's life. But it was hardly your decision to come here. And Agatha has never been a happy woman.'

'I can see that. It is sad that a woman who admires her ridiculous husband — I beg your pardon...!'

'No, Cedric is quite ridiculous.'

When Eliot laughs thus with me, I adore the warmth in his eyes.

'I should not say so. I am as bad as Berthe, who was also reprimanded for personal remarks,'

'You only say so to me, since we are friends.'

Every time this word came up between us, we somehow looked at each other too long, and I could feel an exquisite consciousness and embarrassment, and a mortifying blush begin. I want, at these moments, to know how he feels. But I merely said, 'Well, but it is sad that she seems to love, and be unloved. Every time he utters one of those effusive epithets, I wish to hit him in the nose with whatever comes to hand, it is cruel — he draws everyone's attention to how much he laughs at her.'

'Well, do not say anything to her of that, it will only pain her. As a family we have come to ignore it, I fear.'

'Well, the memory of her unhappiness will help me be better at an honest apology.'

'You did rather speak disrespectfully about the challenge.'

'Well ... no, you are correct. It is beneath me as mama says, to confront the countess who cannot quickly defend herself.'

'Because she is too stupid?' Eliot's brows raised in mock inquiry.

'Eliot...!'

'I only say so before you, my friend.' His eyes were like a puppy dogs, falsely sorry for stealing a treat, and the absurdity made me laugh again.

I steeled myself for my duty, somehow buoyed by Eliot's nonsense.

I found the countess in a little room with large windows, where she worked on a pair of slippers for her husband.

'Countess ... how exquisite your work is,' I began. 'I could never produce such even stitches, or such a heavenly design.'

'No. It requires time, discipline and application, as well as some sensitivity to beauty. Your family have none of these attributes.'

I was there to apologise, and I believe, I truly believe, that if her words had been addressed to me only, and not to my family, I should have succeeded. 'My mother has more discipline than any creature I know, Lady Tremaine. That is how she stops her mouth when you are unpleasant to her children. She also has a great sensitivity to beauty and has preserved many of the relics sewn by the Marchmont ancestors, by virtue of that appreciation. My sister Phoebe has artistic sensitivity in abundance ... perhaps if you asked, she might draw you a pattern for your next embroidery. Her rendering of all wildlife is exquisite. My sister Stephanie is a master of application and discipline as she challenges herself to new athletic achievements constantly. She can shoot arrows to the centre of the target from further each day, she can climb higher and run faster than most men. She is a gifted rider and can tool a team with ease. This all takes time, discipline and application.'

The countess, who was enraged, said, 'Thus applying herself to a life unsuited for a genteel female.'

I was rather brought up by this, in fact. Stephanie had no interest, it was true, in the feminine virtues, or wifely arts. What would become of her? Mama's wealth made this outcome easy to consider after that moment — the answer was ... whatever she desired. I breathed a little more easily as I thought so. 'I do not think time, discipline and application is quite sufficient in every case, however. Only think of Roseanna and Queenie, they are disciplined in practice of the feminine arts, and all of <u>their</u> application leads to indifferent outcomes, I fear. Mine too!'

'Do not speak of my family in your spurious and impudent response.'

'But <u>you</u> may use your tongue on <u>mine?</u> That does not seem just.'

'You have no respect for your elders! You are an impudent, arrogant girl, dull and with no claim to beauty, who uses her tongue to insult her hosts.'

'You are correct in all counts, countess. I came here not to increase my impudence, but only to apologise to you. I have committed a further offense, as I admit.'

She looked at me coldly, a curling lip suggesting that she believed me insincere.

'My family are here for reasons that I do not know, but it is true this is your house, countess, and you should not have to face the sharp tongue of an arrogant female before dinner. I heartily apologise to you.'

'Are you here at your mother's bidding? Does she fear ejection from my house?'

At this I smiled to myself. 'I hardly think so. But I am here at her bidding, for she has shown me that I should not be one who adds to the atmosphere of carelessly harsh remarks. She abhors my lack of politeness, and wishes me to make amends. I agree with her and I am ashamed.' Ashamed, I thought, because you are too easy to attack.

'And will she send Phoebe to apologise to me?'

'I do not suppose so. I do not remember Phoebe saying anything disrespectful to you last evening.'

'Her words and her tone were vastly different.' The countess said this, and then met my eye. Though I said nothing in reply, I could not help my eyes saying, If we are to talk of "tone", Lady Tremaine...!'

In the end, I felt that while my job had been done I did not feel clear of conscience. I am not Mama yet. I am still an impudent, arrogant young woman in my heart.

The letter reached him, and Eliot's hand trembled as he opened it. He sat, crushed, as he read it. He was, it transpired, a gamester indeed. The ship was missing, presumed sunk, with no survivors.

Eliot thought of the captain and mate, whom he had met, and it sobered him. They had been fine men both, and part of the reason he had invested. He might cast his money on the will of the sea, but that was all. They and their shipmates had lost their lives at its bidding.

Queenie, who had taken to doing Eliot some little services to show her gratitude, came in with a tisane she had made herself and said, 'Oh, Eliot, whatever is wrong?'

He found his hand was shaking, the paper fluttering, but looking up at Queenie's concerned eyes, he pulled himself together. 'Not so lucky this time, Queenie. Our home must wait!'

'Oh, Eliot. Does that mean the ship ...!'

'Lost at sea!'

'What ship?' said Berthe's carrying voice. After the kite making incident, she sometimes attached herself to Queenie, as a giver of boons. She had already gleaned two sugared almonds, a cake, an especially made pudding prepared by Queenie herself (since she remembered liking it when she was a girl, she said) plus a ribbon for her hair, a ring with an inlaid shell that she had begun to wear on her thumb as it was too big for her. Queenie had shown her how to wrap the ring with wool to make it fit her tiny finger. 'Lost?' said Berthe with too much interest, 'Does that mean that there are *bodies*?' Again this was said with too much relish, and Eliot, remembering the captain and his mate, twitched.

'Berthe, dear, you must not speak of this to anyone, at least anyone in my family,' Queenie saw Berthe's eye was alight with this chink of permission, but she was too concerned about Eliot's shock to think carefully. But she did see the problem and so she added, 'and if you must tell Tabitha or someone, do so asking them not to say a word! It is Eliot's secret, and as his friend, you must keep it.'

'A secret!'

'Yes,' said Eliot eying the little dark thing with intelligence. 'But not such another as you can use against me, you horror!'

'As though I would!' said Berthe with dignity, taking herself off.

Queenie brought a chair from the wall and brought it to sit next to him, taking his hand tentatively. This was not a usual intimacy between the brothers and sisters of this house, she must have been very young indeed since Eliot had led her by the hand. It was only when she had been overcome with gratitude at their liberation from care given by their generous independence, that had first let her touch him. And now he needed comfort, it was plain.

'You must be so disappointed, Eliot! But we will not starve, you know!'

'I know, my dear, and I assure you I placed the bet with every knowledge that I might lose. But Ness ... I met the captain and the mate ...' his head lowered.

'Ah! How dreadful! Are they dead?'

'It seems likely. There has been no sighting of the ship.'

'Now I see why you are so upset.' She picked up the tisane and said, 'drink some, Eliot dear! It is beneficial, I assure you.'

He put a hand over hers as she gave him the little bowl, an earthenware one from the kitchen, he supposed, that the countess would disapprove of showing its face upstairs. 'There!' he said having drunk, 'I took it, Ness. It was surprisingly delicious. I had forgotten you like to cook.'

'Oh, Agatha forbids me the kitchens these days as beneath me, but sometimes I still slip down to talk to Cook you know. She always asks after you!'

'I should go down and see her more often. I suppose she was rather fonder of me than my brothers, because I haunted the kitchens for food.'

'Yes. Charles eats a lot, but would never go below stairs. And you were more athletic and needed more sustenance than the other brothers, except Dorian. Cook asks after him, too, but I can never tell any news, except when we see him in London.'

This was a diversion, but now Eliot met his sister's eye. 'Thank you, Ness, you have been a comfort. But I want to sit a while, if you don't mind, and think a little.'

'Of course!' said his sister.

'If you tell Ophelia, do not do so now. I really want some peace for a little.'

Queenie left silently, and Eliot gave a sad smile after her. She was just as preened today as ever, in a muslin that had been sewn so that the garish green stripes made chevron patterns at bodice and on the skirt, and her hair was as usual full of tight ringlets that sat on her forehead, unable to budge an inch, her topknot full of coils and plaits, but her eyebrows had been strange, like little beard barbs above her eyes, growing into definite shapes. He supposed Ophelia had succeeded in forbidding the shaving. But there was no doubt she would look odd for some days until it grew out. Even then, he thought, the tight curls would fight with the brows and cause a dispute. He would trust Ophelia to deal with that problem when it occurred.

His eye encountered the letter again, and he sighed, looking into the fire as he silently prayed for the souls lost at sea.

Berthe found Naomi in the library.

'Is that a true account of our time here?' she said, leaning over her sister's shoulder.

'My thoughts only. Perhaps you should write more Berthe, I could make you a little journal of your own.'

'Really? And will it be bound with Morocco leather?'

'No. But I could make you a pretty cloth binding, rather than a paper one,' offered Naomi, hiding her journal page from Berthe's inquisitive eye, and getting ink on her hand in consequence.

She touched her quill to Berthe's nose as reprisal and Berthe said 'ouch!' as the sharp quill touched her. But it was a half-hearted complaint, for she had other business with her sister.

'Well, *my* journal would have secrets in it you would never guess, Naomi!' Berthe danced off to lean over the other side of the desk in a meaningful way.

'No doubt! Raids on the kitchen, going places you should not be...' Naomi replied without much interest, reading back the last line in her journal.

'...*hearing things* I should not hear!' Berthe said, with emphasis.

Naomi looked up at this, but seeing her sister's face nearer to her than she expected (for Berthe's whole body was leaning over now, legs dangling off the floor) and wearing her smug look, Naomi pulled back. 'No, I do not wish to hear tales, Berthe, so you should take yourself off.'

Berthe's smile was smugger still and she merely kicked her legs playfully in the air, not moving her leaning body position, 'Not even if it is about *Eliot*?'

'No,' said Naomi testily, even though she did wish to know, 'if you listen in on things, I shall tell Mama!'

'I did not eavesdrop, that is vulgar!' said Berthe in a saintly voice, jumping back onto her feet. 'I just followed Queenie into the green salon and we found him sad and he said ...!'

Naomi screamed, 'Berthe!' with her hands to her ears. But her sister had continued talking and she just heard "ship lost" and removed one hand.

'A ship lost?' she asked. 'Has he a friend aboard?'

'I do not know, but he had just received a letter.'

'*Say nothing* of this, Berthe. Mind, I'll make you pay if you do.'

'Of course!' Berthe's saintly tone had returned. 'I only told you because Eliot owes you!'

'What does he owe me?'

'Never mind!' said Berthe, and skipped away.

Naomi followed, heading for the green salon. He did not hear her come in, and regarded the fire as though he saw some scenes enacted there. Naomi stood looking on, unable to stop herself regarding him, knowing she should make a noise to alert him to her presence. But she stood and saw him cover his face with his hands at one point, looking the spirit of sadness. She wished to rush to him to sit on the arm of his chair and put a comforting arm about him. But she could not. So she said, 'Eliot, it is fine, and I feel like a walk. Will you come?'

He looked up, surprised. 'What about the noticing eyes?'

'Let them notice today. You have walked with Phoebe, after all...'

'Very well, but I am not so sociable today...'

'Then we can be silent...'

'I'll meet you at the stable block. We can walk from there.'

'*Eminently* discreet,' she approved, teasing him. She was glad to see him smile a little at this and went to fetch her old tweed cape.

'I suppose that is warm, but is it not heavy?'

'I'm used to it. But when it rains I can hardly carry it back!'

'I'm sure!'

'Pray do not make small talk, I told you already you may be silent.'

They sat on the high bank by the brook and looked down silently at the foliage below. After some minutes, he said, 'Berthe told you.'

'Yes.'

'It is an investment I made, but that is not why ... You see, I met with the captain and the mate ...'

'Oh! How dreadful!' she said, grasping his sleeve, 'Do you want to be alone?'

'I thought I did. But now I know I wanted *you* all along.'

She took his hand, 'Oh, Eliot!'

He held her hand more tightly. 'Today's doings mean I should not do this..' He held up their clasped hands, '...but just for a moment, Naomi!'

'Oh, Eliot!' she said again.

He pulled his hand away and she saw there were two others on the path opposite. 'Oh,' he said casually, 'Look! It is the most ridiculous friendship in the world!'

She stiffened. *What ...!*

'Ah! Roseanna has stumbled, and now Queenie helps her and now they are apologizing to each other...' he said in delight.

She glanced over and saw it was true, the girls were in a pantomime of hand gestures of apology, smiling and fawning on each other. It was quite ridiculous. He was looking at her for a shared amusement, but she was still considering his earlier remark, and had to fake a smile in return. They got up and went behind the screen of trees to walk back to the house. She was silent. When the house was in sight, he touched her arm to hold her back. 'Naomi, are you upset?'

'Of course not. Go back to your green salon, I'll see you at dinner.'

She needed to find the horrible child. 'Rich, seen Berthe anywhere?' she said to her brother, who was coming down the stairs.

'She went out with Phoebe, I think. She's found a good climbing tree at the back of the house to show off to Stephanie. Phoebe goes with her to see it first.'

'Very well! Thanks.'

He moved along, but looked over his shoulder as Naomi went towards a back door, 'Do I need to know what she has done?' he asked.

'She might not be guilty! I'll let you know.'

He went on his laconic way towards the green salon. 'Rich!' she called. He turned back. 'Oh, never mind!' Eliot Marchmont could ask him to leave if need be.

She went off to look for her errant sister.

The door to the countess' sitting room was ajar, and that lady said to her sister-in-law, who was sewing at her side. 'Do you see why I am angry? They are just everywhere in the house, shouting. Why, when they have a perfectly good wing of their own. Why must I see and hear them?'

'It wasn't a perfectly good wing until Lady Eleanor saw to it,' said Ophelia. 'Have you visited it? It is charming!'

'I have not. I do not wish to see what wreckage that woman makes of my house.'

'You cannot say that improving the roof is wreckage. And the place shines with an old world charm.'

'All that work for the servants.'

'But they are her servants, not yours. One can tell by their dress.'

'Yes, and why did she do that? Now all my maids look dowdy by comparison. Whoever heard of dressing the maids uniformly in the country?'

'Well, the footmen have livery, why should not the females be similarly united?'

'You dispute me on everything. Now I shall have to clothe my maids, at great expense, only so her servants are not ranked above them.'

'I suppose you will!' agreed Ophelia. 'Perhaps you could apply to Lady Eleanor for compensatory payment.'

'Ophelia! I cannot talk to you!'

'I do feel for you somewhat, countess. I daresay I should not like my own fiefdom to be so invaded, but your anger does you a disservice, sister. She is not at all moved by it. And it is all Cedric's doing after all! Be angry with *him*.'

'I will not. He is master here and can do as he wills. Only, I cannot conceive of why he should have permitted that family to come here!'

Ophelia raised a brow, 'Really, Agatha? You *really* cannot conceive of why he might have permitted them to come?'

The countess' face closed. 'I do not know what you mean.' She said and pursed her lips.

'My esteemed brother does nothing without gain for himself. Did you think him suddenly compassionate? You especially must know that to be unlikely.'

'You shall not say so! My lord is kindness itself.'

'Very well,' said Ophelia, setting a stitch, 'pretend you do not know why Cedric sent for our bills.'

There was silence in the room while the ladies sewed on.

Chapter 16
Truth Discovered

Phoebe threw herself on Naomi's bed, watching for a moment as her sister sat with a hovering quill over her journal.

'Is that your journal? Do you write nothing else these days?' Phoebe asked.

'Apart from the tale of the lady who bit a villain in the middle of a party, no!'

'You exaggerate as ever! I bit him while in a *corridor*, not in the midst of the company.'

Naomi turned around in her chair, one arm on the scrollwork back, looking earnestly at her sister. 'I *do* exaggerate, do I not? I think I do so even in my journal.'

'Do you? You will never permit me to read it!'

'It is to exercise my own private demons, which *you* do by biting baronets.'

'Only one so far, but Mama worries about my Season.'

'She is right to worry.'

'That is what I came to speak with you about, Naomi. It seems to me absurd that I should have been led on by such a man.'

'You are not sad anymore?'

'No just angry. With him, for being such a low fiend, but more with myself, for feeling so towards him. *I kissed his hand*!'

'You did?'

'*Ridiculous*, isn't it. Only because he told me I was beautiful and that he had never before felt such a pull of attraction—'

'The cur!'

'And he looked at me so ... I cannot explain it, but I felt the same, I thought, and so I kissed him.' She laughed. 'He was shocked. I think I had turned the tables on him somewhat.'

'Oh, Phoebe!' Naomi rose and joined her sister on the bed, her hand about Phoebe's waist.

'Eliot saw it, and he told me it was the fault of Barclay. That he led young ladies on like this frequently. Apparently, after he rejected me, I was supposed to be silent and go into a decline.'

Naomi was upset at Eliot's name, but she was glad that now Phoebe was free enough of the pain to tell her story. So she scoffed, '*Ha!* But you did *not!*' and they giggled.

Phoebe pulled away. 'But the thing is, Naomi, now I am afraid.'

'No! Not you, Phoebe!'

'I have always trusted my instincts, and acted on my true feelings. And now, Barclay seems like such an *insect*, and yet I passionately inclined to him.'

'I understand. But he deceived you, Phoebe. You cannot blame yourself for *trust*.'

'Ah, trust is a trap I thought *Roseanna* might fall into, not you or I.'

Naomi was not at all sure she had not fallen into just such a trap, so she closed her lips.

Phoebe's eyes shone. 'But Naomi, if I can no longer trust my instincts, how can I go on and still be *me?*'

Naomi needed some wisdom here, and naturally thought of her mama. 'Do you remember when you approached a fire when you were young, ready to touch the bright end of the poker?'

'I do. And Mama held my hand towards it until it was uncomfortable!'

'Yes. When we are inexperienced we go towards the flame without knowing one can be hurt. Sir Osbert Barclay was your flame, Phoebe. Your instinct has learned it already. Our instinct must be tutored, too, I think.'

Phoebe sighed, relieved, and kissed her sister's cheek. 'You are the most like Mama of us all.'

'Berthe thinks *she* is.'

'Berthe is the *wicked* side of Mama!'

'*Cunning*,' laughed Naomi, 'not *wicked*.'

Phoebe said suddenly, remembering Naomi's earlier remark. 'What is this about *exaggerating* in your journal? Can you read that part to me?'

'No. It is just ... well, imagine you had written your thoughts on Sir Osbert before you knew enough to bite him, and someone...' here Naomi had difficulty speaking, '...read it.'

'Oh, do *not*!' Phoebe's cheeks were aflame even at the thought.

'*Indeed!* A journal records one's thoughts at the *time*, but should never be...'

'I will *never* attempt to read yours, exaggeration or not!' Phoebe said so with fire in her eyes, gripping Naomi's hands. 'I would *detest it* if someone read my unguarded thoughts!'

'Exactly!' said Naomi, a little grimly. Then, shaking herself said, 'Shall we drive to the village? I have not driven the new pair yet.'

'Yes! If Stephanie is not before us.'

'Or Rich!'

They went to the stables together, donning old short capes and worn half-boots as they left the house by the boot room.

There Mama, passing with a basket of wild flowers just picked, said 'What state are your boots in?'

Phoebe looked down. 'It hardly matters, Mama, we are just about to muddy them more!'

Lady Eleanor nodded and entered the house.

The butler was summoned to Lady Eleanor's apartment in the west wing by a maid in the Wild's uniform. Godwin, considerably put out by this summons, began to refuse it, but he thought better of it when he remembered the Scottish lady's eye. Also, there was more that he had heard and deduced that made it unwise to refuse the lady.

The maid, Maude, seeing capitulation in the butler's eye, led the way with a very straight back. There was in this house, *two* households; and though its ownership was not in dispute, there was more and more evidence that *her* lady, the lady of the west wing, was winning the battle. The flood in the attics of the main house, and the arrival of the other maids in *their* attic rooms, so much more comfortably appointed, it seemed, than the staff attics in the main house, had softened the war in the kitchens. Their mistress had instructed the maids to be of use to Mrs Peters or the Cook whenever they may, and to be polite at all times with the other staff, even if they did not meet with equal kindness. This had resulted in a cold war, but the proximity at night was warming up the maids' relations to the point that Becky, an upstairs maid in the main house had helped Maude finish polishing the long corridor during the Wild's breakfast. Maude and her friend Sarah had agreed to help Becky finish the giant ballroom the next week. Since the footmen, with rags on their feet, had helped them with the polishing, it had meant a unification of the two sides, the footmen teasing the new maids equally, as they did their old friends, during this long task.

But Godwin the butler did not fully approve the new treaty, and looked on at the Table grimly when the staff chatted across household boundaries during their dinner. Now, thought Maude, might be his comeuppance.

Lady Eleanor did not look up as Godwin entered, continuing with her papers at her desk. Godwin waited while the quill scratched on, and eventually said, 'How may I help you, my lady?'

'I passed through the bootroom, Godwin, and it appears that my family's boots are not cleaned.'

Godwin was silent. Lady Eleanor looked up, meeting his eye. 'If I were to give you instructions to have it done, it would put you in a difficult position, would it not?'

Since the butler had been specifically instructed, by the jealous countess, to do nothing for the other family beyond serving dinner and breakfast, or meet her wrath, the butler stiffened.

Lady Eleanor sighed. 'A footman, then! Do you think blue livery will be enough of a distinction?'

'Not a footman, my lady, I beg you!' said Godwin, almost in a panic.

'Then what should I do, Godwin, *clean them myself*?'

He blinked. But she did not, this lady, look entirely unsympathetic to his problem. 'Madame, if I might suggest ...'

Lady Eleanor raised her brows.

'I will have them seen to without it needing to be ...' the word *known* hung in the air. Lady Eleanor nodded, dismissing him. But Godwin was thinking. 'Your family's boots will be in the cupboard in the bootroom. If you could let them know, my lady.'

Lady Eleanor had gone back to her quill.

Godwin hesitated, wondering how this lady managed to rent his imperturbability on every occasion. He was trapped between two mistresses, and he had to decide whether to favour the one who had employed him, or the one, he suspected, who paid him. Loyalty said he must put the countess in premier place, but that lady did not understand his dilemma and only issued impossible orders to him, instructing rudeness to the other family. He sighed, deciding to deal with this problem today, if he could.

'If there is anything else of that nature, my lady, then perhaps you could have, eh, Maude, mention it to me, so that I may deal with the matter, eh ... *quietly*, to your satisfaction.'

Lady Eleanor put down her quill. 'I do not wish you to disobey your orders from your mistress, Godwin. This is, of course the house of the earl and countess, which I respect. But I will not have my children *demeaned* in pursuit of peace. Neither do I wish to confront Lady Tremaine with each and every petty domestic detail that might have been ... *overlooked*.' She added ironically. 'By bringing in more staff, I think I have proved that I do not wish my family to be a burden on the household, but neither will I have them *despised*.'

'I understand, your ladyship!' Godwin bowed.

'If your loyalty should trouble you, remember that we are guests of the *earl*. I do not think that *he* wishes me displeased.' The butler nodded. 'That will be all, Godwin,' said the magnificent lady, returning to her papers.

As he left, Godwin reflected that she might have set one of her maids to clean the boots. But she was making a point about the divide. The offer to appoint a new footman would drive the countess to distraction. Different livery, too! It would be war declared. She was quite capable of it, and would win, perhaps. But it was a butler's duty to run a smooth household, and so he would discretely perform, and have his footmen perform, such duties as were usual for guests, without distinction, and keep it from the countess as long as he could. It should not be too difficult. He suddenly realised that the friendship between the two household's staff was to be encouraged. They could thus help each other behind closed doors.

The thing was, not to get caught by the countess.

At dinner that night at The Table, the intelligent Maude, who had been desperate to know why the butler had been interviewed by her mistress, saw the fruits of it. For Mr Godwin no longer frowned down the talk across the two staffs. She saw him speak quietly to Ben, one of the footman she had polished the ballroom with. When she got a chance, Maude leant over and asked him, 'What did Mr Godwin want?'

'Asked me to clean your Family's boots. I would have, but he told me *not to* before.'

'I expect it was orders.'

'But I've to put them in the cupboard.'

Maude frowned. 'So Your Family can't see them?'

'It is only my mistress who would care, I think.' He grinned at Maude. 'Your mistress is a bossy one!'

'No more 'n yours,' shot Maude back.

They smiled the complicit smile of servants the world over.

Naomi had not been herself on the drive to the village. But she hid it well, laughing with Phoebe about Stephanie's anger when she saw them pass in the phaeton. Stephanie had called, '*I* was about to drive!'

'Drive Berthe's pony and trap!' called Phoebe over her shoulder, and Stephanie had shouted back, but they were too far off to hear.

The village had the attraction of the new to them: they could not believe that the children, Berthe and Tabitha, had been before them. They looked in every shop (which did not take long) and only purchased a custard tart each which they ate at a table set up outside the inn. A serving boy asked what they desired and when they were told no tea was to be found here, they ordered a cordial each, made, said the boy, by the landlady herself. They complimented that lady as she emerged to look at them. But the dame sniffed, regarding their tarts and said rudely, 'No nuncheon then? You only order cordial?'

'Yes,' said Naomi, amused, 'and as I said, it was delicious.'

'If you come again,' said this most inhospitable of hosts, who had introduced herself as Mrs Poffit, 'order nuncheon at least.' She looked them up and down, from their straw bonnets, dull dresses to their shabby boots. Ladies, she concluded, but of that order of gentry with less than she in their purses. They could come again, but little profit would she make.

Phoebe, like Naomi, did not resent this female, but found her amusing. Discerning her opinion of them, she took out a half sovereign and gave it to the dame. 'For our next nuncheon, Mrs Poffit!'

The woman put the coin in her pocket and smiled more benignly. 'Certainly, ladies! Come again soon!'

They laughed as they went back to the stables. 'But the poor ladies without money must meet with insult there, indeed!'

'Oh, she is not the worst.'

And so Naomi's day passed, hardly allowing her thoughts on today's shock to be considered. On the way back she let Phoebe talk, and the idea plaguing her since this morning took root again. *'The most ridiculous friendship in the world,'* he had said. It was not too far-fetched an idea for one so like her in opinion, or so odd an expression, she told herself. She had almost reassured herself on the drive that the words had been but a coincidence.

But not quite.

Berthe was, Godwin informed her, in the blue salon with Miss Roseanna and Miss Clytemnestra. They were engaged in tying bows onto a kite string, and all three looked up as Naomi entered, smiling. 'Berthe, can you come with me a moment?' asked Naomi. Berthe ran to her, and Naomi smiled at the others and took her to the library.

In the hall they met Charles, who inquired after Queenie. 'She is in there, tying kite bows. You could help us, Crown Prince!' said Berthe brightly.

'Help...?' drawled Charles almost as faintly as the earl. He took a handkerchief edged in lace and held it to his brow affectedly to express his disgust at this idea, and headed in the opposite direction.

Berthe said, 'Isn't he *funny?*'

As they entered the library, she said, 'Did you find Eliot? Did he tell you about the lost ship?'

'Why? Do you wish to put it into your new journal when I make it?'

'Well, perhaps!' said the child, 'It would be a good story to start with.'

'Well, I shall not tell you, infant. It is Eliot's secret.'

'*He* might tell me!'

'You may try!' Naomi wandered to the shelves and picked up a book, 'Here Berthe!' she said, giving her the copy of Robinson Crusoe that she had found, 'you might like this book!'

Berthe opened it and read the first line:

I was born in the year 1632, in the city of York, of a good family, though not of that country, my father being a foreigner of Bremen, who settled first at Hull.

'It does not sound much!' Berthe said, her nose wrinkled.

'It gets better. Just skip the tedious parts.'

'Very well, thank you, Naomi.'

'By the by, child, where did you find my journal that day you brought it to me?'

Berthe stilled, but not for long. 'Oh ... in this room!' she said cheerily.

'*Where* in the room?'

Berthe squirmed a little. 'Oh, around.'

'On the desk, or on a shelf?'

'Em...'

'And it was early when you gave it to me ... did you find it that morning?'

'No. At night,' said Berthe, looking at her toes.

When Eliot took over the library.

Naomi looked at her sister, who had just developed a fascination with the volume of *Robinson Crusoe*. She did not wish to speak. Naomi's bosom heaved. It was *true*, what she feared! What Berthe's reasons were, she did not seek to know. There would have been some profit for her, though goodness knew what. She remembered the child saying that Eliot *owed* Naomi. It had troubled her at the time, but Berthe's little schemes were so numerous that one ignored them.

'Off and read your book, Berthe.'

'Oh,' said Berthe, relieved, 'I shall show it to Queenie!'

Naomi sat heavily, thinking what this meant. Soon, she flew to her room, taking the journal from her desk drawer. *How much did he read...? What on earth had she written...?* She sat on her bed scanning the pages, giving little squeals as she read each description of Eliot. It was *too* humiliating! And more ... she had thought he had understood her, as she did him, in an almost magical way. Well, the magic was dispelled at a stroke. *Of course* he knew her! He had read, like a villain, her inner thoughts. How *could* he? How *dare* he? He *knew!* He knew *everything*! Rage, betrayal, humiliation and despair took her in waves. She curled herself on her bed and gave way to hot, confused, tears. He was not her best friend, he was an insect, the flame she had unwittingly gone towards, just like the loathsome Sir Osbert Barclay was for her sister.

Phoebe, upstairs to dress for dinner, found her there and took her in her arms. 'Naomi! Whatever...!' she began.

'Can you *kill* someone for me, Phoebe? Or hold him while I do so myself?'

'Certainly!' said Phoebe with gusto. 'Who?'

'Eliot Marchmont...'

'Eliot?' said Phoebe amazed. 'Not *Eliot*?'

'He has read it!' she said holding up the red Morocco. 'He has read *everything!*'

Phoebe, remembering their conversation this morning, said '*No!*' understanding the hideousness.

'*Look!* He read *this*'! she said, pointing to a passage with her fingers.

Phoebe read gingerly, muttering aloud, '*His face is rather more like Richard's too, in that it is handsome, chiselled from fine marble by the ancients, almost.* Oh my goodness!' she looked in horror at Naomi.

'I *know!*' squealed her sister.

Phoebe read on, appalled. '*sulky mouth...look better with a smile ... a man not a fribble! ...overwhelmingly handsome face...* Oh Naomi!!!'

Naomi's face burned, but she manically turned the pages again. 'And look!' she said, frantically, 'This too!'

Phoebe read on: *I made a mistake today. It does not seem possible as mistakes go, being so utterly stupid. I was beneath my reading tree, a good deal away from Roseanna and Tabitha, who were sketching. I was reading an amusingly awful passage, and when I heard someone come up towards me, in my distraction I thought it was Richard, and held out my hand without looking around. There is no way to explain this. We had just seen dear Rich off on his travels. I knew it. How could I make such an error?*

Someone grasped my hand and I pulled him down to share the book. I even leaned in further and virtually forced him to be close to me. Suddenly, it felt strange. I turned my head and it was Eliot Marchmont, His face turned too, only inches from mine.

Phoebe read, seeing her sister's trembling body, and feeling the rage for her. It was terrible for Naomi. But also, as Phoebe held Naomi's trembling form and dried her eyes of tears made of rage and hurt, she saw something else. All the things that Naomi had not shared. Before Barclay, Phoebe would have been hurt that Naomi held back with her. But after Barclay she understood. When one is encountering attraction for the first time, one has no words to describe it to another. This was why Eliot's sin was not to be forgiven. Naomi had tried to describe these feelings to an inanimate object first, the journal, to explore their meaning for herself, and it was no one's business to intrude on this. Again a wave of nausea overtook Phoebe at the thought that Barclay could have read such a journal of hers. But Eliot was not such a one as Barclay, Phoebe was sure. Still, he must be punished.

Naomi, broken hearted, was saying, 'I thought he understood me, Phoebe ... but it's all a *lie!*'

Phoebe lent back on the pillows holding Naomi close. 'We shall kill him later, Naomi, but first we will *trap* him!' she said, with relish.

'I cannot go to dinner!' cried Naomi.

'You certainly can. Are you not the daughter of Mr Julian and Lady Eleanor Marchmont? Are you not directly descended from the houses of earls and dukes?'

'I am!' said Naomi, sitting up. 'But I did not think you cared for such things, Phoebe.'

'I do not, as a whole, but when I need to be given courage, as when I had to face Barclay again, it helped to remember it.'

Naomi nodded, shoulders straight. 'What trap do you propose?'

CHAPTER 17

The Trap

Phoebe and Naomi came down into dinner dressed in their violet muslins that night, which their mama raised her brows to see. Eliot, looking his admiration to Naomi, found Phoebe's eye instead. It was a little cold and a little jeering, he thought. Naomi's eye was always elsewhere. Eliot was surprised. For all they sought to avoid speculation, they usually managed one or two complicit, affectionate looks to each other.

Her hair was different too, it was not in its simple coil, with the messy waves at the front. The waves were now ringlets, the coil now a topknot from which more ringlets fell. Eliot looked at her covertly, admiring the becoming style. He took it, without quite understanding why, as a compliment to himself. She had perhaps, tried to look pretty for him, and he was proud. But in the next moment he wished she would not. She was already too beautiful for him to be able to stand their distance from each other.

'You are, at least, dressed appropriately this evening, Naomi!' said the countess, in that voice that turned compliment into an insult.

'Oh, so are *you*, countess!' said Phoebe, claws showing even as her mouth spoke in a honeyed tone.

Phoebe was rather quick to protect on so slight a provocation, Eliot thought. He looked at her, considering. The girls were lively tonight, talking along the line of their siblings, without keeping to the rule of addressing only the person on either side.

'Did you finish your kite string?' asked Naomi to Berthe.

'No, but we will tomorrow. I asked the Crown Prince to aid us, but he did not,' Berthe replied.

The earl looked over at his brother at this, 'Ah, Charles, you disappoint me,' he drawled ironically, 'The age of chivalry is dead indeed!'

Charles and the countess laughed at this pleasantry, but Berthe said, in her friendliest voice, 'Oh, then *you* can help us tomorrow, King!'

The earl shuddered and turned to Lady Eleanor. 'Can you kindly instruct your child to give me my proper appellation. I do not think it too much to ask...' This was said in the faintest voice, full of complaint, and the Scotswoman gave him the smallest of bored nods only in reply.

Berthe looked at him, thinking about his appellation. 'Your highness?' she ventured.

Ophelia gave a bark of laughter at this, and said, 'Oh you might as well give up, my lord earl, for you will never best her!'

Roseanna, the peacemaker explained, 'She is reading a book about a king you know, my lord, and has mistaken ...' she turned her face to Berthe's, touching her head. 'Do you not remember, dear, that I said you should respectfully address the earl as *my lord*?'

'Oh!' said Berthe, 'but is not Your Highness *more* respectful?'

Ophelia giggled and Eliot gave her a disapproving look.

'Oph-el-ia!' screeched the countess.

'You see,' began Queenie helpfully, '*Your Highness* is only more respectful if one *has* the title—'

'Stop! That is quite enough...!' said the feeble voice of the earl. 'My head, my head, with all this useless prattle!'

Naomi's eyes lit up, Eliot saw, and he wanted to catch her eye. But she looked to Phoebe instead to exchange smiles hidden by their hands.

The table was silent until Lady Eleanor inquired of her son. 'Have you word from the patent office?' It was said in a low tone and would not have been heard by the rest of the table but for Cedric's imposed silence.

'Do not speak of anything so vulgar as *business* at my dinner table!' said the countess.

'Quite right!' sniffed Charles, in a superior tone.

'*You* discipline *my mother?*' said Richard to Charles in that frozen voice he had once used to the earl.

Charles jumped, eying the young man with trepidation.

'Let silence reign!' said the earl, almost shrill. 'My poor head!'

And, for what was left of the dinner, it was so.

Berthe had escaped once she wolfed down an *Île flottante,* and returned just before the table broke up. She went to the earl's chair and he eyed her warily. She held something out to him and he took it despite himself. It was a little cone, which he looked at without comprehension.

'It is a pastel,' she informed him. 'It is what Mama burns when anyone among us has a sore head.' She looked up at him smiling. 'It works! Really it does. It is for your poor head.'

She tripped from the room, grasping Richard's hand as she did so, and the earl looked after her, then down at the pastel. 'Dispose of this, Godwin!' he said to the butler, at his most disdainful.

'My lord!' said the butler, bowing. Just as well the naughty child had not seen it. She was a handful, but she was kind. It occurred to the butler that the earl had not spoken until the child left the room. But perhaps he was thinking too much.

***

Eliot, in bed, was a little concerned. Naomi had been unbelievably pretty this evening, and also distant. Not from others, and not, he thought, angry. But put simply, they had not connected by word or deed. He had been going to pull away a little himself, but gradually so that she would feel no hurt. Never let her know that he was doing so. He knew that today's letter meant that he had not the means to ask her ... well he was very clear now what he wished to ask her. But with only his income, and hoping to keep two sisters also, Eliot felt he had little to offer. It seemed, perhaps, that Naomi had funds of her own, or at least that her mother might dispense funds upon her marriage. His conversation with

Lady Eleanor had suggested she despised his holding back. But was it not to be a *fortune hunter* to ask for her hand?

He had funds enough to live simply. Even to support a wife and two sisters simply. But wild as they were, the other Marchmont family had never known want or debt and thus could hardly understand him. His brother owned a wealthy estate, and two others not so wealthy. But Cedric was in the process of ruining all. Eliot wondered if stopping this wreckage might be the purpose of Lady Eleanor's removal of her family here. It was evident she did not need shelter. Perhaps she sought to save her husband's rightful inheritance, perhaps too, she planned it for her son.

From something Cedric said over port, he thought that Lady Eleanor had tightened the purse strings. He was inclined to whine, and Charles with him. But Eliot had no time for that. She had paid the servants, as well as all the outstanding bills of Cedric and his siblings, fixed the roof, saved a crumbling wing of the house, and added to the stables. What had his brother, Eliot asked him, to complain of?

'This was all done in the interests of her *own family*, cannot you see?'

'Paying servants who are loath to serve her? No, I do not see!'

'You are a turncoat, Eliot! Cedric is right!'

'Whatever improvements she has made to the roof and the West Wing are in your interests, no?'

'In her interests, and the estate may eventually benefit, I suppose. But the price? I have to listen to my angelic countess complain to me daily about her affronted dignity.'

'She has too much of it in any event,' said Eliot cynically.

'How can you say so?' complained Charles. 'Her nerves are strained at the presence of the others.'

'We only see them at dinner.'

'But they are always there, laughing in the garden or the hall, making kites with my sisters.'

'*Ophelia* made a kite?' Eliot said, astonished.

'But that is not my point. They invade the place. Do not stick to the West Wing.'

'Cedric may simply tell them to *go*.' Eliot said, as a taunt. 'It can hardly be accounted cruel by the World, since Lady Eleanor has a great many houses she might choose to live in.'

'How many?' asked Charles avidly.

Eliot ignored him. 'Just tell them to leave, Cedric!' The earl sunk his chin into his cravat, ignoring him. 'You will not, in case the lady should open her purse again.' He scoffed. 'Why not just pay attention to your estate and live within its ample means, brother?'

Cedric gave him a glance of dislike. 'You have never partaken of gentleman's pleasures, have you Eliot? You have always been the weakling of the family, adjuring safety and caution, not living as a true Marchmont at all.'

'There were many true Marchmonts in the past who *increased* the family fortune, and did not ruin it.'

'You have always been dull, Eliot!' said Cedric, dripping disdain. 'I pity you.'

The great earl then rose and left the room in as stately a fashion as a bottle and a half of port would permit him.

But with this background how could Eliot go to Naomi. And in what? With a begging bowl? The thought repulsed him.

He pictured, for a moment, love in a cottage with Naomi. He did not think she would much mind it. She was not so attached to fashion as his sisters and had not yet had the time to be attached to London diversions. If he asked her now, just to come to him, with only a trunk of clothes, would she do so? He could tell her that whatever her fortune, he did not want it, but she must keep it for her own amusements. And if she had none, that they should not seek money from her wealthy mama.

He longed for her. He almost went to her room to ask her now, but it was absurd. He would see her before breakfast for their secret walk. It was only six hours away now.

The time of the walk came, and there was no Naomi. He began to think that last night's distance was no mistake, but he could hardly credit it. Yesterday they had held hands, she had comforted him, and now... perhaps she was ill.

He sat on his bench for an hour before he saw her pass, riding with her family on the before breakfast ride. They were laughing and Stephanie was trying to provoke a race, but the others did not push beyond a canter. Richard rode behind beside Berthe on her pony (not the Shetland one) and the others took turns to fall back too. Eliot wanted to jump up from his bench, but the party took a fork in the road, and disappeared from view. He was tempted to get a horse and join them, but Naomi had warned him about inciting interest in their families, and so he did not. If he had he would have pulled his horse beside hers and asked what was wrong.

He went back to the house and waited for breakfast. He was first at the table, and the servants, not yet prepared, tried to scramble to find him something to eat, but he told them he would wait. He was thinking, he said. This was odd behaviour, but the Quality were odd, so they left him sitting there for forty minutes until he was joined by his two sisters. He was bad company, and spoke little though encouraged to do so. Queenie ventured that he was still upset about the captain and his mate, and Eliot realised he had not thought of them since dinner last night. He was, he thought, a shallow person. Ophelia stopped her sister's mouth and talked amusing inanities until they heard the Wild Marchmonts in the hall.

They came in as a bunch, laughing, and Eliot was glad when Queenie asked Roseanna, 'Have you not lost one of the party?'

But it was Phoebe who answered, 'Oh, her horse stepped into a deeper puddle than she thought, and now her entire body is splattered in mud! I will compose a plate of good things for her and take it upstairs after she bathes.'

'Naomi looked so funny, Eliot!' said Tabitha in her quiet voice, but smiling. So disappointed was he that he could not smile in return. When, then, might he see her?

'She was in such a dream, I suppose it is because *Robert* wrote!' said Phoebe to Roseanna, while making the plate.

'Did he?' said Roseanna, 'she has been expecting his reply.'

'She is *over the moon* to receive it.'

Roseanna, Eliot thought, looked confused at this. 'I knew she would be happy, but I did not think that she would be so moved by—'

Phoebe interrupted. 'She wrote avidly in her journal all night after it was delivered.'

'Really? It means so much to her?''

'No one but her journal knows Naomi's true heart.'

'I often think so,' agreed Roseanna.

'I think she is in a quandary now,' continued Phoebe, 'I do not know why. After all, the fate of Naomi and Robert has long been determined.'

Eliot became stone.

'Pardon?' said Roseanna.

'Do you want to go to the Fair?' Phoebe asked brightly. 'I heard there is a traveling show, as well as wares from all over the county.'

'A groom told me there is a dancing dog!' said Berthe.

'Let us take the coach and the phaeton too. Do come Ophelia, Queenie.'

'Well we shall, and take our own coach in case Agatha should wish to come.'

'Mama will not,' said Tabitha. 'She says she has a great deal to do.'

'Well let us meet in a half hour, so that Naomi has time for breakfast.'

Richard, who had been reading over breakfast as usual, looked up, 'Tabitha, Berthe, stay close to me today. Some people sell *women and children* at these Fairs.'

'*No!*' said Tabitha, shocked.

But Berthe only asked, 'What about Phoebe and Stephanie?'

'Oh, they can sell them for all I care,' said Richard and took a buffet to the head from Stephanie, eating at his side.

Eliot supposed Naomi was not here to insult.

'Will you come, Eliot?' asked Phoebe.

'I too have a great deal to do.'

'My dull brother has never cared for these things,' said Ophelia, dryly.

'But it will be *fun,* Eliot!' protested Berthe.

'No! Do you not think I deserve some peace from you, dreadful child?'

'Oh!' said Berthe, 'but the king, no, the earl does. I shall tell him we will be away today, for his poor head's sake.'

She headed for the door, and Stephanie said, 'Do you think we should stop her? She will go to his room, you know.'

Richard grinned. 'I know!' he said.

CHAPTER 18

The Trap Sprung

Eliot, unable to eat, went to the library to wait, his head spinning. Who was Robert? What fate was determined? He might follow her to the Fair and ask her, but he felt that last night, this morning, and breakfast was all too much of a coincidence. She had received some letter after meeting him, and then she had avoided him. She had not looked cross with him last night, not like last time she had distanced herself, so prickly and on her dignity. No, she had looked happy last evening, she had just not shared it with him. She had avoided him, and done so twice this morning. If she felt as he did, she could *never* have done so. Though he knew he should not, he could not keep away from her. He ached to connect with her again, to know they were ... special friends. He sometimes thought there were stars in her eyes when she looked at him, was it not so?

He must know the answer, and his instinct told him that she would not say.

They would go soon, all of them from the West Wing. He would be able to ... see the journal. Just one more time. He had to know who Robert was, what fate... why she avoided him. She would not hide it, would she? Not in her room surely. There were no interlopers in the West Wing to worry about.

It would be despicable, dismal behaviour, but he must read what she had written all night.

What kind of man have you become, Eliot Marchmont? he thought to himself. But his resolve did not waver amidst the self disgust.

He heard the general commotion of leaving, and from the library window he saw Phoebe and Naomi get into the phaeton which a groom had brought around from the stables. Strange, he thought, the girls usually go to the stable block themselves and exit through the bootroom. He watched them until they reached the bend in the carriage path, and then went to the West Wing.

As he reached the first floor, he remembered that Lady Eleanor was still here, as well as sundry servants. They must be attending other duties, or some given leave to visit the Fair, for he was able to enter her room with ease. He looked around at her things and leaned up against the door, a new wave of self-disgust hitting him. He could smell a faint scent of her. What he was doing was despicable, he thought again, but two things stopped him turning back. The first was the name *Robert* that rang in his ears, and the second was the journal itself, lying on her desk, open, the quill diagonally across the pages as though she had just left off writing.

He felt the guilt of a criminal as he moved the quill to its stand and picked up the journal. He sat on her bed as he rifled the pages. There were a few more entries since his last look. Much as he wanted to know what she thought about their conversations recently, or their held hands, he skipped these entries. He found the last entry, some pages long, which began, *'Robert wrote to me at last...'*

Eliot's heart sank. He was sick, but he must read on.

...his letter was more than I could have dreamed of. Since I left him in Scotland he had promised me he would write, of course, but while I waited for a word, there was so much happening in Tremaine Towers that I almost forgot his vow to me. I had just come from a walk with Eliot, I felt so sorry for his loss. But then there were the strange actions between us, some looks, some words that vaguely suggest Eliot has feelings for me.

Robert's letter put everything in that friendship into perspective instantly. It was so direct, so full of statements that could not be clearer, sentiments precisely expressed. All came back to me in a rush, all our old conversations and the decisions we made together. Of course, I was young then, and Mama did not quite approve, although Papa was always on Robert's side. He had to go to Europe, I knew it, and saw him off on the great ship. As he left I thought, 'Robert, in two days you will be in France and who knows when I will see you again!'

He told me he would write to me, but only upon his return, since only then could he tell me everything he wished to say. And so I waited, all this time, and now he has written, and in such terms! Was there ever a girl as fortunate as I? He will come soon, to speak to and reassure Mama, and I await him eagerly! I shall keep Robert's letter hidden and safe forever.

His words contrasted so strongly with Eliot's on our walk today that it seems the time I have spent with this strange friend is only a dream.

Eliot put his forehead in one hand, hardly able to believe what he was reading. *A dream? The most real days of his life?*

As I look at these pages, I see that I was carried away by Eliot's good looks which is a base reason to feel affection, I feel. Robert too, is handsome, but it is his decisive nature that excites my admiration. Eliot's nature is well enough, but not firm. Any inclination he feels towards me would be short-lived, I fear. Perhaps, but for my pact with Robert, I might have taken the lead towards more than the friendship that was all he offered me, but the letter has thrown the scales from my eyes. I shall tell Robert about my friendship with Eliot. He is a Scotsman and will take it stoically. I have done nothing, after all, to dishonour him. No promises were made.

I shall still be friends with Eliot, but in a different way, perhaps. It was, after all, only a dream...

A voice said, 'Caught you, Eliot Marchmont!' Eliot looked up, confused, the journal in his hand, forgetting his shame in his misery. Phoebe stood pointing like a goddess of retribution, but her face fell. Naomi stood behind her as she said, 'Oh Naomi! *Eliot...!*'

Naomi came forward and saw him. His face looked up at hers like a child and copious tears fell from his eyes. 'Naomi!' he cried, 'Oh, my Naomi!'

She knelt beside him and held his hands, 'Eliot, Eliot, do not!'

When Phoebe heard a wracking sob, she left quietly, pulling the door behind her.

Naomi was touching Eliot's face, wiping away his tears with her fingers, 'Oh Eliot, do not!'

He seemed to come to himself from a nightmare and he grasped her shoulders, not daring to look away from her eyes, now weeping like his own. 'It wasn't a dream, Naomi, it was never a dream!'

'I know, I know, my darling Eliot, it was never a dream!' she soothed, hardly knowing what she was saying.

'Do you? Do you know how much I love you, how I have longed to ask you to marry me almost from the start?'

He was still weeping. The wryly amused, urbane, strong man she knew was weeping still.

'I know, that is, I *almost* know. You never said...'

'The life I have to offer you is too simple, but it is all I possess. How *could* I speak?'

'You hinted as much, but I am quite wealthy, you know.'

'What has that to do with *me*?'

'And so you will let me go?' Naomi asked, her eyes bright.

His passion pulled her to him, and he said, 'No, no! He shall not have you!'

Naomi was smiling to herself, crushed to his chest. The chin against her forehead was wet. 'But my previous arrangement...' she said.

Eliot stilled. He had heard that note in her voice before. 'What did you call me before? Your *darling* Eliot?' He held her off to look at her, his crying ended abruptly.

'I *could* not have said so!' she told him with laughing eyes.

'Yes you did!' he told her severely, looking at her as though she were a puzzle. 'Who is Robert?'

'My literary agent.'

'And what is your arrangement?'

'Why, to sell my books to the highest bidder of course.'

'There is more than one?'

'Yes. I write a great deal.'

'And he is handsome?' Eliot pursued.

'For a man of his age, very. I suppose he must be nearly sixty now.' She smiled, 'But as I said, Eliot dear, appearance is a base reason for choosing a mate. Which thought you ought to know, since you are a vile thief of secrets.'

He looked ashamed, at last, so she kissed him. 'Naomi!' he protested. 'You are just like your sister!'

'You do not mean Phoebe has kissed you...' she teased him.

'Come here!' he said and kissed her again and again. 'I was so unhappy.'

'So was I, when I discovered you had read my thoughts.'

'It started as an ungentlemanly caprice — you wrote so entertainingly about my family! But then you wrote about me...'

'Don't!' Naomi hid her head in his coat.

'And I knew I should never know these things ... but it became a drug of some sort. I could not ...'

'Do not!' she said again, 'I cannot think of unhappy things just now. We are to be married and I shall have time to torture your perfidy for a lifetime.'

'Married?'

Naomi pulled away with violence.

'Now that is *quite* enough! You cannot weep and kiss me and then tell me that we are not to be wed!' She was seriously angry, her eyes like her virago of a sister's.

'Naomi, it is just ...'

'I do not wish to hear it. Or I shall marry Uncle Robert truly.'

He laughed. 'Oh, darling!' he went towards her holding out his hands. She stepped back, still angry. 'Let me hold you!' He spoke into her hair with a laugh. 'Are you perhaps, wealthy enough to house my sisters, too? They are very expensive, you know.'

'Are you quite finished with your stupid pride?'

'If you forgive me for reading your journal.'

'I shall not forgive that yet. I had a great scheme planned with Phoebe, of catching you read, and then hating you forever, but now it has all come to nothing.'

'Such a shame it came to nothing!' He was twisting his waist as he held her tighter and tighter, swaying together happily.

'But I shall forgive your pride on one condition.'

'Which is?' he said, pulling away to look at her again.

'We shall post the banns on Sunday.' She gave him a strange look. 'Is it,' she said in a little voice, 'too soon?'

He looked at her seriously. 'Not too soon ... but *why* Naomi?'

'Because I am afraid your pride will return, and you will blow hot and cold.'

'You said I was an indecisive man, and your mama said I was a ditherer.'

'She did? How wonderful!' she laughed.

'But I decided very soon, and there was little dithering. It was only...'

'Don't commence again!'

'The banns will be posted on Sunday. If your mother permits.'

'She married a penniless inventor, so she will have no objections. But let us go to her now.'

Since they found Lady Eleanor and Phoebe together, his formal proposal was not so unexpected as it might have been. But before he could begin, Phoebe ran to them and hugged them. 'But do not think, Eliot Marchmont,' she said, in pretend wrath, 'that your sins are all forgiven you. The punishment is to come.'

'Sins?' inquired Lady Marchmont with only a little interest.

But Eliot was replying to Phoebe, 'You may as well just bite me now.'

'Lady Eleanor,' he then began with a bow towards Naomi's mama. 'I wish...'

'Yes, yes, Eliot you have been wishing for Naomi for some time now, and you have had those silly kinds of reservations that gentlemen hold on to. Ophelia and Clytemnestra anticipated this union, and sought me out a week ago, to tell me what you have *already* done for them and plan to do. Who would not wish for such a responsible son-in-law? Permission granted.'

'Really? But...'

'I cannot abide buts, Eliot.'

'Good, Mama!' said Naomi, excited, 'Then the banns will be posted on Sunday?'

'So soon?' said Phoebe.

'She's afraid his qualms will get the better of him. Very well. Though we shall have to go to Town to order your trousseau. It interrupts my plans somewhat.'

'I have plans, too Mama,' said Naomi warmly, 'but let us discuss them later.'

'Outdoors, now, you two!' said Lady Eleanor picking up her stitchery, 'you were too long in Naomi's chamber. I almost sent Phoebe for you.'

As they left the room, Phoebe opened the door with a sweet smile and handed Eliot a handkerchief. 'Just in case you have the vapours again, dear Eliot.'

'And so, the punishment begins!' Eliot sighed.

Phoebe looked over his shoulder, 'Mama, do you have a vinaigrette with you?'

'Never use one.'

Phoebe looked sadly at Naomi. 'You'll just have to hope he doesn't faint, Naomi dear.'

Naomi tried not to smile, and Eliot pleaded, holding out an arm, 'Bite me, *please*, Phoebe!'

Phoebe smirked. 'Not just yet, Eliot, not just yet.'

Eliot took his betrothed for their walk, and they ran for the shelter of their bench. But now, he thought happily, he did not need to hide his love.

'Oh Eliot,' she said for him, 'I am so happy!'

As he drew her down to sit, he took her into his arms. 'I do not know why your Mama should suppose the open air will be any restraint to us. I can kiss you just as easily here.'

'Oh, I should suppose Mama would suppose so!' said Naomi, wickedly.

Chapter 19

Lady Eleanor's Plans

Eliot Marchmont was not quite dressed as there was a faint knock on his door. 'Wait!' he ordered, as he put on a waistcoat over a shirt still open at the neck.

'Come!' he said, the door opened softly, and an upright female figure entered.

'Lady Eleanor!'

'I shall close the door, Eliot, since I should like a word with you.' He looked around his room, strewn with various garments since he did not have a valet of his own, and the maids tidied later.

'Shall we go elsewhere?' he said picking up the most embarrassing items and thrusting them into a cupboard.

'No. And do not tie your cravat as yet, dear boy, since I know it takes gentlemen some time to do so.'

'Not I!' he said.

'No, you have much in common with my son.' She took a seat by the fire that was laid, but not lit, and Eliot took the other, wondering what hour this was to be paying a visit.

'There are some practical things we might discuss, Eliot, and I hope you will not find me intrusive.' She smiled at him. 'I have talked with Naomi, and your sisters, too. You want a house, for them and for your wife, and felt you could not ask Naomi the interesting question until you could offer more than you can now afford.'

Eliot could think of no more to say than 'Yes!' His fists clenched, for he believed his future mother-in-law was about to offer him largess. 'But I cannot accept...!'

'I said I detest *buts*, Eliot.' She said severely. 'I believe, from your gains already, that it will not be long before you achieve your goals, Eliot. But now you will marry Naomi in six weeks, and we must plan.'

Eliot, who had done nothing else all night, said 'I can afford a house, but it may not be ...'

'It must have occurred to you, Eliot dear, that I possess many properties. To be frank, they are a burden to me, and it would be a blessing if you, Queenie and Ophelia took up your home in one of my estates and took care of it for me.'

'That is very generous,' said Eliot, barely biting back the 'but' that Lady Eleanor so disliked.

'It is not. I have no doubt you can put much in order. Nothing is so desirous as a *present* landlord.'

'It is a roof over our head, and a welcome one, but I cannot...'

'Your investments will pay off, Eliot! I offer you a way to enrich yourself in the *meantime*, to pay for the London Season.'

'I could not accept estate profits from something of yours.'

'I am not so despising of business as your sister-in-law, Eliot. I offer you a deal. If you were to move to Cameron Court in Surrey, for example, you can have any *increase* in profits that you make from last year. This costs me *nothing*, as you see, and if you choose to move to your own home, I shall possess an estate that has increased in value. It is called *investing* Eliot. I shall invest in *you*.'

Naomi had always said, and he had already divined, that her mother was intelligent and capable. And now he saw her delicacy.

'It might be a solution.'

'There is another for you to consider. The Dower House.'

'Here? It has not been lived in for fifty years.'

'I think I may put it to rights, and by the time you return from your wedding trip.'

'Impossible!'

'Perhaps. You might have to live here a while longer.' She sighed. 'I considered the place for my own family, of course, but separation was not the point of my stay.'

'And what *is* that my lady?'

'I shall not say as yet. I suppose you might guess something of it.'

'You wish Richard to inherit?'

'Perhaps. But this was my husband's home. I do not intend that it is wrecked by one generation. Unfortunately, the earl's present heir is no more responsible than himself ... but he may not live much longer than his brother.' She lifted her brows. 'I am sorry. I am a harsh woman sometimes.'

'You want *me* to inherit?' he said, incredulously.

'It is a long way off, but only you or Richard are able to assume the responsibility fully. I had this notion before I saw your interest in Naomi, Eliot.' She looked off. 'I think of the future generations, so that you and Richard are free to be self-made men when you are young.' She laughed. 'Neither of you want it, I know. But saving one's heritage for one's children is no bad thing.'

'The dukedom is gone,' said Eliot, suddenly seeing it, 'but there is still the earldom.'

'Yes ... and no. I do not covet it for Richard precisely. But I wish for the estates to be well managed and preserved for the next earl, whoever he may be.'

'You are doing so for your own estates, and now you take on the extra burden of Cedric's.'

'It *is* a burden. But you could help me, Eliot!'

'But the Dower House...!'

'That is because ... Naomi will miss us terribly.'

Eliot knew it. Had thought of it at night. How on earth could he replace that unit that was the Wild Marchmonts? The playfulness, the shared affection, the united entity that was her family.

'Grand houses are made to accommodate extended family, I think. But I must admit I may become bored here and move off elsewhere. Being at odds with your family brings *ennui.*'

'Perhaps we will *all* move to Surrey. Your family, my sisters and I, too.'

'Perhaps! But I have plans for the earl before I go. They may succeed. It depends on events...! So perhaps first, your little family could live in the Dower House.'

He saw it at once. Ophelia and Queenie removed from the daily tongue lashings, far enough away not to hear it, not so far as to excite the comment in society that Cedric would hate. He and Naomi close enough to the Wild Ones to let her keep her family. 'Yes, the Dower House, if Naomi agrees. And later, we shall all discuss it more fully.' Eliot said earnestly. 'I have been, a little included in your family, my lady, and it has warmed me to feel part of it.'

'Yes, the proximity part of my plan may have caused problems but has borne much fruit already. And it is by no means finished.' She smiled, 'Now do you see, Eliot, how your petty concerns have been vain?'

'Yes, my lady.'

'You have given me a great gift, Eliot.'

'*I* have?' said Eliot, amazed.

'Yes! Naomi is the happiest I have seen her since my husband's death.'

'My lady. I am happy too. The most perfect woman has agreed to be my wife, and I have the richness of her family, also.'

'Your mama has arranged all!' He informed Naomi at their walk the next day, brazenly holding hands.

'She did? I mean, I thought you would not permit her...'

Eliot shrugged, resigned. 'I am no match for her. I am to be made richer at no cost to her, it seems, but instead will deliver great benefits. I graciously agreed to enrich myself at no one's cost at all.'

Naomi laughed at his ironic tone, but on regarding him closely understood that he was more amused then annoyed. 'Oh, mama is wonderful! Your pride is not hurt?'

'I have given it up. If Lady Eleanor disdains my pride, I do too,' he said comfortably. 'We are to start off in the Dower House.'

'Oh, let us go and see it now!' she pulled his arm in the direction, and he suggested going back for their horses.

'You need a better mount to keep up with mine,' said Naomi, preening with pride as she toyed with her mare Precious, looking at Eliot's serviceable hack with exaggerated pity.

'No doubt your mother will supply one. At no cost to her, I'll be bound. I will be doing her a favour.'

'You sound reconciled to wealth.'

'No, I have just submitted to the goddess.'

'Should not your goddess be I?' Naomi said pertly.

'I shall not change my religion. You are my equal, my love. Goddess Eleanor is my spiritual refuge.'

'*Idolater!*'

The Dower House, said the attendant there, had thirty rooms. There were some holes in the roof, but very few, there was a great deal of ivy blocking the light, but it turned out to be, 'Just perfect!' said Naomi twirling in the marble hall. 'But will your brother permit it?'

'I don't suppose your mother will tell him until the day we are installed!' remarked Eliot.

'Very likely!' laughed Naomi. 'Let us ride back to Tremaine before we see the upper rooms!'

'Why?'

'We should fetch Ophelia and Queenie to see. It will be their home, too!'

He took her shoulders. 'Do you mind?'

'Not at all! Did you see how they both welcomed me as a sister last night? I was moved to see Queenie crying — and Ophelia secretly held my hand.'

'Ophelia did?'

'I expect your brother will be furious if his sisters set up home with us.'

'Not from affection, but only from being bested.' As they rode back, he said. 'I was wondering how we are to manage London. Do we all reside at Tremaine House there with Cedric and Agatha, or do we have a separate fate?'

'What do you think?'

'It may suit Cedric to accommodate us all, I do not quite know. If he does, I imagine the main expenses of the Season will fall upon—'

'Mama! She will not mind that, but she may have other plans.'

'I shall leave it all to my goddess. I am sure she has it in hand.'

'It is addictive, is it not, depending on Mama to know what is best?'

Eliot knew that there were many barriers he would not cross in this regard. He was laughing at his own capitulation, but it came of trusting his mother-in-law to make him *earn* his gains. To understand what he would and would not take, and his own determination to make a fortune by his own investments, however they should diversify. His capitulation was also based on the belief that the goddess knew that he would do so. She believed in him. A wise elder who did so had been absent from his life, and her trust had disarmed him at a stroke.

And he still had a hope. His smaller second investment, from his grandmother's legacy, had failed. But there was still the larger, the £5000 invested in a ship that still had many weeks of voyage. If this ship came in without loss, he would be a wealthy man indeed. Would he still help with the estate in Surrey in that event, or would he force his independence? He realised suddenly, that it would not matter then. Whether they lived in Surrey, the Dower House, or an estate he bought. He hoped, he realised, to live with all his family, (his sisters and the Wilds, at least) wherever it was. It might even be excessive, he grinned to himself, to add to the number of properties that already existed in his family.

It was as though Naomi divined his thoughts. 'I know you have your own plan, Eliot.'

'I still do. I have many. But we shall speak of it. Your mother has shown me it is right to discuss one's plan with a partner. It changes, perhaps, but for the better. So, your plan, too, Naomi, will become part of ours.'

'And Queenie's and Ophelia's too!'

Queenie and Ophelia when informed, while roaming around the Dower House, that they had to speak their plans, had various reactions.

Queenie, who thought women must follow the plans gentlemen make, was astonished.

'What is it *you* wish to do, dear Queenie?' asked Naomi.

'Oh, I have no notion!'

'You shall think about it some more — you might do whatever you wish to in our home here,' said Naomi.

Seeing her sister's abject fear at having to venture an opinion of her own and seeing that a mounting pressure was in her chest, which Queenie clutched, Ophelia suggested, taking her sister's hand. 'Well, you may see to the domestic comforts of our home, do you not think?'

'But that is for Naomi...' began Queenie timidly.

Naomi, catching Ophelia's eye and reading the message there, said, 'Oh, but I have no interest in domestic details. I just want to write, you know, and hitherto all such things were arranged by Mama.' She grasped Queenie's hand, 'If you could just order the menus, and deal with the housekeeper, it would be such a boon to me.'

'Oh, I shall, with pleasure!' said Queenie.

'But of course, I shall have to learn the housewifery tasks, to become a good wife, and I shall rely on you to teach me!'

'Oh, of course!' Queenie saw a new life before her, a useful one perhaps, adding to the comforts of her dear brother, and now two sisters. It seemed delicious.

Ophelia nodded to Naomi in gratitude for these words to her sister and said. 'As to me, I have never thought of a life beyond fashionable indolence, since it was all that was before me. I shall have to consider what my desires truly are.'

'I too!' said Naomi. 'Beyond the pen and my family, I have never given anything else a thought. But now, for example, Mama will demand colours from me ... help me, Ophelia! I shall decorate Eliot's study and my own, and I have an idea for the main salon, but beyond that I have no fashionable taste as yet.'

'Leave it to me!' said Ophelia. 'I know all the latest modes.' She looked critically around the second salon. 'Although I do not think we should fight the Rococco,' she considered.

'The original style? Oh, I think you are very wise. It is so pretty, but everywhere needs fresh paint and hangings.'

'A project!' said Ophelia. 'I shall give my plans to your mama for her ultimate approval. To make it easier I suggest a *restoration* rather than a *renovation.* We may use the present colours in most cases.'

'Eliot ...' said Queenie, drawing him apart, 'is it quite right that the cost of the renovation should fall on your betrothed's Mama? Can I not give you my trust money to use in the meantime?'

'Ah! You little understand Lady Eleanor. She does not do this for *us*, but for the estate. Have you not seen the work she has done everywhere to improve it?'

'Well, yes!' agreed Queenie.

'This is more of the same, and she desires we live here for the present so that we might improve the land, at no cost to her at all.' This was said ironically, but Queenie did not perceive so.

'Oh, Eliot, in that case ...!' Queenie frowned, more obvious now that her brows were growing in. 'But why does Lady Eleanor wish to do so much for this estate, when it is Cedric's.'

Ophelia, who came up behind with Naomi unnoticed, said, 'Is Richard, as I've heard from an estate worker, *indeed* the *true earl*?'

Queenie was shocked as Naomi and Eliot told his sisters the true story.

As they left their future home Eliot was hardly shocked when men began unloading slates at the side of the house. His mother-in-law was a force to be reckoned with.

Ophelia looked amazed. 'I shall finish my plan for the inside tonight,' she said, 'and show it to you and your mother. Otherwise, Lady Eleanor may reprimand me for tardiness! No doubt the wallpaper will arrive tomorrow...'

'Perhaps! I was going to choose rose silk for the main salon, but it may make Eliot uncomfortable. He will have enough femininity to deal with. Now I think ... French green. It is the original colour, perhaps, but it may be renewed in silk.'

'Silk moiré would be prettier,' said Ophelia.

'You are quite right.'

'And the rose can be in the little salon where we ladies might sit to work. Or perhaps you never set a stitch?'

'I do!' Naomi assured her, 'Mama instilled it in us all. Let us do what she did and look in the attics. There may be many things we can preserve of the past.'

'That is for later, surely!' said Eliot. 'It will be enough to make the place habitable for now!'

'Hush!' said his sister and betrothed both, and Eliot understood this was not his dominion.

'I wonder,' said Queenie pensively, as she mounted her horse, 'where the kitchen garden was previously located?'

Eliot smiled at his Naomi as they rode ahead. *A home!* His sisters were part of it, and already were feeling its pull. A new life. They had chosen rooms, and now all the other notions of comfort were to be thought of. Naomi, open and inclusive to his sisters, as with her own family, had given the key to unity.

They would be happy.

CHAPTER 20

The Family Informed

Though it diluted his happiness somewhat, Eliot visited the rooms of his brother the earl. He found Cedric at his toilette, a long procedure, Eliot knew. His Italian valet Guido was peeling a hot towel from the noble jaw, and as the earl was shaved he regarded Eliot in the mirror.

'You are the *second* unwelcome visitor to my rooms today, dear brother,' he informed him. 'Forgive my brutal honesty, I must have caught it from that appalling child.'

'Berthe visited you?'

Guido the Italian, sniffed at his side, as though disgusted at the mere mention of the child. He looked rather like a swarthy ruffian whom Eliot had relieved of a stiletto one evening in a London alley.

'She did. To inform me that everyone was going out to the fair. She thought I might like to rest my ... eh ... poor head.'

'*Bambino insolente!*' hissed the valet.

'You too, are insolent to talk of the earl's relative so, Guido!' shot back Eliot.

The earl groaned at this.

'I used to think the Towers...,' bemoaned Cedric in that faltering voice Eliot loathed, '...a *vast* house, but now it seems this tiny spot,' indicating the commodious apartments (which would make four of Eliot's large room) with a negligent hand, 'is my last refuge, and *still* you bring conflict here. Do not upset Guido when he has a *blade* at my throat, I pray you!'

'I am here to deliver good news, my lord.'

'*Sarcasm...*' said the earl faintly.

'No indeed. I am to be married, and I thought that I should inform the head of my family with all dispatch.'

The earl pushed away Guido's blade and regarded his brother from hooded eyes. 'Ha!' he scoffed, 'I always thought you the *cleverest*, Eliot. So, you fill your pockets with the Scottish woman's guineas!' The earl gazed off theatrically, to indicate thought, then turned back to look at his brother through the looking glass. 'It cannot be the pretty, vapid female or the redhead who climbs trees.'

Eliot had not been expecting to enjoy this interview, but he was moved to cold anger at his mention of Stephanie, a child, as someone he might profit from.

'I have written to Dorian, to tell him that he should catch a rich treat before their Season, if he can stomach their *appalling* dress and manners, but he has been silent by return.' Cedric's poison was dripping. 'It cannot be that you take on the beautiful, biting, hellcat? You will *certainly* earn your keep if you do so!'

Eliot was cool. 'I am to marry Miss *Naomi* Marchmont.' However angry he was, the very words lifted his spirits.

'Which one is *she*? The least pretty, with the sharp tongue? Well, I don't suppose you could set your sights too high.'

'I leave you brother,' said Eliot bowing. 'But I advise you not to talk in such a tone before my betrothed, for I shall not spare you. If Richard Marchmont does not get to you first.'

'You are braver now,' hissed the earl, 'that you have riches behind you.'

Eliot instructed Godwin to divert his sisters to the Chinese salon before dinner.

Naomi and he had missed the arrival of the fair party, who were rushing upstairs, happy and bearing any number of parcels, to get dressed for dinner, as they were late. Naomi scrambled to follow, them on the stairs, anxious to impart their news, but Berthe had seen her and grasped at her.

'Oh Naomi, you should have come! There was no dancing dog, but a great bear who danced instead.'

'There was?' laughed Naomi.

'Yes,' said Tabitha, 'but afterwards I saw the owner beat it and I cried.'

'Oh, how dreadful!' said Naomi.

'Not really, for then Richard *bought* it.'

'A *bear*! *Richard*!' called Naomi to him, at the head of the throng on the stairs.

'Now it is our very own!' said Berthe happily.

'I have told you, Horror, that it is not a pet, and that I shall find it somewhere better to live.'

'But meanwhile it will arrive in a crate tonight,' said Phoebe, who had visited the fair after the betrothal.

'*No!*' said Naomi.

'Eliot!' Richard called down to him, 'Have you any idea what to feed a bear?'

'Berthe, I should think!' said Eliot.

There was general laughter at this, and Eliot held back Naomi. 'It looks as though Phoebe held her tongue. Let us tell them all at once, in the Chinese salon before dinner!'

Eliot and Naomi entered the Chinese salon last, as was their plan. Her mother looked up smiling as they came in arm in arm and then a series of shrieks greeted them.

Eliot's sisters were the first to reach them. 'Oh darling, Eliot, dearest sister Naomi!' said Queenie, shedding tears. 'Roseanna, your sister is mine now, too!' she said to her friend, who beamed back. Queenie's weeping seemed copious. Something, Ophelia thought, had occurred to her sister at the fair, but that was for a later consideration. For the moment Ophelia glowed at her brother and said, 'You fortunate dog!' in a low voice. He smiled and Ophelia turned to Naomi who was being squeezed by a weeping Roseanna.

Richard shook Eliot's hand. 'Welcome to the family! We are out-numbered, but at least there are two of us now.'

'You do not mind?'

'Like Roseanna and the children, I had no idea. But I trust Naomi. She would not wed a fool.' He clapped Eliot on the shoulder, and Eliot suddenly saw one of the things Lady Eleanor had tried to tell him. He had a role to play here. He could share Richard's burden of protection, at least. His qualms melted even further away.

'Oh Eliot!' said Roseanna suddenly around his neck, 'I had no idea! But I am *so* happy!' Berthe was simultaneously pulling at his pantalons, saying 'You are my brother now, Eliot. So, you *have to* speak to me!'

He looked down, not yet free of Roseanna's arms around his neck and suddenly he could picture himself on the floor by the fire in the library, in a pile of bodies who clung to him. He looked over at Naomi, whose lovely face was glowing with happiness and his eyes were showing mock panic and a call for salvation from her sisters' manhandling. She smiled back ironically, understanding, from the bottom of her heart, how truly happy he was to be amidst the throng.

In the earl's withdrawing room the Royals, depleted in number because of the unaccountable absence of their sisters and Eliot, exchanged only desultory conversation. They heard, in the distance a number of squeals and a great deal of laughter, which seemed to contrast to the dull, empty room even more.

'At least,' said her lady ship, 'we are free of the rowdy and the vulgar this evening.'

'Wherever are Queenie and Ophelia?'

'I might hazard a guess,' the earl drawled.

'Then do so!' said Charles, testily.

'You will both be informed quite soon, I imagine,' said Cedric with disdain, looking down at the book he was not reading as a dismissal.

The countess looked worried about any new threat to her dominance and Charles looked surly at being kept from Cedric's confidence. His brother was irritatingly smug at times.

When at last dinner was served, Charles rose with alacrity to escape Cedric's bitter depression and Agatha's resultant anxiety.

It was, they found, as they entered a dining room and encountered a group of people already in a festive spirit, much worse than the two uninformed Royals could have imagined.

'Eliot... to be married ... to *you?*' said Lady Tremaine with obvious shock and disgust.

It was such an exaggerated reaction that Naomi giggled.

'Eliot ... *rich?*' said Charles hitting his own concern with accuracy.

Cedric's eye glittered and Eliot caught his gaze in warning. Richard Marchmont sat on the other side of his sister, and so the earl held back, only permitting himself a quiet scoff of agreement. 'Strive to contain your expressions of delight, my family, and let us eat.'

'*How did this happen...?*' said Charles still shocked and confused.

'He's really pleased, is he not?' said Berthe to Naomi with childish sincerity. She turned to Charles. 'Well, since it is no longer a secret, Crown Prince, *I* think it happened because of the *purloined journal*...!'

'Can no one stop the child?" said Charles, pulling back a lace ruff that Richard regarded with horror.

'You will *like* the story, Crown Prince. *I* am the heroine, who meted out *horrible* punishment to Eliot and ...'

'No,' interrupted Richard, regarding Berthe and then answering Charles, 'I do not suppose anyone *could* stop her.'

'I thought it was just a story of theft, but it might be more...'

'Oh Naomi! ... and so Eliot read the words of love you dare not speak?' said Roseanna, in a dream of romance .

'*No...!*' protested Naomi blushing.

'Prob'ly. I haven't *read* it,' admitted Berthe.

'He should *not* have read it,' said the ethical Tabitha.

'Eliot, I am shocked...!' said Lady Tremaine.

'It was despicable, and I shall be punished,' said Eliot piously, directing a raised eyebrow to the smug Phoebe.

'You will be,' said Phoebe. 'But you cannot deny that it brought you together.'

'It did.'

'*Must* we...?' pleaded the earl.

'How did you discover I had read it, darling?' asked Eliot quietly to Naomi.

Naomi looked at Queenie and Roseanna, both too close for comfort and whispered, 'I will tell you later.'

'Read the book and saw an innings, then,' said Charles sarcastically. 'Mightily clever, Eliot!'

Lady Eleanor who had sat quietly content, smiling occasionally, now entered the conversation. 'My lawyers are not quite done with our business Charles.'

Charles jumped. 'I quite thought they were.'

'I delayed them...' Lady Eleanor continued, raising her fork and eating with great attention to the *morceau* of veal she had speared.

'Why?' asked Charles looking at her cravenly.

'For just such an occasion as *this,*' she said sweetly. Then a trifle more dryly she added, 'Control your unpleasant tongue!'

Charles nodded and became quiet, glancing fearfully at Cedric.

But Cedric was ignoring the proceedings, Queenie and even Ophelia seemed taken by the general delight, and the countess was left quite alone to swallow her bile.

Thoroughly outnumbered now, with the evident defection of Eliot's sisters, the remaining opposing Royals could only look on at the general delight, bitterly.

Berthe continued her tale of the purloined journal, and Eliot's punishment, which her mama applauded with, 'How clever of you, Berthe! He must have suffered!' Eliot touched Berthe's head calling her *dreadful child!* which made her smile at him sunnily. Naomi looked, Charles had to admit, very beautiful as she smiled so widely when she looked at his brother that her face might crack. Perhaps it was not a marriage for profit after all, he concluded seeing Eliot's rare answering smile.

But still, he was jealous, and Eliot's hands in the pockets of the dreadful Scotswoman were to be envied. His stomach had almost turned with it until the dreadful child saved him.

'What one needs at a celebration is cake!' Berthe said, with relish. 'I saw cake in the kitchen this afternoon.'

What a good idea, considered Charles.

'I had it made,' said Lady Eleanor and the countess's bile at this was ignored by all.

'Godwin,' said the terrible child, in the commanding accents of her mother, 'Have them bring the cake now!'

The countess choked.

CHAPTER 21

Epilogue

Naomi and Eliot sat on their bench, and only Berthe had come to interrupt them, not stopped by Phoebe's cry of, 'Do not disturb them, ragamuffin!'

'*Why?*' demanded Berthe, squeezing herself between the couple, looking up at Eliot trustfully.

Richard arrived before Eliot could answer, lifting the child up and putting her, squealing, over his shoulder, her black curls hanging, 'Sorry, Eliot,' he said, walking off, 'I'll find a pigsty to shut her in.'

'Thank you,' said Eliot sincerely. He took Naomi's hand again and they looked at the view of the running family playing. He said, 'I wanted to ask you how you discovered I had read the journal?'

'*The most ridiculous friendship in the world*, you said.' She informed him.

'Ah! It was a quote! How could I be so empty headed as to give myself away? I was probably distracted because I held your hand or some such thing.'

'*Is* that so distracting?' she teased him.

'Yes! *Hours* worth of distraction.' He replied, teasing her in return. Then he sighed, 'You must have been furious with me.'

'Furious and hurt. I thought our connection made by God, but it was only because you stole my thoughts.'

'I assure you, after reading what you said of me at first,' Naomi's face contorted in the attempt to recall, 'that I was dull, but my face should be rendered in marble...' She cringed and hid her head on his arm, '...my conscience *did* smite me terribly. And I tried to resist temptation any number of times. But failed. '

'Sinner!' she said, pertly. 'You ought to carry chains about your body all day, like the penitent monks.'

'I endured Berthe's penance!' he said in self-defence, 'It may have been worse.'

'It was your *honour* to converse with my family, not a *penance*!'

'You would not say so if you knew as much as I now do about gears. Since I am male, like Richard and your Papa, Tabitha naturally assumes I will be as interested as they. She talks my ear off. For a reserved child normally, she has remarkable animation.'

'*Poor* Eliot!'

'And our connection *is* made by God, for if I had not wished for the volume of Donne, and your journal was not made of red Morocco, I should never have discovered you! That was certainly divine intervention. I have been a surly fellow, I suppose, and I may have kept my conversations with your family to no more than civilised exchanges once a day.'

'I remember our first conversations as curt, not civilised.'

'I fear you are correct. I have been civilised by you, my sweetheart.'

'Do not! You sound like Sir Osbert Barclay might when flirting with females.'

'No, Cedric!' said Eliot, adding in his brother's faintly deprecating accents, '*My Celestial Angel of Wisdom!*'

'Urgh!' said Naomi. 'But I do not think you would have resisted us Wild things forever. Berthe alone would not have permitted it.'

'You may be right, but it was my introduction to you all in the journal that broke through my reserve and enticed my interest from the first line.'

'I intend to purchase a locked box for it, for I shall tell you what I *wish* you to know, and no more.'

'*Quel dommage!* I know that is correct, but I will miss your lively accounts of our daily lives. Your pen is quite wonderful!'

'Perhaps I may read you extracts after our marriage, but you must promise ...!

'I shall never purloin your journal again.' He stood. 'Shall we walk to the Dower House?'

'Mama says we must not. She says it is all in hand and will be a surprise for us on our wedding day!'

'As my deity decrees.'

Naomi stopped, causing him to look down at her. 'I do not care how you knew me anymore, Eliot, for I am sure you were designed *just* for me.'

'Darling, you *darling*.' He kissed her face and hands and stood back to catch his breath, pulling her hand through his arm. 'By the way, I will have a gift made for your writing desk, Naomi!'

'Really?' she said, walking at his side again. 'A new journal?'

'Not at all! It is my head, rendered in a marble bust...'

As she tried to slap his back for this, he ran ahead, and she chased him, squealing, until he caught up with the wild Marchmonts, and ran into the midst of the throng, snaking through bodies with a laughing Naomi trying to catch him.

As Charles scoffed at a salon window, Queenie and Ophelia came to take a look. They exchanged smiles, and Queenie said to her sister, once Charles had flounced off, 'Do you think that we, *too*, might ever be that happy?'

Ophelia linked arms with her sister, quite as if they had been Wild Marchmonts instead of Royals. 'We have a new life beginning, Ness. Can't you feel it?'

In the distance Eliot was caught again, and after assault, he took his betrothed's hand as they headed back to the house with the others. Suddenly Naomi saw the sisters at the window, and she raised her hand and jumped a wave. In return, the free hand of each raised high and waved back.

Charles, appalled, said, 'What *are* you two doing?'

He watched as they walked back to the sofa together and he looked at their arm lock with distaste.

Ophelia replied, '*Doing?* Oh, just beginning to be happy, Crown Prince.'

About the Author

Alicia Cameron lives between her homes in rural Scotland and rural France. She reads avidly, laughs a lot, and is newly addicted, unfortunately, to Korean Dramas ... for which she refuses treatment. Here is a link to get **Angelique and the Pursuit of Destiny** for FREE! https://BookHip.com/XSNQVM It puts you on the list to receive Alicia Cameron's book news and offers, occasionally.

All Alicia books are available on Amazon and as audiobooks on Audible. Some are available in several languages, German and Spanish especially.

You can find out more here :

The website https://aliciacameron.co.uk

Facebook https://www.facebook.com/aliciacameron.100

Twitter https://twitter.com/aliciaclarissa2

Bookbub https://www.bookbub.com/authors/alicia-cameron

Also By Alicia Cameron

Regency Romance

Angelique and the Pursuit of Destiny: (A short story) getbook.at/Angelique

Angelique was named by her French grandmother, but now lives as Ann, ignored by her aristocratic relations. Can she find the courage to pursue her Destiny, reluctantly aided by her suave cousin Ferdinand?

Beth and the Mistaken Identity: getbook.at/Beth

Beth has been cast off as lady's maid to the pert young Sophy Ludgate, but is mistaken as a lady herself by a handsome marquis and his princess sister. Desperate to save the coach fare to London, she goes along with them, but they do not let her escape so easily.

Clarissa and the Poor Relations: getbook.at/Clarissa
Clarissa Thorne and her three friends have to leave their cosy School for Young Ladies after the death of Clarissa's mama. all must be sent off as poor relations to their families. However, Clarissa suddenly inherits Ashcroft Manor, and persuades the ladies to make a bid for freedom. But can she escape their unpleasant families? The Earl of Grandiston might help.

Delphine and the Dangerous Arrangement: getbook.at/Delphine
Delphine Delacroix was brought up by her mother alone, a cold and unloving childhood. With her mother dead, she has become the richest young lady in England, and is taken under the wing of her three aunts, Not quite trusting them, Delphine enters a dangerous arrangement with the handsome Viscount Gascoigne - but will this lead to her downfall?

The Fentons Series (Regency)

Honoria and the Family Obligation, The Fentons 1
https://getbook.at/Honoria
Honoria Fenton has been informed that the famous Mr Allison is to come to her home. His purpose? To

woo her. She cannot recall what he looks like, since he made her nervous when they met in Town. Her sister Serena is amused, but when Allison arrives, it seems that a mistake might cost all three there happiness.

Felicity and the Damaged Reputation, The Fentons 2 https://getbook.at/Felicity
On her way to London to take a post as governess, Felicity Oldfield is intercepted by Viscount Durant, who asks her to impersonate his cousin for an hour. When, in an unexpected turn of events, Felicity is able to enjoy a London Season, this encounter damages her reputation.

Euphemia and the Unexpected Enchantment, The Fentons 3 https://getbook.at/Euphemia
Euphemia, plain and near forty, is on her way to live with her dear friend Felicity and her husband when she is diverted to the home of Baron Balfour, a bear of a man as huge and loud as Euphemia is small and quiet. Everything in her timid life begins to change.

Ianthe and the Fighting Foxes: The Fentons 4 https://getbook.at/Ianthe
The Fighting Foxes, Lord Edward, his half-brother Curtis and Lady Fox, his stepmother, are awaiting the arrival from France of a poor relation, Miss Ianthe Eames. But when Ianthe turns up, nothing could be further from their idea of a supplicant. Richly dressed and in high good humour, Ianthe takes the Foxes by storm.

The Sisters of Castle Fortune Series (Regency)

Georgette and the Unrequited Love: Sisters of Castle Fortune 1 https://getbook.at/Georgette
Georgette Fortune, one of ten sisters, lives as a spinster in Castle Fortune. She refused all offers during her London Seasons, since she fell in love, at first glance with the dashing Lord Onslow. He hardly knew she existed, however, but now he has arrived at the castle for a house party, and Georgette is fearful of exposing her feelings. She tries to avoid him, but Onslow treats her as a friend, making Georgette's pain worse, even as he makes her laugh.

Jocasta and the Cruelty of Kindness: Sisters of Castle Fortune 2 https://getbook.at/Jocasta
At a house party in Castle Fortune, Jocasta's beau had fallen for her sister, Portia. Now Jocasta is back in London and has to suffer the pity of the friends and family that care for her. Only Sir Damon Regis treats her without pity, and she is strangely drawn to him because of it.

Katerina and the Reclusive Earl: Sisters of Castle Fortune 3 https://getbook.at/Katerina
Katerina Fortune has only one desire, to avoid going on her London Season altogether. On the journey, she hears of a recluse, who dislikes people as much as she. Katerina escapes her father and drives to offer a convenient marriage to the earl, who refuses. But an accident necessitates her stay at his home, and

they discover they have more in common than either could have believed.

Leonora and the Lion's Venture: Sisters of Castle Fortune 4 https://getbook.at/Leonora
The pretty Fortune twins come to Town, and Leonora has only one object in view: The Honourable Linton Carswell. But Foggy Carswell is too craven to be caught – he is not a marrying man. While trying to save her twin Marguerite from the results of her own romantic naivety, Leonora has her work set for her. But a number of family alliances begin to aid the unlikely pairing.

Marguerite and the Duke in Disguise: Sisters of Castle Fortune 5 https://mybook.to/Marguerite
Marguerite Fortune, bereft of her newly married twin Leonora, is heading back to her Castle Fortune home with only her two unsympathetic male relatives for company. At an inn she meets another Leo, this time a man mountain, who saves her from harm. When her father diverts their journey and abandons Marguerite to make a match at Dysart manor, Leo arrives too. They are soon embroiled in awful plots, kidnap and even murder.

Edwardian Inspirational Romance
(typewriters, bicycles, and leg-of-mutton sleeves!)

Francine and the Art of Transformation: getbook.at/FrancineT

Francine is fired as a lady's maid, but she is a woman who has planned for every eventuality. Meeting Miss Philpott, a timid, unemployed governess, Francine transforms her into the Fascinating Mathilde and offers her another, self directed life. Together, they help countless other women get control over their lives.

Francine and the Winter's Gift: getbook.at/FrancineW

Francine and Mathilde continue to save young girls from dreadful marriages, while seeing to their own romances. In Francine, Sir Hugo Portas, government minister, meets a woman he could never have imagined. Will society's rules stop their union, or can Francine even accept the shackles of being in a relationship?

CHAPTER 22

Chapter of Honoria and the Family Obligation : The Fentons Book 1

G Getbook.at/Honoria

Chapter 1

'He has arrived!' said Serena, kneeling on the window seat of their bedchamber. She made a pretty picture there with her sprigged muslin dress foaming around her and one silk stockinged foot still on the floor, but her sister Honoria was too frozen with fear to notice.

'Oh, no,' said Honoria, moving forward in a dull fashion to join her. Her elder brother Benedict had been sitting with one leg draped negligently over the arm of the only comfortable chair in the room and now rose languidly to join his younger sisters. After the season in London, Dickie had begun to ape the manners of Beau Brummel and his cronies, polite, but slightly bored with the world. At one and twenty, it seemed a trifle contrived, even allowing that his long limbs and handsome face put many a town beau to shame.

Serena's dark eyes danced wickedly, 'Here comes the conquest of your triumphant season, your soon-to-be-fiancé.'

Dickie grinned, rather more like their childhood companion, 'Your knight in shining armour. If *only* you could remember him.'

'It isn't funny.'

Serena laughed and turned back to the window as she heard the door of the carriage open and the steps let down by Timothy, the one and only footman that Fenton Manor could boast.

'Oh, how did it happen?' Honoria said for the fifteenth time that morning.

Someone in the crowd had said, 'Mr Allison is approaching. But he never dances!' In confusion, she had looked around, and saw the throng around her grow still and part as her hostess approached with a tall gentleman. With all eyes turned to her she stiffened in every sinew. She remembered the voice of Lady Carlisle introducing Mr Allison as a desirable partner, she remembered her mother thrusting her forward as she was frozen with timidity. She remembered his hand lead her to her first waltz of the season. She had turned to her mother for protection as his hand snaked around her waist and had seen that matron grip her hands together and glow with pride. This was Lady Fenton's shining moment, if not her daughter's. Word had it that Mr Allison had danced only thrice this season, each time with his married friends. Lost in the whirl of the dance, she had answered his remarks with single syllables, looking no higher than his chin. A dimpled chin, strong, she remembered vaguely. And though she had previously seen Mr. Allison at a distance, the very rich and therefore very interesting Mr Allison, with an estate grander than many a nobleman, she could not remember more than that he was held to be handsome. (As she told Serena this later, her sister remarked that rich men were very often held to be handsome, strangely related to the size of their purse.)

There was the waltz; there had been a visit to her father in the London house; her mother had informed her of Mr Allison's wishes and that she was to receive his addresses the next afternoon. He certainly visited the next afternoon, and Honoria had been suffered to serve him his tea and her hand had shaken so much that she had kept her eyes on the cup for the rest of the time. He had not proposed, which her mother thought of as a pity, but here she had been saved by Papa, who had thought that Mr Allison should visit them in the country where his daughter and he might be more at their leisure to know each other. 'For she is a little shy with new company and I should wish her perfectly comfortable before she receives your addresses,'

Sir Ranalph had told him, as Honoria's mama had explained.

Serena, when told, had thought it a wonderful joke. To be practically engaged to someone you could not remember! She laughed because she trusted to good-natured Papa to save Honoria from the match if it should prove unwanted; her sister had only to say "no".

'Why on earth do you make such a tragedian of yourself, Orry,' had said Serena once Honoria had poured her story out, 'After poor Henrietta Madeley's sad marriage, Papa has always said that to marry with such parental compulsion is scandalously cruel.'

And Honoria had mopped up her tears and felt a good deal better, buoyed by Serena's strength of mind. To be sure, there was the embarrassment to be endured of giving disappointment, but she resolved to do it if Mr Allison's aura of grandeur continued to terrify her.

'And then,' her sister had continued merrily, 'the rich Mr Allison may just turn out to be as handsome as his purse and as good natured as Papa - and you will fall head over heels with him after all.'

The morning after, Honoria had gone for a walk before breakfast, in much better spirits. As she came up the steps to re-enter by the breakfast room, she carelessly caught her new French muslin (fifteen and sixpence the yard, Mama had told her) on the roses that grew on a column. If she took her time and did not pull, she may be able to rescue herself without damage to the dress. She could hear

Mama and Papa chatting and gave it no mind until Mama's voice became serious.

'My dear Ranalph, will you not tell me?'

'Shall there be muffins this morning, my dear?' said Papa cheerfully.

'You did not finish your mutton last night and you are falsely cheerful this morning. Tell me, my love.'

'You should apply for a position at Bow Street, my dear. Nothing escapes you.' She heard the sound of an embrace.

'Diversionary tactics, sir, are futile.'

Honoria knew she should not be privy to this, but she was still detaching her dress, thorn by thorn. It was incumbent on her to make a noise, so that they might know she was there, but as she decided to do so, she was frozen by Papa's next words.

'Mr Allison's visit will resolve all, I'm sure.'

Honoria closed her mouth, automatically continuing to silently pluck her dress from the rose bush, anxious to be away.

'Resolve what, dearest?' Honoria could picture her mama on Papa's knee.

'Well, there have been extra expenses – from the Brighton property.' Honoria knew that this was where her uncle Wilbert lived, her father's younger brother. (Dickie had explained that he was a friend of the Prince Regent, which sounded so well to the girls, but Dickie had shaken his head loftily. 'You girls know nothing. Unless you are as rich as a Maharajah, it's ruinous to be part of that set.')

Her father continued, 'Now, now. All is well. If things do not take with Mr Allison, we shall just have to cut our cloth a little, Madame.' He breathed. 'But, Cynthia, I'm afraid another London Season is not to be thought of.'

Honoria felt instant guilt. Her own season had been at a rather later age than that of her more prosperous friends, and she had not been able to understand why Serena and she could not have had it together, for they borrowed each other's clothes all the time. Serena's intrepid spirit would have buoyed hers too and made her laugh, and would have surely helped with her crippling timidity. But when she had seen how many dresses had been required - one day alone she had changed from morning gown to carriage dress to luncheon half dress, then riding habit and finally evening dress. And with so many of the same people at balls, one could not make do - Mama had insisted on twenty evening gowns as the bare minimum. However doughty with a needle the sisters might be, this was beyond their scope, and London dressmakers did not come cheap. Two such wardrobes were not to be paid for by the estate's income in one year. Honoria had accidentally seen the milliner's bill for her season and shuddered to think of it - her bonnets alone had been ruinously expensive. She had looked forward to her second season, where her wardrobe could be adapted at very little cost to give it a new look and Serena would also have her fill of new walking dresses and riding habits, bonnets and stockings. If she were in London with her sister, she might actually enjoy it.

'Poor Serena. What are her chances of a suitable match in this restricted neighbourhood?' Mama continued, 'And indeed, Honoria, if she does not *like this match. Though how she could fail to like a charming, handsome man like Mr Allison is beyond me,' she finished.*

'Do not forget rich,' teased her husband.

'When I think of the girls who tried to catch him all season! And then he came to us – specifically asked to be presented to her as a partner for the waltz, as dear Lady Carlisle informed me later - but she showed no triumph at all. And now, she will not give an opinion. She is strangely reticent about the subject.'

'Well, well, it is no doubt her shyness. She will be more relaxed when she sees Allison among the family.'

'So much rests upon it.' There was a pause. 'Dickie's commission?'

He laughed, but it sounded sour from her always cheerful Papa. 'Wilbert has promised to buy it from his next win at Faro.'

'Hah!' said Mama bitterly.

Honoria was free. She went towards the breakfast room rather noisily.

'Are there muffins?' she asked gaily.

'How on earth do you come to be engaged to *him*?'

Honoria was jolted back to the present by Serena's outcry. She gazed in dread over her sister's dark curls and saw a sober figure in a black coat and dull breeches, with a wide-brimmed, antediluvian hat walking towards the house. She gave an involuntary giggle.

'Oh, that is only Mr Scribster, his friend.'

'*He* you remember!' laughed Serena. 'Is he as dull as his hat?'

Honoria remembered Mr Scribster's long, miserable face, framed with two lank curtains of hair, at several parties. She thought it odd that a gentleman so patently uninterested in the events should bother to attend. And indeed her mother had whispered the same to her. Honoria must be present where her parents willed her - but surely a gentleman should be free not to? But Mr. Scribster attended in company with Lord Salcomb or Mr Allison with a face suitable for a wake.

'Yes,' said Honoria. 'He never looks happy to be anywhere. And generally converses with no one. Though occasionally I saw him speak to Mr Allison in his grave way and Mr. Allison *laughed*.'

'Maybe it's like when Sir Henry Horton comes to dinner.' Sir Henry was nicknamed among the children "The Harbinger of Gloom". 'Papa laughs so much at his doomsday declarations that he is the only man in the county that actually looks forward to him coming.'

Honoria spotted another man exiting the chaise, this one in biscuit coloured breeches above shiny white-topped Hessian boots. His travelling coat almost swept the ground, and Serena said, 'Well, he's more the thing at any rate. Pity we cannot see his face. You should be prepared. However, he *walks* like a handsome man.' She giggled, 'Or at all events, a rich one.'

The door behind them had opened. 'Serena, you will guard your tongue,' said their mama. Lady Fenton, also known as Lady Cynthia (as she was the daughter of a peer) was the pattern card from which her beautiful daughters were formed. A dark-haired, plump, but stylish matron who looked as good as one could, she said of herself, when one had borne seven bouncing babies. Now she smiled, though, and Honoria felt another bar in her cage. How could she dash her mother's hopes? 'Straighten your dresses, girls, and come downstairs.'

Benedict winked and walked off with his parent.

There were no looking glasses in their bedroom, so as not to foster vanity. But as they straightened the ribbons of the new dresses Mama had thought appropriate to the occasion, they acted as each other's glass and pulled at hair ribbons and curls as need be. The Misses Fenton looked as close to twins as sisters separated by two years could, dark curls and dark slanted eyes and lips that curled at the corners to give them the appearance of a smile even in repose. Their brother Benedict said they resembled a couple of cats, but then he would say that. Serena had told him to watch his tongue or they might scratch.

The children, Norman, Edward, Cedric and Angelica, were not to be admitted to the drawing room - but they bowled out of the nursery to watch the sisters descend the stairs in state. As Serena tripped on a cricket ball, she looked back and stuck her tongue out at the grinning eight-year-old Cedric. Edward, ten, cuffed his younger brother and threw him into the nursery by the scruff of his neck. The eldest, Norman, twelve, a beefy chap, lifted little three-year-old Angelica who showed a disposition to follow her sisters. On the matter of unruly behaviour today, Mama had them all warned.

As the stairs turned on the landing, the sisters realised there was no one in the large square hall to see their dignified descent, so Serena tripped down excitedly, whilst her sister made the slow march of a hearse follower. As Serena gestured her down, Honoria knew that her sister's excitement came from a lack of society in their neighbourhood. She herself had enjoyed a London season, whilst Serena had never been further than Harrogate. She was down at last and they walked to the door of the salon, where she shot her hand out to delay Serena. She took a breath and squared her shoulders. Oh well, this time she should at least see what he looked like.

Two gentlemen stood by the fire with their backs to the door, conversing with Papa and Dickie. As the door opened, they turned and Honoria was focused on the square-shouldered gentleman, whose height rivalled Benedict's and quite dwarfed her sturdy papa. His face was nearly in view, Sir Ranalph was saying, 'These are my precious jewels!' The face was visible for only a moment before Serena gave a yelp of surprise and moved forward a pace. Honoria turned to her.

'But it's you!' Serena cried.

Everyone looked confused and a little shocked, not least Serena who grasped her hands in front of her and regarded the carpet. There seemed to be no doubt that she had addressed Mr Allison.

Honoria could see him now, the dimpled chin and strong jaw she remembered, and topped by a classical nose, deep set hazel eyes and the hairstyle of a Roman Emperor. Admirable, she supposed, but with a smile dying on his lips, he had turned from relaxed guest to stuffed animal, with only his eyes moving between one sister and another. His gaze fell, and he said the most peculiar thing.

'Blue slippers.'

Printed in Great Britain
by Amazon

45135855R00188